Emily squared her shoulders.

"Are you interested in the job or not?"

He paused a long moment before answering. "Yes."

"In that case, I'll let you know tomorrow whether I've chosen your company to do the work," she informed him coolly. "Is there anything else you need for your estimate?"

"No, that's complete."

She conducted him to the door and shut it behind him, relieved. Trent Hawkins might be near perfection in the appearance department— the perfect image of a rugged Western male— but he was also rude and pushy. She wasn't sure she liked him, and was definitely sure he made her nervous.

Before he'd come, she had made up her mind that if the estimate was reasonable, she'd go with Big Sky because of their reputation. They really were the best. But now she needed to think it through again. It gave her a peculiar sensation to know Trent wanted the house for reasons he refused to explain.

Dear Reader,

One of my dreams is to buy an old house and discover a forgotten treasure in the attic, such as an artifact from the Titanic or a previously unknown Rembrandt painting. So for my loner hero, Trent Hawkins, I couldn't resist pairing him with Emily George, a cheerful, new-age city woman determined to renovate his childhood home.

Trent isn't sentimental about Wild Rose Cottage, as Emily calls it, but he doesn't want a stranger tearing the place apart and discovering some of the dark, hidden secrets of the Hawkins family. He hadn't known the property was for sale, and Emily won't sell, though he makes an offer that few people would refuse. So when she chooses his construction company to do the renovations, he decides to supervise the job himself.

I hope you have fun reading *At Wild Rose Cottage*. Writing it indulged my dream of finding treasure, because while Trent and Emily don't uncover a Rembrandt, they discover something worth far more...each other.

I enjoy hearing from readers and can be contacted c/o Harlequin Books, 225 Duncan Mill Road, Don Mills, ON M3B 3K9, Canada.

Callie Endicott

CALLIE ENDICOTT

—

At Wild Rose Cottage

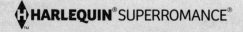
HARLEQUIN® SUPERROMANCE®

Recycling programs
for this product may
not exist in your area.

ISBN-13: 978-0-373-60963-5

At Wild Rose Cottage

Printed in U.S.A.

As a small child **Callie Endicott** was fascinated that little squiggles on the page of a book could actually tell tales of faraway places and people. So naturally, she grew up wanting to use those squiggles to share the stories she made up in her head. Callie is grateful for laptop computers, which allow her to indulge one of her passions and still write...travel. At the same time she loves home and her guy, along with her cats, walking on a beach or hiking a forest trail.

Books by Callie Endicott

HARLEQUIN SUPERROMANCE

Montana Skies

Kayla's Cowboy

That Summer at the Shore
Until She Met Daniel

Other titles by this author available in ebook format.

To my dad's father, who worked with his hands.

CHAPTER ONE

EMILY GEORGE STROLLED downtown to her new store. What a treat to take a leisurely ten-minute walk instead of fighting Los Angeles traffic for an hour.

It still seemed incredible that she'd bought the Emporium. She'd passed through the town of Schuyler while exploring Montana and had acted totally on impulse. Of course, being impulsive wasn't strange for her, but usually it wasn't regarding something so huge. After all, people said she was the "smart George sister," while her sister was the pretty one.

But four months ago she'd thrown caution to the wind and made an offer on the business. Well, it wasn't as if she was risking everything—her shop in Los Angeles was doing ridiculously well. Even after hiring a manager, she had ample income each month to do whatever she wanted, and that wasn't counting her savings and investments.

"Good morning," a friendly voice called as she entered the store.

"Hello. Back already?" Emily greeted the woman who'd visited the shop the previous day.

As far as she knew, it was the first time she'd met a member of the prominent McGregor family.

Sarah McGregor had spent two hours searching for the perfect present for her son and daughter-in-law, and they'd gotten into a fascinating conversation about the town's history. Later her manager had explained that when Sarah and her husband got married, it had ended the rivalry between the two biggest ranching families in the area. Emily had instantly envisioned the Western range wars of Hollywood legend, but apparently it hadn't been quite that dramatic.

"I thought you found the anniversary gift you wanted," she added, "but we're happy to take returns."

"It isn't that. I just kept thinking about how nice it would look in one of these polished wood boxes. They're so elegant and simple. And I asked my son, the one I told you about… Oh, there he is." Sarah stopped and smiled as a tall, rather forbidding man entered the shop. "Over here, Trent," she called.

Emily's own smile became strained. She'd made the mistake yesterday of mentioning her new house—desperately in need of renovation—only to have Sarah McGregor begin raving about her eldest son's building skills. Emily had manufactured an excuse to duck out of the conversation, wondering when she'd learn to keep her mouth shut.

It seemed as if half the women in town had talented sons capable of tackling repairs. *Plumbing?*

The dear unstopped my plugged sink in nothing flat. Electrical? You should see the way Joey rigged my broken vacuum cleaner. Drywall? I swatted a spider and knocked a hole in the plaster, so Carlton just covered it with masking tape and painted right over.

Supposedly some of them were licensed contractors, but Emily needed more than a mother's say-so to trust her home to them.

"Are these the boxes you wanted me to check?" asked the man as he approached. He looked absurdly out of place in the gift store. It was a large building with high, old-fashioned ceilings, but he seemed too powerful and intense to be confined inside four walls. With his green eyes and dark hair, he made her think of Irish adventurers braving the seas for fame and fortune.

"Er...yes, dear."

He lifted one of the wood boxes and turned it over, carefully examining every aspect of its construction, not seeming to notice the awkward silence that had fallen. A second and third box were inspected with equal care.

"These are finely constructed, all hardwood, and the price is acceptable for the level of workmanship," he said at length. "I'm surprised you wanted a second opinion."

Bright flags of pink appeared in Sarah's cheeks. "You're the expert. Let me introduce you to Emily, the new owner of the Emporium. Emily, this is my son Trent."

Trent flicked Emily a cool look. "Hello." If he was aware that his mother was trying to introduce a potential client, he wasn't using charm to clinch the deal.

"Hi."

"Emily just bought a house that needs renovation," Sarah explained gamely.

"That's nice. I should get back to work," Trent said to Sarah. "I'll see you at Sunday dinner." He gave her a kiss on the forehead and strode out.

He seemed to suck up all the oxygen in a room, and Emily felt the need to gulp a lungful of air after the door closed behind him.

Sarah let out a sigh. "I'm sorry. You said your new place is pretty bad, and I thought you could get some advice from Trent. What did you say— that the roof was in danger of falling down around your ears? It sounds as if you're living the Montana version of *Under the Tuscan Sun*."

Emily couldn't suppress a laugh. Her "new" house might be in even worse shape than a sturdy Italian villa that had survived centuries of use. "I suppose it does."

Except for the romance part, she added silently. The character in the movie had wanted a man in her life, but Emily wasn't interested in romance. And it didn't seem likely, in any case.

"You should consider having Trent's company

do the work. Not that I'm trying to drum up business for him, or that he needs it," Sarah added hastily. "He's terribly independent—when he was starting the business he wouldn't take anything from us. Not even..." Her words trailed and there was a hint of frustration in her tone.

Emily understood how Sarah's son must have felt. She often wished she had refused a loan from her parents when starting her boutique in Southern California. She'd long since paid it back, with compounded interest, but they rarely failed to refer to their role in her success.

"I'm planning to call a number of contractors for bids," Emily said, hoping Sarah would drop the subject.

"Then I'm sure you'll call Big Sky Construction, too. Trent is the top contractor for miles around. Their bid may not be the lowest, but I know they'd do the best work. They don't cut corners."

Emily's eyes widened. Big Sky Construction had a great reputation. "I hear good things about them," she said in a noncommittal tone, "but I thought the company was owned by someone named Hawkins."

Sarah nodded. "Hawkins is Trent's last name. We raised my husband's nephew and niece after their parents died in an accident, but Trent and Alaina are our children, the same as the others. We just didn't think it was right to change their surnames when we adopted them."

"I see."

From what Emily had heard of Trent Hawkins, the man was formidable, and his construction company was in demand across a large section of Montana, thanks to the construction yards he'd opened in other communities. Yet in a way, Big Sky's size and popularity was a potential drawback. She'd dealt with large companies and they weren't always attentive to smaller jobs. Still, this wasn't the city, so it might be all right, and there had to be a reason Big Sky was doing so well.

As if realizing she'd pushed hard enough, Sarah gestured around the Emporium. "Everybody loves the changes you've made. Until now we had to go to Billings or Helena for a really special gift."

It was the sort of comment Emily had heard often since buying the large gift shop. Tourists were flocking in, but it was the locals who'd recognized the upgraded stock and weren't shy about complimenting her choices. Their down-home friendliness was refreshing. Between her Rodeo Drive boutique and the people she knew in the fashion industry, she'd spent too much of her life with men and women who knew they were beautiful and subtly lorded it over anyone whose birthright didn't include a gorgeous face and body…and they hadn't always been subtle.

Emily squirmed at the thought. Maybe she'd been the problem; in a way she had always felt like a fraud running a boutique when she wasn't that interested in clothes and makeup. A gift shop specializing in Montana products was a much better fit, though being a city gal, her move to a small town in Montana seemed just short of crazy, even to her. Still, crazy or not, she'd needed the change after ending her engagement to a cheating skunk.

"How do you like Schuyler?" Sarah asked after making her purchase.

It was another query Emily had received numerous times. Folks were friendly and while they couldn't possibly know everyone in town, they seemed aware that she was a newcomer.

"I love it here."

Sarah tucked the credit card receipt into her purse. "I hope you feel that way after dealing with your disastrous house."

"Me, too, but something about it called my name. I couldn't resist."

As the morning wore on, Emily stewed about the home she'd bought. Sarah McGregor's remarks about her son's construction business had made her realize she shouldn't wait any longer to find a company to do the renovations. It could take a while to decide on the right contractor and get them to schedule Wild Rose Cottage, her name for the neglected Arts and Crafts–style house.

After her employees had taken their lunch breaks, Emily returned home, determined to start setting up appointments to get bids on the renovations. Stopping on the front walk, she wondered if she *had* been a little insane to buy it. The place needed a new roof and windows, a full paint job, the front porch replaced…and that was only on the outside. 320 Meadowlark Lane had suffered from over forty years of careless renters.

She'd driven by it often since moving to Schuyler, feeling drawn to the house, then a month ago had spotted a for-sale sign on its weedy lawn. After a quick look inside, she'd purchased it the following day…possibly the second-most-impulsive decision of her life.

Emily didn't admit it to most people, but she often got feelings about places; she felt as if this one had a sad history and deserved a brighter future. Besides, the house had actual wild roses growing up its trellises. How could you beat that?

Inside, she grabbed a phone book and thumbed through to the small contractor's section, then checked online. The sensible way was to get competing bids, compare reputations and decide on the best company to do the job. After she'd made a number of appointments, she sat down with a notebook. To compare the bids they would have to cover the same specific pieces of work, so she began to write down everything she wanted done.

It was a long list.

Over the next few days she interviewed several contractors. Trent Hawkins' representative from Big Sky brought a printed record of recent jobs they'd completed, phone numbers for each client recommendation and copies of letters from satisfied customers. It had seemed like overkill until she'd asked for references from a different company. He'd dragged his feet before finally giving her a few names. Another one promised to email a list, but after five days and two calls, she had stopped hoping it would come.

One bright note had come out of the meetings. The consensus of everyone who'd looked at the house was that it was structurally sound.

Six days after her interviews she had jumbled estimates from two of the contractors. Nothing from Big Sky, though the representative had said it might take up to ten days to ensure it was thorough. Plus, an estimate required final approval from his boss.

It was a good thing she was a patient woman. A fleeting thought of Dennis crossed her mind and she shrugged. Actually, she'd had too much patience in that regard, but at least she'd learned her lesson.

LATE THE FOLLOWING Wednesday morning Trent drove to the construction yard, tired but satisfied. One of his mares had foaled in the middle of the night and he'd stayed with her to be sure everything went well. He didn't consider himself a rancher like the McGregor side of the family, but when the Balderdash Ranch had come up for sale, he'd decided to indulge himself. The Balderdash was small, more of a hobby ranch than anything, but it had enough land for horses and a few head of cattle.

Of course, the house wasn't much, but "home" didn't have much meaning for him. For years he'd lived in a back room at the construction yard. He could get by as long as he had basic bathroom facilities, a microwave and a mattress.

And since the Balderdash was adjacent to his cousin's spread, he could ride for miles without having to stop and speak with anyone. Around Schuyler nobody objected if you rode on their land so long as you closed gates behind you, but he preferred solitude and Jackson's hands knew to leave him alone.

"Alaina told us about the foal. Aren't you handing out cigars?" the yard foreman called as Trent swung out of the truck and started for the office.

"I'll bring two when the next one comes," Trent promised. He walked toward the structure that had replaced the rickety building he'd used when starting the business. The older structure had served his purposes, but a well-built administrative center was good advertising.

When he'd called Alaina to tell her he would be late, she had told him there was a stack of estimates waiting on his desk for final approval, so he started working on them.

Now that Big Sky Contractors had grown to its current size, with five satellite construction yards, he had a full-time employee who met with potential clients throughout their service area and put the proposals together. Kenny was good at his job and it usually didn't take long to approve the estimates. But two thirds of the way through the stack, Trent stopped and stared at one for 320 Meadowlark Lane.

When had old man Webber decided to fix up the place?

Checking the estimate, he saw the owner listed was Emily George rather than Bob Webber. How did that happen? He'd asked his real estate agent to let him know if the house ever came up for sale.

Grabbing his cell phone, he dialed Garth Real Estate and asked for Steve Sheldon.

The agent came on the line. "Steve here."

"Steve, this is Trent Hawkins. When did 320 Meadowlark Lane come up for sale?"

"It did? Let me check and I'll call you back."

Trent drummed his fingers on the desk as he waited. Ten minutes later his phone rang.

"Yes?"

"Sorry, Trent. Webber put the place on the market while I was on vacation and it was purchased less than forty-eight hours later by Emily George, the new owner of the Emporium. Who could have guessed with the state of the place?"

Trent recalled the young woman Aunt Sarah had maneuvered him into meeting.

"I've met her. While there was a mention of her having renovation needs, I didn't realize it was the house on Meadowlark Lane until a few minutes ago."

"I understand Ms. George hails from Los Angeles and is doing well with the old gift shop."

"With a new business it's hard to imagine she has time to deal with the renovations needed at that…uh, house." Trent had almost called it a dump, which was accurate, but since he'd been trying to get the property for years, the description might raise questions.

Steve snorted. "It's a terrible investment except for someone who can do the work personally—it'll cost more than the house is worth. Maybe she'll be willing to sell."

"It's a possibility," Trent agreed. "I'll see if we can work something out."

That was the solution. He'd meet with Emily George and propose a business deal.

After finding her number on the estimate, he punched it into his phone.

"Hello?" Her voice was warm, with a pleasant timbre.

"Ms. George, this is Trent Hawkins of Big Sky Construction. We met at your gift shop a couple of weeks ago. There's a matter having to do with your estimate that needs to be resolved. It would help if we could meet."

"Sure. Anything to move things ahead will be great. It's pretty grim living here under the circumstances."

Her eagerness didn't bode well for his cause. On the other hand, if she was already living in the house, it wasn't surprising she wanted to get things going. But she couldn't possibly realize how costly it would be to do everything listed on the estimate. Surely she'd sell once she saw the bottom line.

"I understand," Trent said. "Where shall we get together?"

"Don't you want to come to the house?"

320 Meadowlark Lane was the last place he wanted to go. But he couldn't tell a stranger something he'd never told anyone else.

"That's fine," he agreed. "What time is good for you?"

"Later this afternoon, or whenever you like tomorrow."

Trent didn't want to wait another day. "How about today at four?"

"Terrific. I'll see you then."

It wasn't terrific. As a rule he no longer met with customers; he'd discovered the business did better if other employees handled contacts that required diplomacy. But the situation was different with his childhood home, and he would do whatever it took to get what he wanted.

EMILY ENDED THE CALL, a little surprised by the conversation with Trent Hawkins. From what she'd seen and heard, he was an odd duck.

Oh, well, she wasn't looking for a friend; she wanted to get her house fixed. But it was strange that the head of such a large company wanted to meet personally.

The representative from Big Sky had been extremely thorough and hadn't anticipated any problems. Emily had contacted a number of their references and they were all quite satisfied. The conversations had taken a while, since a lot of them wanted to chat—something she'd learned was typical of people in Schuyler. Most said they'd never dealt directly with the owner of Big Sky. A few knew Trent Hawkins through community contacts or his family, but their vague comments gave her the impression of caution, as though they considered him a slightly dangerous enigma.

One retired schoolteacher had mentioned that she'd taught most of the Hawkins and McGregor kids in her classroom, but had never understood Trent.

"At first glance he reminded me of his father," she'd said. "But Gavin was such a bright, charming man. Trent isn't as…cheerful. Of course, losing his parents that way has to affect a child. It's probably no surprise that he was socially awkward."

Emily had found the comment irrelevant. Trent Hawkins's charm, or lack of it, wasn't important.

It was his company's skill and honesty that she cared about. Nonetheless, the opinions expressed by other Big Sky clients certainly jived with her own brief impressions of him.

The doorbell gasped out a disgruntled squawk at precisely four o'clock and Emily realized that was one repair that had failed to make her list of improvements.

She opened the door and though she'd already met Trent Hawkins, almost gasped herself. While she wasn't short, he seemed to tower over her in the doorway.

"Hello, Ms. George," he said politely.

"Uh, call me Emily," she returned, taking an involuntary step backward. "I'm from Southern California. We're informal there."

He hesitated a moment before nodding. "Emily, then. Call me Trent."

She led him into the living room where she'd set up a card table and folding chairs. That, along with the air mattress in the back ground-floor bedroom, made up her current furniture. She'd bought them in Schuyler since most of her belongings were staying in California until she was completely settled.

Trent barely glanced at anything.

"Is there a part of the house you need to look at?" she asked, his silence making her nervous.

"No." He seated himself and she sat across from him. Pulling a sheaf of papers from a folder he pushed it toward her. "You can see from the estimate that any renovations will be extremely expensive. Some might even say prohibitively expensive. So I have a proposal. I'd like to buy the house. I'll pay ten percent over your sales price and reimburse your moving and closing costs on a new property. There are some nice homes on the west end of town you should consider purchasing."

Surprise shot through Emily. "Do you do this often?" she asked. "I mean, try to buy a house instead of contracting to fix it up?"

"Generally, no."

She leaned forward. "I don't understand. If you were interested in Wild Rose Cottage, why didn't you make an offer when it was for sale?"

"Wild Rose Cottage?" Trent repeated, staring at her as if she was batty.

It wasn't a new experience to Emily, but this time it bothered her more than usual. Maybe it was the other, less defined emotions in his eyes that were getting to her. It was almost as if he'd been reminded of something both pleasant and deeply disturbing. On the other hand, he was hardly a touchy-feely sort of guy, so she might be projecting her own reactions onto him—she'd always had an active imagination.

"That's my name for the house," she said, lifting her chin. "There are wild roses growing everywhere. Someone must have loved them. There are even wild roses etched on the glass in the front door. Anyway, supposedly I was the only interested buyer."

"I didn't have time to learn it was for sale. The property was on the market for less than forty-eight hours," he returned sharply, and this time his mood was unmistakable—pure annoyance.

Emily restrained a tart remark. She had no intention of letting Trent Hawkins guilt her into selling Wild Rose Cottage. It wasn't her fault that he hadn't known it was for sale, and considering the state of the place, she could hardly have expected someone else to be interested.

"So what do you want with it?" she asked.

"That's my concern," he answered in clipped tones.

Her eyebrows shot up at the bald response. Then all at once he took a deep breath and smiled, except his smile looked more like a dog lifting its lip to snarl.

"I beg your pardon," he continued, "that was rude. It's simply that my reasons are personal and I'd rather not discuss them."

While his explanation had begun in a more genial voice, it ended in the same tight tone as before. Oddly, Emily didn't think he realized how he sounded.

The intensity of his gaze bothered her, so she dropped her attention to the proposal and started going through it, page by page. It was thorough and organized. The prices were higher than the other estimates she'd received, though not ridiculously so. She'd had more costly work done on her home in California.

"Are you saying that you aren't interested in renovating Wild Rose Cottage if it belongs to me?" she asked finally.

"You can see how expensive it will be."

"I'm not an idiot. I expected it to run high."

Trent shook his head gravely. "Housing values in Schuyler will never escalate enough to make it a feasible investment, not if you have to pay a contractor to do it."

Plainly he was suggesting that fixing up the house made sense for him, and not for her, since he wouldn't have to pay himself for the work. But she couldn't shake the conviction that he had another agenda altogether.

"I'm not interested in selling," Emily said, her obstinate nature kicking into high gear. "I like this house and want to fix it the way it should be fixed."

His jaw went tight and hard. "It isn't worth the investment," he repeated.

"This isn't an investment, it's a home. For me. And I don't want to live on the west end of town. I enjoy being able to walk to my store in a few minutes and still feel as if I'm living in a nice neighborhood."

He seemed to be breathing very carefully, perhaps controlling a deeper reaction. Anger? Exasperation? Hope? What was it about this particular house that interested him?

Since moving to Schuyler she'd heard a fair amount of gossip about the McGregors. They had piles of old money, some coming from Texas and Oklahoma oil. On top of that, Trent Hawkins was the most successful contractor in the area. He'd been in business for over fifteen years and had gone from a small operation in Schuyler to having numerous branch offices. 320 Meadowlark Lane could only be a blip on his radar.

Emily squared her shoulders. "Are you interested in the job or not?"

He paused a long moment before answering. "Yes."

"In that case, I'll let you know tomorrow whether I've chosen your company to do the work," she informed him coolly. "Is there anything else you need for your estimate?"

"No, that's complete."

She conducted him to the door and shut it behind him with relief. Trent Hawkins might be near perfection in the appearance department—the perfect image of a rugged Western male—but he was also rude and pushy. She wasn't sure she liked him, and was definitely sure he made her nervous.

Before he'd come, she had made up her mind that if the estimate was reasonable, she'd go with Big Sky because of their reputation. They really were the best. But now she needed to think it through again. It gave her a peculiar sensation to know Trent wanted the house for reasons he refused to explain.

But surely he would do a good job, regardless. Or rather, his employees would. It was just as well, because she'd rather not deal with the owner of the company in person again.

TRENT'S JAW ACHED with retraining his frustration as he drove back to Big Sky. He'd been certain Emily would sell the house to him. What kind of idiot hung on to a wreck when offered a profit after only six weeks of ownership?

It didn't make sense.

By all accounts she was a successful businesswoman, and he'd offered her a sweetheart deal. She should have snapped it up, no questions asked.

Trent let out an impatient breath and tried to sort out his impressions of Emily George. Medium brown hair, and he thought her eyes were brown, as well. She was around thirty and attractive, albeit somewhat nondescript, with loose clothes that concealed her figure. A huge point in her favor was that she hadn't come off as a single woman on the prowl.

She was stubborn, though. It was obvious from the way she'd reacted when urged to sell the house to him. He should have just told her that he'd lived there as a kid. She probably would have assumed he had a sentimental reason for wanting the place;

she seemed the type to sympathize with that sort of thing.

On the other hand, she might have raised unholy Cain later, when she saw what he really wanted to do with the property. Besides, he wasn't good at subterfuge.

His thoughts continuing to churn, Trent walked into the office and saw his sister.

"Hey, what are you still doing here?" he asked, trying to sound normal.

"I'm taking care of some things for the Firefighters Auxiliary. You said it was all right to use the photocopier and office supplies."

Trent shrugged. "Sure, just don't ask me to get involved with that silly bachelor auction they hold every year."

"It's for a good cause."

"No, thanks. I'll make my usual donation and leave it at that."

Alaina looked wistful. "You'd make such a wonderful bachelor for the fund-raiser."

For some reason Trent thought of their new client and how poorly he'd handled his meeting with her. Granted, by a purely business standard she ought to have accepted his offer, but he hadn't been at his best. The loud screech of the doorbell alone had evoked a flood of sensations, none of them positive. And it had been worse after he'd walked into the living room. Strange, how clearly the memories had come back. And he hadn't been there since he was ten.

"You're forgetting my terrible social skills," Trent told his sister.

"Then it's a good thing you have me to run your office," Alaina told him brightly. "I'm great with people."

"True."

Alaina was another puzzle Trent hadn't figured out. Why had she come back to Montana? After graduating with honors from Stanford with an MBA, she'd been recruited by a large New York firm and had risen rapidly in its ranks. Then a year ago, when his old office manager had announced she was retiring soon, Alaina had begged Trent for the job, saying she was homesick. He wasn't sure he'd gotten the whole story.

Nevertheless, she *was* terrific with people. She had all the social skills he lacked, though he worried that she let herself be too vulnerable and it was hard not being overprotective. Still, she had to make her own decisions, which Trent hoped would be better than those their mother had made. Why *had* she stayed with such a lousy husband?

Trent's mouth tightened. He'd wanted to protect his mom as well, and childhood conditioning was hard to escape. He still felt the old instinct, the urge to rush in and save people, but he'd discovered that some women were willing to use those instincts to their advantage. It hadn't taken long before he'd got tired of the games.

His sister looked at the clock and began gathering her belongings. "Much as I'd love to stay and convince you to get involved with a worthy cause, I have a meeting to attend. See you tomorrow."

"Be safe."

Dropping into his office chair, Trent pulled out the 320 Meadowlark Lane estimate. A lot of work was needed on the place and other things would undoubtedly crop up along the way. All of Big Sky's estimates included a warning to that effect, and advised clients there was often a 20 percent, or higher, overage. His estimate consultant tried hard to check everything ahead of time—even doing a quick termite inspection—but something always got uncovered in such a large renovation.

Uncovered.

Damn.

Emily wanted walls removed. Depending upon which walls and how curious people were about what they might find, a lot of questions could be asked.

Trent rubbed his temples. It had been years since he'd taken the lead on a construction job. He checked on crews and sometimes lent a hand for a day or two, yet being the company's owner gave him less and less time for work at a basic level. But he would take the lead on 320 Meadowlark Lane. That is, if Emily chose his company to do the renovation.

A cold sensation went through Trent and he had a sudden impulse to reduce the estimate, anything to convince her to sign a contract with Big Sky Construction. But it would seem suspicious after his offer to buy the place, so he'd have to wait and hope.

CHAPTER TWO

AFTER SLEEPING ON the subject and looking around the house in the early-morning light, Emily was almost ready to tell Trent Hawkins that he could have it after all. Then she saw an early rose blossom dangling over one of the living room windows and decided nothing had changed. Besides, with both of her businesses doing well, she could afford the indulgence.

At 8:00 a.m. she phoned Big Sky and the office manager promised to have the contract ready by the end of the day.

When Emily arrived at Big Sky Construction the following morning, she found the office building to the right of the gate. It didn't surprise her to see that it was built to last, but the nicely maintained flowerbeds were unexpected—Trent Hawkins seemed a no-frills kind of guy.

The door opened as she walked toward it.

The woman holding it ajar smiled at her. "Hello."

"Hi, I'm Emily George. I'm here about the contract on my house."

"Nice to meet you. I'm Alaina Hawkins, Big Sky's office manager."

Trent's sister. He and Alaina shared the same dark hair and green eyes, except Alaina projected far more warmth than her brother.

Alaina took a sealed envelope from her desk and handed it to Emily. "Go ahead and take this home to read and digest. There are two copies. When you're ready, sign each of them and initial the pages. I'll make copies of both for your records after Trent signs." The office manager grinned. "We're kind of redundant at Big Sky."

"I'll read it here if you don't mind," Emily replied. "I'm really anxious to get this going. Until the house is done, I'm only camping out. A little of that is okay, but…"

"It wears thin before long?" Alaina finished.

"You bet."

"You're welcome to read the paperwork here, but Trent has to approve any changes."

Sitting in the comfortable chair next to a small table, probably used for customer consults, Emily started reading the contract. She took a pad from her purse and jotted notes for reference. A few minutes later Alaina set a tray on the table; it held a steaming cup, with cream and sugar on the side.

"I thought you could use some coffee," she said.

"Decaf?" Emily asked.

"Sorry, no."

"Good, because while reading the most boring literature in the world, I need my potions fully leaded."

Alaina laughed and went back to her desk.

Emily stirred a generous amount of cream and sugar into her cup. The coffee surprised her with its quality—she'd halfway expected sludge.

With a sigh she continued reading the legal-sounding language, though it wasn't as complicated as some of the contracts she'd signed in Southern California. It was straightforward, providing protection for Big Sky and some for her, as well. That impressed her. She'd fought for similar protections in the past and had been prepared to do the same in Schuyler. But it wasn't necessary. Everything her lawyer had said she needed was set out clearly.

One other thing surprised her. Trent had already signed the paperwork.

After two hours and three cups of coffee, Emily put her signature on the final page of each contract and carefully initialed the others.

"You can make the copies now," she said, handing the sheaf of paper across the desk, along with a deposit check. "Trent already signed."

The office manager's eyes opened in obvious surprise. "Wow, that's a first, but I guess he knows you're anxious to get started."

Alaina made copies and put them into a manila envelope, along with one of the originals.

Emily's toes tingled. Before long she was actually going to see Wild Rose Cottage turning back into a home.

"Thanks for the coffee," she said.

"My pleasure."

As Emily opened the door of her car outside, a voice startled her.

"Good morning, Ms. George."

She wheeled and saw Trent Hawkins gazing at her with a sharp, inscrutable expression.

"It's Emily," she reminded him, no longer sure she favored informality. For the first time she was realizing that polite titles could maintain a desired distance. Come to think of it, perhaps the infuriating, self-anointed mavens of society she'd encountered at her boutique would have had more respect if they'd had to say "Ms. George."

"Is something wrong?" Trent asked.

"Excuse me?"

"I asked a question, but you didn't seem to hear me."

Drat, her mind had gone merrily wandering again.

"I'm sorry," she apologized. "My brain occasionally travels south when it's supposed to be headed north. Of all things, I was considering the merit of polite society."

"I see."

"What were you were saying?" she asked, wondering if it was her imagination that he was so tense. He practically radiated the focus of a cat on the prowl.

"I asked when you expect to return the contracts."

She waved the envelope Alaina had given her.

"Actually, I stayed and read them, signed on the dotted line, got my copies and am heading home to assure Wild Rose Cottage that its neglected days are over."

His eyebrows lifted a half inch, then his face smoothed. "In that case, the crew will begin work on Monday, Ms.— Emily."

"That soon?" Her toes fairly danced in excitement.

"You seemed anxious. Is 7:00 a.m. too early?"

"Nope. The house and I will be ready and waiting for your guys to start."

Emily slid into her car and he politely closed the door for her. She breathed a sigh of relief as she fastened her seat belt. Trent Hawkins may or may not have been suffering from tension, but her entire body had tightened as soon as she'd heard his voice. It would have given her second thoughts about having Big Sky do the renovations, but it was silly to regret the decision, especially so soon after making it. Anyway, it was probably the last time she'd see him.

With a business the size of Big Sky, Trent Hawkins would be too busy to think about a single house under contract, much less its not-so-memorable owner. Emily knew from experience that guys as gorgeous as Trent Hawkins automatically dismissed ordinary women. And if she'd ever cherished illusions about fairy-tale possibilities, her former fiancé had drummed the fantasy out of her.

Oh, well.

Emily shrugged as she drove toward the grocery store. She'd concentrate on the good feelings she had about her new house. It was as if Wild Rose Cottage had whispered in her ear and begged for a second chance. And its chance was coming even earlier than she'd expected.

That was something to celebrate.

TRENT WATCHED EMILY'S car disappear down the road and suppressed the adrenaline surging through his veins. He wouldn't get to bulldoze 320 Meadowlark Lane into toothpicks, but at least had a chance to salvage the situation.

Turning, he strode toward the office.

"Hey, Trent," Alaina greeted him as he came through the door. "Did you intend to sign that contract with Emily George before she saw it?"

"Er...yeah."

"Okay. She didn't ask for any changes, so it'll save time. You never said somebody asked for an estimate on our old house."

He hadn't considered the chance Alaina would figure it out.

"You remember the address?" he asked.

"No, but Mom has mentioned Meadowlark Lane, so I checked and it's the same one. I can't recall anything about the place." She bit her lip. "I wish I could remember something about our parents... I mean, our first mom and dad."

"You were pretty small when they died. What... three and a half?"

Personally, Trent was relieved Alaina didn't remember anything about them. He had few pleasant memories himself, though life with their biological father had taught him valuable lessons—mostly that people couldn't hurt you if you didn't let them get close enough to do it. Long before he turned ten, he'd known that he had to protect himself.

"You've got good memories from the rest of your childhood, right?" he asked.

"Sure, but sometimes I think I can remember the early stuff, though it's hard to sort out what's a real memory and what's just something I've been told." Her face was pensive. "Tell me a story from back then."

Trent hated disappointing her, but he couldn't manufacture a nostalgic tale when there weren't any.

"There isn't much to tell. I prefer the present. Who do you have on the crew schedule for next week so we can start on Emily George's job?"

"You're starting so soon?" she asked, clearly surprised. "I mean, there's a four-week leeway in the contract and I thought some other jobs would go first."

"The client is living under difficult circumstances until the work is completed, so I've decided to put her contract as a priority. And since the house is such a wreck, it gives us an extra month in case we run into complications."

"That makes sense. I'll have to see who's available as foreman."

"No need," Trent cut in swiftly. "We're unusually tight right now, so I'm taking the lead."

Her head cocked in puzzlement. "You haven't done that in years."

Trent managed to chuckle. "I never planned to be more of a businessman than a contractor. To be honest, I'm itching to get my hands on a hammer again—I don't want my skills to get rusty."

"Okay. It will make scheduling easier. I'll get a crew together. And I'm sure Emily will be thrilled you're starting quickly. She seemed nice."

"I suppose," Trent muttered, sorting through a stack of letters Alaina had laid out for him. He made notes on several and gave them back to her before heading out again. Generally he tried to visit the various sites his company worked on at least once, so he had plenty to do before he could concentrate on Meadowlark Lane.

ALAINA WATCHED HER brother leave, both puzzled and sad. It always seemed as if there was an invisible barrier between them, and she knew the rest of the family felt the same way. She couldn't blame them for being concerned—he was even more reserved with the rest of the McGregors than he was with her. And despite her hopes, working together hadn't changed anything.

She filed the contract on 320 Meadowlark Lane, along with a pile of other papers. Until a week ago she'd had a secretarial assistant, but Tamara had come down with the intestinal bug going around… or at least that's what Tam had *thought*. It turned out that after giving up hope of ever getting pregnant, Tamara and her husband were finally going to have a baby. But it was a high-risk pregnancy and the doctor had put her on bed rest.

Alaina was happy for Tamara, but couldn't keep a thread of melancholy from going through her. When would she have her own happy ending?

She pressed her lips together and determinedly focused on the filing. The stomach flu making the rounds was nasty. It could take close to a week to stop feeling washed-out and rubbery—she knew from experience. They would have a challenging couple of months if it spread among the construction workers.

Studying her charting schedule and Emily George's estimate, she began making notes. It was best to keep the same guys on a job, because it saved time and made the finished product more consistent. Fortunately, their usual summer employees were starting to become available.

A smile curved Alain's lips. The school year had ended on Friday, which meant Mike Carlisle might be interested in a job. Picking up the phone, she dialed his number.

"Hello," he answered.

"Hey, it's Alaina," she said.

"Yeah, what's up?" he asked with his usual lack of charm. No, not usual; it was only usual since the accident that had ended his major-league baseball career.

"Are you free to join a construction crew next week?"

"I suppose, but I might have to work a half day to clean out my classroom."

"Did you have a good year?" she asked.

"Same as always, I guess. There's nothing new or exciting about teaching."

That annoyed her. Teaching was a wonderful career. Kids were important and a teacher could make a huge difference in their lives. So what if a teacher didn't get cheered the way Mike "Lightning" Carlisle had been cheered by his fans?

"How did your students do this year?" she asked, trying to be tactful.

"They passed their finals, so presumably they did all right. Where do you need me next week?"

With a silent sigh, Alaina gave him the address and reminded him to pick up a time card.

Resisting the urge to slam the receiver down, she sat back in her chair and decided to sulk for an entire five minutes. She only allowed herself one sulk-fest a day, being a woman who preferred action over just sitting.

Drat Mike, anyway.

As if she cared that he had a limp and never became known as the fastest base runner in major-league history. She'd been wild about him ever since she was a flat-chested, awkward kid and he was the star player on the school baseball team. The future looked bright for Mike—first he'd scored an athletic scholarship, followed by a major team recruiting him when he graduated from college.

Mike had really been going places. He was traded to another team for his contract two years later and adoring fans had called him Lightning Carlisle, the same nickname he'd earned in Schuyler. Then came that awful day when he'd dived into the stands to catch a fly ball...and never played again. After three knee operations he still limped, but the worst part was seeing how much he'd changed in other ways—he rarely smiled any longer and was as much a loner as Trent.

Alaina tossed her pencil onto the desk. She might as well admit that Mike was acting like a grizzly bear with a mountain-size chip on its shoulder. But that hadn't kept her from moving back to Montana, hoping he might finally notice her... and feeling utterly stupid for doing something so ridiculous.

And, so far, zilch.

Damn it.

Of course, she could always return to New York. She was still doing freelance work for her company and they kept saying they wanted her back full-time. But she wasn't going to give up on Mike. There had to be a way to crack his shell.

She looked through the estimate again on Emily's house and dialed her cell number.

"Hi, Emily, it's Alaina Hawkins at Big Sky Construction."

"Don't tell me, you aren't coming on Monday after all." Emily's dismay was apparent, even over the phone.

"Not at all, you're still scheduled," Alaina said hastily. "How did you know a crew was coming?"

"I ran into Trent on my way out."

"Oh. Well, I'm still figuring out who will be assigned to work on your house, but in the meantime I wanted you to know a chemical toilet will be delivered for the crew."

"Ick. There's a small half bath off the kitchen that they could use instead."

"Okay, but I'll tell them to clean it every day and provide their own soap and stuff. Personally, I wouldn't touch a toilet used by construction workers—their aim is terrible. I make the guys working in the construction yard use one in a separate building."

Emily laughed. "I'll let you know if it gets too bad. Anything else?"

Alaina checked the notes she'd made when writing up the contract. "I'm also ordering a large Dumpster. Is there space in the yard where it can go?"

"There's room in the front or on the driveway. It's wide and I can always park somewhere else if necessary."

They finished their call and Alaina went back to thinking about ways to catch Mike's attention. You'd think in such a small town they'd run into each other more. Nevertheless, she was determined to come up with a workable plan, which shouldn't be impossible for a woman who'd earned an MBA.

But she had an idea. Mike would be a great addition to the annual auction for a "dinner with a bachelor or bachelorette."

She planned on making sure she was the committee member who approached him…and still needed to figure out the right way to ask. Everyone knew where he lived and it shouldn't be difficult to come up with excuses to visit the Meadowlark Lane job site, either. He couldn't duck her that easily at work, and any contact with him would be better than nothing. Besides, she *wanted* to visit the house and see if it jogged any memories.

Pleased with her new plan, Alaina grabbed her pencil again and returned to the scheduling chart.

Okay, she'd put Mike on the crew, along with Eduardo, Vince and Caveman…she erased *Caveman* and wrote *Chuck*. Chuck *was* a caveman, but her brother didn't think it looked professional to have nicknames on the official schedule. With those guys and Trent, they'd be able to handle the range of work required. Emily needed everything from a new roof to all-new plumbing, along with a restoration specialist to help preserve the historic character of the classic Arts and Crafts–style architecture.

Oh.

Alaina blinked. Perhaps that was why Trent had decided to be the foreman…he was an expert at restoration. But it was still strange that he was moving so fast on the job. As for taking the lead? He'd made it sound as if he did nothing except push paper. Hardly. Maybe he didn't wield tools all day, every day, but did go out and work alongside everyone else when needed.

With any other guy, Alaina might have thought he wanted to impress the client, but Emily wasn't Trent's type—he went for flashy women who were okay with short-term affairs, the same as her brother Josh. Her other brother, Jackson, had been the same…until he'd met an old flame from high school and got knocked on his ass. Kayla had been good for Jackson, but Alaina didn't expect Josh or Trent to change—lightning didn't strike that often.

Perhaps Trent was handing the job this way simply because it was their childhood home and he wanted to be there to fix it up. Well…it would be nice to think so, but that didn't sound like him, either.

EMILY BOUGHT GROCERIES, then couldn't resist stopping at the hardware store to look at paint samples. She had always loved the paint department at home improvement centers…the rows and rows of swatches ranging from light to dark. You could practically get drunk on all the color. And she could pick anything she wanted. One of the hard parts of selecting stock for her boutique was restricting her choices to the "fashionable" colors for that season.

"Shopping for paint again?" asked a pleasant voice.

Turning, Emily saw the woman who'd helped her on several prior occasions. The clerk had been knowledgeable and patient…the way someone was patient with an impulsive child. Emily was used to that. Most people thought she was quirky and "New Age-ish," though she wasn't sure that Schuyler was in tune to New Age culture. That was fine; she disliked labels.

"Is there something I can do for you?" the clerk prompted.

Emily jumped. Cripes, she'd let her mind wander into never-never land again.

"Sorry," she apologized. "I'm really excited today."

"Let me guess…you decided to paint the Emporium a different color than the one you finally selected."

Emily made a face. Picking the right color for

the interior of the gift shop had taken a while. She'd gotten the paint tinted, only to change her mind. So she'd bought more paint. But her final choice had turned out great, so it was worth it, and she'd donated her original purchase to a local church, so that had worked out equally as well.

"Nope," she said, "but I'm starting all over again, this time for my new house."

"Congratulations."

Beaming, Emily turned back to the paint samples. "It's like being at Disneyland," she said. "All the colors and possibilities are spread out in front of me. The renovations haven't even started, so it's a long way from getting painted, but I thought I'd get sample strips."

After picking out a huge selection of color samples, Emily headed home to start thumbtacking them to the walls.

"Don't worry," she assured the house, "better days are coming."

ON MONDAY MORNING Emily couldn't believe that she'd overslept when she woke up at 6:30 a.m. Of course, she'd been working at her computer until after 3:00 a.m., so that probably explained it. The Big Sky crew was arriving soon, so she bounced out of bed and dressed fast. The doorbell squawked and she ran barefoot to open the door.

Trent Hawkins stood on the porch.

"Uh, hi," she said. "Is something wrong? Oh,

don't tell me your crew can't start today. I mean, I know you have four extra weeks, but…well, if you can't, you can't. When—"

He held a hand up and Emily stopped talking. She knew she was babbling, but it had been a huge shock to see him.

"We're still starting today and the rest of the crew will be here shortly," Trent told her.

"The rest of the crew?" she repeated, foggy from her short night of sleep.

"I can't do it all myself."

"But I didn't think you'd be working here." Emily stopped, realizing how dismayed she'd sounded. "I mean, you own the company and must have other things to do."

If Trent had recognized how she felt, nothing showed on his face. "This is the busy season for construction companies, so I'm taking the lead on this job. But don't be concerned. I'm fully qualified."

"It isn't that."

Emily didn't doubt his qualifications—she just didn't want him around. So far he'd acted rude and pushy. Of course, she shouldn't assume rude and pushy was his true personality…he might be chauvinistic, bad-tempered and obstinate, as well. While Schuyler obviously respected Trent as a contractor, nobody seemed comfortable with him.

Still, the renovations might get done faster if he was the foreman, and his employees would be on their toes under the boss's gaze, so it could work out for the best.

With that conclusion, she stood aside to let him come in.

"Which area do you want tackled first?" he asked.

"Um…the kitchen is hideous. I barely go in there because the floor is sagging so badly. But I don't know if I'll be doing much cooking anyway, not with dust and stuff flying around. So start wherever you think works best."

He nodded briskly. "We'll hang plastic sheeting to help contain dust, but it will still be a problem. You might want to find another place to live while the work is being completed—or at least during the initial stages while we're tearing stuff out."

Emily shook her head. "Not a chance. The room I'm using as a bedroom is at the back and has a bath connected, so if I keep the door closed, it shouldn't be too bad in there. After everything else is finished, I'll move, and leave that room and bath free for the work *it* needs."

"If you say so."

She had a strange feeling he was disappointed and she told herself not to take it personally; he was just thinking about making things easier for his crew. Anyway, it was her fish to fry if she wanted to stay.

The doorbell squawked again and soon four more men stood inside her living room.

"This is Eduardo, Vince, Mike and Cav… Chuck," Trent told her.

"Great to meet you."

She watched as Trent efficiently assigned tasks.

Eduardo was a silver-haired man with a jolly expression. Trent sent him to examine plumbing issues. Vince was tall and skinny, with long fingers that carefully began removing the older light fixtures she hoped to preserve. Mike looked vaguely familiar, so she might have already seen him around town. He walked with a limp, but seemed quite strong as he went through the kitchen's swinging door to start removing the ancient painted plywood cabinets.

The last one, Chuck, had a round, solid build. Before he went to check the basement—a dismal space that had never been finished—he nodded to her and said, "Pleased to meet you, ma'am. Everybody calls me Caveman."

Caveman?

Emily tried not to laugh. He looked like a caveman with his bushy hair and beard, but she suspected he'd earned the moniker for reasons that went beyond his appearance.

Trent consulted a diagram on his clipboard and began tapping on the downstairs wall that Emily wanted removed. "There's no need for you to be here," he told her over his shoulder. "Why don't you go out to breakfast or head to your store?"

She hesitated. "Maybe later."

Despite the early hour, she could always find something to keep her busy at the Emporium. Breakfast also sounded appealing and there was a café near her shop. The dust and noise would be unpleasant while the construction crew was working, so it really didn't make sense to stay. But Trent's presence made her uncomfortable. While she knew construction companies were busiest in summer, she didn't think that was the sole explanation for him being at Wild Rose Cottage.

Trent Hawkins had another motive.

AS TRENT CHECKED the wall, his gaze flicked over the spots he had patched as a kid. The house had been a war zone when he'd lived there. His dad would walk in the front door, drunk, and before long he'd start punching—furniture, walls, his family, it hadn't made much difference to Gavin Hawkins. He'd been known for his charm all over Schuyler, but he'd never brought it home with him.

His mother had been afraid that people would guess, and that the landlord would throw fits at the damage, so Trent had learned to repair whatever got broken.

It turned out that holes could disappear faster than bruises. His first patching jobs had been rough, but he'd quickly become skilled at covering up the evidence of his family's rotten little secret.

Now it was years later and a number of walls were scheduled to come down, along with all the crap he'd stuffed inside of them. But he wasn't going to start while Emily was watching, so he went into the kitchen to help remove cabinets. They couldn't be salvaged, having being poorly made and abused for decades.

Normally Trent deplored not being able to recycle, yet there would be a curious satisfaction in ripping them down and sledgehammering them into pieces.

He just wished his memories could be disposed of so efficiently.

CHAPTER THREE

MIDMORNING THE SQUEAL of brakes signaled a large truck had stopped outside the house. Trent went to look through the front windows and nodded with approval. Alaina had arranged for a large Dumpster to be delivered and it had arrived on schedule. He stepped out and gestured to the spot in front of the house where he wanted the container.

Emily had dashed outside as well and stood watching as the large metal box was put in place. She winced as a lilac bush was crushed.

"Sorry about that, ma'am," the truck driver said when he came around to check the container's placement.

She sighed. "I guess there wasn't any other good place for it."

"No, ma'am."

"Let's shift it out a little and the bush might come back," urged the second employee, who gave Emily a broad, appraising smile. Trent had seen Billy come on to women often enough to recognize his typical moves.

Annoyed both by the delay and Billy's propensity to waste time flirting, Trent waited while the two city employees shifted the container. It seemed unlikely the mangled bush would survive, but Emily appeared to appreciate the gesture. Then he opened the end of the Dumpster and lowered the wall, hinged at the base, to the ground. This way, much of the debris could be walked in and stacked.

Trent took the clipboard the truck driver offered and signed for the unit. Big Sky owned a number of roll-away containers for use at commercial building sites, but Schuyler required city-owned Dumpsters to be used in residential areas.

Billy was still courting Emily's attention. "Say, are you new in town?" he asked.

"About four months," Emily told him.

"Don't know how I missed such a pretty newcomer."

"That's nice of you to say."

Her tone was neutral and Trent couldn't tell if she was buying Billy's line.

"By the way, I'm Big Bill Halloran." He winked at her in a way that suggested the "Big" referred to more than his height. "How about letting me buy you a drink tonight as a welcome to Schuyler?"

"Thanks, but I'm pretty busy right now."

"Another evening?" he pressed.

"We'll see."

The driver cleared his throat noisily, so Billy tipped his cowboy hat, climbed into the cab and the truck drove away.

"In case you haven't guessed it already," Trent

said, stepping closer to Emily, "Billy chases after everything and anything female."

He regretted the warning as soon as the words left his mouth. At times, his protective instincts jumped forward, despite his intentions to keep them contained. But Billy had caused a lot of damage in Schuyler and it didn't seem fair not to warn a newcomer.

"Forewarned is forearmed?" Emily asked, still in neutral tones.

"That always seems best."

"Sure." She turned and headed for the house. Idly he noted that she was wearing a comfortable T-shirt paired with a light full skirt, similar to what she'd worn the other times he'd seen her. It stood out in a town where both men and women tended to don jeans.

Trent glanced at the roof. At appropriate intervals he could send the whole crew up there to work, giving him privacy for what he needed to do inside the house. Granted, it wasn't likely that anyone would even look at most of the things inside those walls—they'd just shovel them into the Dumpster. But what if they *did*, or what if Ms. George got curious?

And then there was his father's old handgun… If someone found that, there'd be questions and possible revelations that could upset a whole bunch of lives. He should have turned the gun into the police when he was a boy, but he'd wanted to protect his family. If he'd had more time to think about it, he might have changed his mind. But Gavin Hawkins had died and nobody could send him to prison posthumously.

Maybe it wouldn't be an issue, though. The estimate showed question marks on two walls—including the one where Trent had hidden the handgun—with the annotation that the client was undecided about which to remove, so there was a chance it would be okay.

On the other hand, if he could pull the wall down and retrieve the gun, he'd never have to think about it again.

BILLY CHASES AFTER *everything and anything female.*

Emily tried not to be offended by Trent Hawkins's blunt statement.

After all, he'd tried to be helpful by warning her about a local good-time boy. But she also couldn't miss the fact that he'd seen no particular reason why Billy would chase her—she was classed with anything and everything female. Nobody would say that kind of thing to her sister, Nicole, or question why a guy would want *her.*

She stopped and looked at herself in the dusty wall of gold-splotched mirror tiles someone had once decided were a good idea for the dining room wall. Medium brown hair, medium brown eyes, medium height, medium everything… She wasn't ugly, but she also wasn't a woman Billy would kick himself for missing. Average was the best description, which should be okay, except that she'd grown up in a world where anything except drop-dead gorgeous was inadequate.

At least she has brains, her mother had sighed to her friends, often when her eldest daughter was within earshot. Paula George embraced the school of thought that it was best to be honest with your children about their limitations, so they wouldn't develop unrealistic expectations. Personally, Emily thought her mother was just secretly embarrassed to have one stunning daughter and one who wasn't, and wanted to acknowledge the contrast before anyone else.

Nicole *was* dazzling. Not that it had given Emily an inferiority complex...or at least not much of one. She was smart and by no means bad looking, but she'd learned that most people preferred the glamorous beauty her sister possessed...including her former fiancé. On the other hand, there were plenty of guys who'd said they liked the person she was, so she should be grateful for small favors.

Emily impatiently pushed the thought away and considered what to do with her morning. Originally she'd expected to leave the Big Sky crew to work on the house while she went to her store, but now she was rethinking her plan. Having Trent Hawkins on the crew made her wonder if she ought to keep an eye on things. It wasn't that she believed Trent or his men would pocket stuff, but after he'd tried so hard to buy the house, it was strange that he'd suddenly decided to be there every day.

Of course, she would have to leave part of the time. There was no way she could stay in the house for the weeks it would take to finish everything. She'd go stark-raving stir-crazy if she tried, but construction workers started early—she could do stuff for the Emporium in the late afternoon and evenings, and work there on the weekends.

"Emily?" Trent said from behind her. "Can we do a walk-through?"

"Sure."

Accompanied by periodic crashing sounds from the kitchen, she followed him into each room and described her ideas of what she wanted done. Upstairs, she hesitated.

"I think there should be a master bedroom suite up here," she explained, "only I haven't decided which two rooms should be combined into one. Your guy who did the estimate said it wouldn't affect the cost, so I could take time to decide."

She showed him the two sets of rooms she'd considered converting into a master suite. The ones in the back had a view of rolling, tree-studded countryside, but she got a weird feeling in that part of the house and the sensation intensified as she noticed the hard-faced way Trent studied the space. It didn't help when an especially loud crash came from downstairs, making her jump. He didn't seem to notice, so presumably there was nothing to worry about, though it had sounded as if half the building had collapsed.

"Are you leaning one way or the other?" he asked in a tight voice.

"No… I've even considered doing both since it would still leave three bedrooms on the second floor. I know that would have to be another contract," she added hastily, "or an addendum to the first."

His nod was short. "Yes."

The last part of the house was the attic. The latch always jammed and Emily was about to explain, when Trent pulled down and then to the left, and the knob turned easily. How odd. But he was probably used to old fixtures.

"I thought this would make a terrific craft or sitting room," Emily explained. "Or a play area for kids."

"You're planning a family?" he asked, his eyebrow arching.

"Not at the moment. Right now I expect to use it as an office. Attics are usually too dark to be living space, but this one is huge and has lots of windows, so someone must have hoped to finish it someday."

Trent glanced around. "I take it the former owner didn't bother to clear anything out of here."

"Nope, but I've always thought it would be fun to poke around an attic filled with years of forgotten stuff."

"You won't feel that way for long. I'm sure it's all worthless junk."

Emily made a face at the back of his head. Trent Hawkins was obviously a pessimist, while she preferred looking at the bright side of things.

The tour over, they descended to the bottom level.

"Thank you," Trent told her formally. "Since I'm foreman for the crew doing the reconstruction, it helps to have an overview."

He disappeared into the kitchen and she peeked in to take pictures, wanting to make a scrapbook showing the whole process. Mike was using a crowbar to pull cabinets off the walls while Trent sledgehammered them into pieces. If it had been the original shelves and cabinetry, Emily might have considered restoring them, but at some point they'd been replaced by cheap alternatives.

The stack of debris grew. Trent grabbed an armload and Emily backed out of his way as he carried it toward the front door. She saw him walk it into the Dumpster.

That gave her an idea…there was something she could do instead of standing around watching. Grabbing as much as she could hold, Emily headed for the Dumpster. On his way back inside, Trent reached for what she was carrying.

"We'll take care of this," he said, his tone bordering on curt.

She stepped past him. "Oh, I don't mind."

"It's best if our rhythm isn't disrupted."

Why was the guy so grim? For Pete's sake, he could give the Three Bears lessons in grumpiness. Perhaps he realized how he'd sounded, because he gave her one of his smiles that wasn't really a smile.

"We're prepared for this kind of work," he told her in a milder tone, "with boots and clothes that won't catch on anything, and even if it does, the damage won't matter. By the way, until we're done, you'll probably want to wear shoes in the renovation areas."

Yikes. Emily had forgotten her bare feet. It just felt so nice not to worry about dressing like the owner of a fashionable clothing boutique. At this moment her suits, hosiery and high heels were languishing in storage. Life in Schuyler was so much more casual and comfortable.

"Whatever you say," she said with false sweetness, not appreciating the way he dismissed her. She dropped the cabinet doors she'd been carrying.

Swiveling, she marched back into the house, but made sure to nod cheerfully at Vince since there was no point in taking her ire out on anyone else. He was examining the fireplace.

"Can any of it be salvaged?" she asked.

The carved mantelpiece was beautiful, but parts were crumbling.

"I'm not sure," Vince told her. "There's significant dry rot, probably from a leak at some point."

Emily laughed. "That always seems like a contradiction in terms, water causing dry rot. But I sure hope something can be done. I've had visions of lining the mantel with pine boughs at Christmas, stockings hanging down. A fireplace is the heart of a room."

"I suppose so," he agreed.

She went to her bedroom to find her sandals. Much as she hated admitting that Trent was right, shoes were a good idea.

And maybe she should wear pants or something more practical than a flowing skirt, which she found more comfortable than most clothes. For a while she needed to keep in mind she was living in a construction zone.

TRYING TO GET into a better position for leverage, Mike positioned his strong leg and yanked at a stubborn section of the kitchen shelving. Pain shot through his left knee, a reminder of everything he'd lost at what turned out to be his final game.

Though he'd told reporters he didn't recall much of the accident, it wasn't true. He remembered every excruciating minute. Most of all, he remembered that there hadn't been any need to make a sensational leap into the stands to catch a foul ball. It was late in the game and they'd been winning by a wide margin, but he'd done it to impress the redhead sitting three rows back.

When had looking good become more important than playing the game the way it should be played?

"I'll get the other side," Trent said, inserting his crowbar at the opposite end of the shelf. With a shriek of nails twisting out of the wall, the unit came toppling down.

Mike ground his teeth. When he'd started to work for Big Sky the previous summer, he had mouthed off whenever someone offered a hand. He didn't need anyone's help or pity. Then Trent had overheard and gotten pissed, saying he expected his employees to back each other up and Mike had better just deal with it.

He'd nearly yelled back and quit. After all, he didn't need to work. He had his teacher's salary and a large chunk of the money from his pro-ball days was still in the bank, but he'd go bonkers without having something hard and physical to do over the summer months...something real that wasn't just make-work. Teaching summer school was out; it was tough enough being around hopeful young-sters nine months of the year.

So he hadn't quit Big Sky or gotten into a shout-ing match. Anyway, it wasn't that easy talking back to Trent when he was wearing his customary steely expression; he'd not only perfected a persona that would unnerve an old-time umpire, they'd also been friends since they were kids. Well...at least as much as Trent Hawkins could be friends.

He'd never been the kind of buddy you'd catch

a movie with, or hang out with at the Roundup Café, admiring girls. Mostly they'd gone riding on the McGregor ranch, though Trent had spent hours pitching baseballs so Mike could get more batting practice. That was when Alaina had hung around the most, dutifully chasing after the balls for Trent to throw again.

A noise caught Mike's attention and he saw their client picking up more debris from the floor.

Trent's mouth tightened. "As I've explained, Emily, it's best to leave that to us."

"And I've decided that since it's my house, I can haul trash out of it if I want to," she informed him.

Mike's lips twitched. Emily George had done what few of Trent's employees had ever dared to do—contradict him. Seizing a chunk of cabinetry, she headed toward the swinging door. Mike glanced at Trent.

"Don't say it," Trent warned.

"Okay. By the way, I thought you preferred staying away from jobs for women…something about your personality being too abrasive?"

Trent's eyes were impassive. "We're really busy now and have crews out everywhere."

"Whatever." Mike quickly focused on his crowbar. It was obvious that Trent wasn't working the job because he liked Emily. Not that there was anything wrong with her. She seemed nice and pretty in a low-key way, nothing like the sexy redhead he'd been showboating for that day. Actually, Emily was the sort of woman a teacher should think about dating.

Maybe he'd ask her out to dinner when he got a chance. He particularly liked that she was a newcomer. This way she couldn't remember him as the local hero who'd come back a beat-up nobody.

TRENT BARELY CONTAINED his frustration as he watched Emily return and grab another load to take out to the Dumpster. At least she'd changed into roomy Levi's and was wearing sandals, though hard shoes covering her toes would be better.

Some customers planned ahead and it was included in the contract that they would do certain aspects of the work. But it made him suspicious when they tried to "pitch in" after the fact. It often led to protests that the bill should be cut because they'd done part of the labor, which was usually about fifteen dollars' worth of effort.

But his real concern had nothing to do with possible disputes over the final invoice; he just wanted Emily to leave everything alone.

He forced himself to relax. It was also common for clients to be so anxious to see progress that they tried to help, with no ulterior motives when it came to the final bill. Usually it didn't take long before they unwound and left things in more expert hands. Besides, he'd much rather have Emily puttering around in the kitchen than doing it somewhere else in the house.

He hadn't enjoyed hearing the enthusiasm in her voice when she'd talked about going through the junk in the attic. Would she be that curious about *everything*?

In the meantime he marched out to his truck and hunted for the smallest pair of leather gloves he could find. "Here," he said roughly, thrusting them at Emily after she'd dropped another load in the Dumpster.

"No, thanks, I'm okay."

"Wear them," he snapped and returned to work, assuring himself that he wasn't trying to rescue her, he was just preventing a delay in case of injury. He stuck a crowbar in the side of another stubborn cabinet and together with Mike, they yanked it off the wall.

Even if he couldn't bulldoze the house into the dirt, it felt good to rip some of it apart.

"Hey, you can leave part of the work for me," Mike chided.

"Huh?"

Emily had stepped back into the kitchen and was curiously looking their way.

"You're going after those things as if the devil was chasing you," he said.

"It just feels good to get back into the physical part of the business. I've been pushing too many papers lately," Trent told him, picking his words carefully.

"If you say so." Mike sounded doubtful and

Trent wondered how much his face had revealed earlier. He didn't like anyone to know what he was thinking.

Eduardo came through the door. "I've checked the plumbing, boss. It's pretty bad—mostly corroded zinc pipes. There've been a few repairs with PVC, but poorly done." He looked at Emily. "I see you want copper piping. It's a good choice, though more expensive."

"Thanks," she told him. "Wild Rose Cottage was nice once and it keeps telling me it can be nice again."

Trent swallowed a snort. She actually seemed to believe that nonsense. But he knew better, because if houses could talk, this one would surely explain that its day was over. Though…considering the things he'd hidden in the walls as a kid, the old place did have a few secrets it could still expose.

"Will it be possible to keep the laundry and the bathroom in the downstairs bedroom running?" she asked. "That's the one I'm using right now. Also, I told Alaina that you guys could use the half bath off the mud porch."

Eduardo nodded. "There will be periodic water interruptions, but we'll try to ensure you have it at night."

"Great."

The bell sounded and Emily headed for the front door. Several minutes later she reappeared, Caveman following close at her heels like a faithful hound dog. A stack of four giant pizza boxes was in her arms.

"I hope you guys don't mind," she said, "but I was hoping you'd help me celebrate the renovations getting started."

Caveman sniffed appreciatively. "We never mind pizza."

"Then I'll put them on the card table in the living room and you can grab some whenever you want."

"Now sounds good. Time for lunch, isn't it, boss?" asked Eduardo.

Trent checked his watch and was surprised to see it was almost 11:30. Because construction crews generally started early in the day, they ate lunch earlier, too. Come to think of it, he vaguely recalled everyone going for a coffee break, but he'd been too distracted to pay attention.

"Sure," he agreed. Having a client provide lunch on the first day of the job wasn't unheard of, but usually they were in financial shock after shelling out the deposit required by the contract.

"Sorry there aren't enough chairs," Emily said as she went back through the hallway into the living room, the scent of pepperoni, onions and peppers wafting behind her.

Trent hurried out the front door to his truck, muttering that he had phone calls to make. It was true enough, but he mostly wanted privacy to regroup. If Mike was picking up on his mood, it meant something was getting exposed that he hadn't intended.

Great. Trent's grip tightened on his phone. He knew he had a reputation for being as hard and tough as a polecat. Most people avoided him and that was the way he wanted it. An ornery polecat knew how to survive, and so did he.

CHAPTER FOUR

EMILY TOOK A slice of pizza and sank down on one of the wood boxes she'd found in the backyard. "I didn't know which pizza joint was good," she said. "Hope this works for everybody."

"They're all decent," Mike replied. "But this one averages out the best."

"Yeah, they put the most meat on," added Caveman.

The corners of Emily's mouth twitched. She bit into her slice of Hawaiian and chewed happily.

It had been nearly impossible to treat her employees at the boutique to meals or snacks. The time she'd brought in a selection of fresh bagels they'd practically fainted in horror. Black coffee or tea had been okay, but even lettuce wraps had been regarded with mistrust in case they contained hidden calories. Ironically, she'd never required her sales staff to be skinny, but that seemed to be the only sort who applied.

"This is real nice of you," said Eduardo. Caveman nodded, his mouth stuffed with pepperoni and sausage.

"I'm just thrilled you're here," Emily told them.

"I'm sure you'll do a great job. It might sound strange to say, but I think the house likes you."

None of them rolled their eyes; in fact, they seemed pleased by her comment, and they settled into serious munching. Emily wondered why Trent hadn't joined them and supposed he didn't like to socialize with his employees, even on a lunch break. But that would be pretty snotty and the construction crew seemed to be on comfortable terms with their boss. Maybe Trent avoided his customers…or just the one who hadn't given in and let him buy the house he wanted.

Aside from not particularly liking Trent, Emily couldn't get any real sense of him. He was too hard, too humorless, too fierce, and he had too many secrets in his eyes—the biggest one being why he was strangely attached to Wild Rose Cottage. Could that be why she had such strong feelings about the place?

Surely not.

She didn't have good instincts about people, or she wouldn't have been engaged for five years to a cheater. Even now she couldn't believe she hadn't recognized the truth. All those business trips Dennis had taken, always with an excuse not to take her with him? And how about the way he'd dragged his feet on planning the wedding? There must have been a hundred little signs she hadn't seen…or hadn't wanted to see. It was lowering to think she'd put up with so much for so long.

What kind of man decided to marry a nice "girl next door" type of woman for home and family, with the plan of having sex and fun on the side? She just hoped Dennis wouldn't break anyone else's heart in the future.

"Hello?" a voice called through the front door.

Emily popped up and found Alaina Hawkins on the porch.

"Hi."

"Hope you don't mind me dropping by, but I'm on my lunch hour and was curious to see this place."

"The more the merrier. Welcome to the construction zone," Emily said cheerfully. "Come in and have some pizza."

Alaina readily followed her into the living room. "Hey, guys." She glanced into the closest pizza box and took a slice of pepperoni. "I didn't expect to be fed."

"It's a celebration for the work getting started," Emily explained, noticing that Vince, Caveman and Eduardo appeared comfortable with Alaina. Mike seemed less so, but she'd already noticed that he was more reserved than the other guys.

The group ate an astonishing amount of pizza, but there was still part of a pie left to put in the wheezy old refrigerator, which had been moved to the mud porch.

The men went outside for the remainder of their lunch break and Emily turned to Alaina. "How about looking around? You can see how the house looks now, and then again after everything gets fixed. Whenever you like."

"I'd love to. We lived here when I was a little girl. That was before...well, our folks were killed in a car accident, so I haven't been inside since I was three and a half. I don't remember it, though. I even had to ask Mom if it was the right place."

Emily was surprised. Was that the big secret? This being his childhood home would certainly explain why Trent appeared so familiar with Wild Rose Cottage, even knowing how to open the funky latch on the attic door.

"It's too bad that the kitchen is already partly demolished," Emily said as they went down the hallway and Alaina peered through the door.

"That's my fault for not coming earlier."

Letting Alaina wander where she pleased, Emily followed as her guest went from room to room, cocking her head and half closing her eyes, as if trying to evoke long-ago memories.

"Gosh," Alaina said as they climbed the stairs. "I was pretty young when my parents died, but you'd think I'd have *some* memories. Do you remember anything from that age?"

Emily winced. Brother, did she ever. And this particular early memory wasn't something nice like a picnic or a trip to Disneyland. No...what she remembered was dashing across the runway and tripping a model as she glided out, wearing the finale of the fashion show.

She relayed the tale to Alaina. "It was horrible and the model was screaming bloody murder because her eye was turning black. I should have felt worse about it, but I kept expecting her to cackle, 'I'll get you, my pretty,' the same as the Wicked Witch of the West."

Alaina giggled. "Did your parents beat her off?"

"No. They were just as furious and the paparazzi were taking pictures right and left. Anytime I was in danger of forgetting, my mother would haul out those photos and remind me of what a mess I'd caused."

"Why would your mother bring you to a high-end fashion show?" Alaina asked.

"Mom and Dad were clothing buyers. I visited fashion capitals like Paris and Milan every year until I went to college."

"It must have been nice seeing such wonderful places."

"Usually I just saw fitting rooms and expensively clad models." Emily didn't explain that one of those models was her sister, Nicole. "But when I was fourteen I rebelled and ran off to check out the Tower of London and see where Anne Boleyn was beheaded."

"What happened after that?" Alaina asked with a laugh.

"I nearly got beheaded myself, but they finally gave in and let me explore."

Alaina seemed puzzled, but didn't say anything.

As they continued looking around the house, Emily hoped that she might be making a new friend. The hardest part about leaving Southern California had been moving away from Lauren, her best pal for over two decades. They talked on the phone often, but it wasn't the same.

Alaina Hawkins was almost as pretty as Nicole, but she didn't seem bigheaded or overly focused on her appearance. Not that Nicole was snotty, but despite them being sisters, Emily had little in common with her.

From an early age Nicole had spent most of her time on the modeling circuit. Emily, on the other hand, had developed a thriving business advising kids how to dress like her sister...and selling Nicole's clothes when she moved on to the next size or style. Opening a boutique had seemed a logical step after graduating with a business degree.

"Wow," Alaina exclaimed, interrupting her thoughts. "The view up here is terrific." They were in one of the rooms where the windows looked past the edge of town at the land and hills beyond.

Schuyler sat on the margin of where rolling prairie gave way to the mountains, rising west to the continental divide. It made for glorious vistas, though Emily had yet to see a part of Montana that wasn't beautiful. The whole state seemed designed for a photographer or artist, though she didn't know how anyone could capture the breathless sensation of endless sky arching over vast reaches.

"I love the view," she said, "though I haven't decided what to do with these rooms."

"This is the first time I've realized how fun it might be to remake a house." Alaina gave Emily an embarrassed smile. "That probably sounds strange since I work at a construction company, but I haven't been at Big Sky for long. Before that I was at an investment firm in New York."

"That's a big switch."

"Yeah, I got homesick." Alaina glanced around, a thoughtful frown creasing her face. "I'll have to ask Trent which room used to be mine and what it looked like back then."

Emily wanted to ask if Alaina knew why Trent was acting so oddly about Wild Rose Cottage, but decided not to say anything. While the brother and sister appeared to have opposite personalities, they might both prefer keeping certain things private.

TRENT'S HEAD THROBBED and he lay in the dark, staring at the moonlight leaking through the broken blind on the window. For two days Emily had tenaciously stuck close to her house, but surely she couldn't stay away from her new business much longer.

He got up and turned on his bedside lamp. The mattress was high quality—he believed in a good night's rest—but aside from a shabby dresser and the lamp sitting on an old wood chair, there wasn't much else in the room.

The floor creaked as he went into the living room where he kept his weight machine. The Balderdash ranch house was old, but it wasn't an architectural treasure... It was barely habitable. He could renovate it or build a new one, but he didn't care what sort of place he used for sleeping. Mostly he kept an eye on whether any part of it was in danger of collapsing.

The family assumed he was just waiting until he found the right woman so he could build a home to suit them both. At least that's how they'd talked since Jackson had married Kayla. Trent smiled grimly. It had been an unholy mess when his cousin-brother had discovered he had a teenaged son with his old high school girlfriend. Now that the truth was out they'd done the practical thing by getting married, and luckily, Kayla was a better sort than Jackson's first wife.

Mom—Aunt Sarah—practically melted whenever the subject of Jackson's wife was raised. She adored Kayla and was more anxious than ever for all her children to find spouses and have kids. How could he tell her that the thought of marriage left him cold? All he wanted was occasional good sex, with a willing woman who had no fantasies about happily-ever-after. Love and family? He'd leave that to people who still had a few illusions.

A lengthy session of weight lifting didn't help and Trent sat in his easy chair staring at an inane television program. Anything was better than revisiting the memories evoked by working on 320 Meadowlark Lane. Actually...he needed to think of it as Emily's house. Yet his gut clenched as he thought about her name for the place. Hell, his *mom* had called it Wild Rose Cottage. Wasn't that a kick in the gut?

Fiona Hawkins had optimistically hoped that things would change in her marriage, and it had killed her. How unrealistic could a woman be? She'd been afraid to go with her husband the night of the accident, knowing how drunk and angry he was, but more afraid to refuse. The only right thing she'd done was leave her son and daughter at home—otherwise they'd all be dead.

Trent dropped his head back with a groan.

He didn't know if Emily had idealistic ideas about relationships, but she was obviously another optimist. A shudder went through him; he didn't *care* if she meant well—the cliché was right, the road to hell was paved with good intentions. Under normal circumstances, he wouldn't go near her.

Trent clicked off the television and padded out to the barn. The animals stirred restlessly until they recognized him. Miranda, his mare that had recently foaled, peered over her stall door and nickered for attention.

"Hello, girl," he murmured, stroking her neck with one hand and feeding her an apple with the other.

Trent liked horses because there were no pretenses with them—they dispensed service and affection in exchange for food and care. It was basically a barter system, and if he held up his end of the arrangement, they responded in kind. The only horse he'd ever had trouble with had been abused before coming to him.

Thinking of which... He approached Speakeasy's box stall, deliberately making his footsteps heavy so the stallion wouldn't be startled. Speakeasy stood in the back, regarding him warily. Trent had bought him at an auction a few months before, furious at the sight of his thin body and half-healed wounds.

"Come here, boy," he said, holding out an apple.

Speakeasy pawed the hay, clearly wanting the treat, but unwilling to come forward for it.

With a sigh, Trent left the apple on a post and stepped away. He could work with the stallion, but it wasn't easy. It would take time and patience before Speakeasy trusted humans again.

After several hours Trent realized it was time to get moving. Perhaps today would go better and Emily would spend the morning or afternoon at her store. That way he could send the crew onto the roof, leaving him to tackle the wall between the living and dining rooms. She wanted it cut down into a low divider to open up the space. If things went well he might even be able to retrieve his father's gun upstairs.

But as the morning began, Emily showed no sign of leaving. Instead, she now wore sturdy new running shoes, an unfortunate sign she might be planning to stick close to home for yet another day. Vince noticed them immediately and grinned.

"They won't stop a determined nail, Em," he informed her in a familiar tone.

"They're safer than bare skin," she returned.

"Boots would be best."

"Gotta get more Southern California out of this girl before I'll be ready for boots. My toes like to breathe."

Eduardo chuckled. "You're too late for the flower child generation, kiddo."

"Better late than never."

They all smiled, even Mike, whose sense of humor had suffered since his accident.

It was disgusting. His crew was rapidly becoming fond of Emily, helped along by boxes of doughnuts and the coffeemaker she now kept filled on the card table in the living room.

The prior morning the crew had quickly served themselves and left. Today they'd arrived earlier than usual, apparently so they could stand around chatting with her. Without coming off as a surly badger, he couldn't refuse joining them for a cup, though he ignored the pastry. And…damn, it was really good coffee.

Of course, Trent encouraged his crews to get mentally together before launching into the day's task. It also fostered friendly relations, which reduced slowdowns from personality clashes. So it was annoying that the coffee klatch bothered him, when it wouldn't bother him anywhere else. The problem had to be because he wasn't sure of Emily's motives in being so accommodating.

"Thanks, that's mighty tasty," Vince said, leaving his cup on the table. "Em, do you want to help me remove that light fixture in the dining room?"

"I'd love to," Emily agreed enthusiastically. "Do you think it can be salvaged?"

"Converted, maybe. They never removed the old gaslight fixture, just cut off the gas."

"Wow."

"Wait," Trent interrupted, then turned to Eduardo. "When you were inspecting the water pipes did you get a chance to evaluate the gas lines?"

Eduardo nodded. "Yep, but I want to double-check everything."

"Good. We can't take anything for granted about this house."

"Absolutely, boss."

The men departed to their various areas and Trent closed his eyes, drawing several deep, calming breaths. When his temper had flared as a teenager, he'd been tempted to hit walls, the way his father had done so often. Trent had also engaged in a number of monumental fights—generally with bullies, figuring they deserved it anyway. It wasn't comforting to remember that he'd deliberately sought them out, wanting to punch and be punched.

Over time he'd learned to control the urge, knowing a man who couldn't manage himself couldn't be trusted to boss anyone else. But he also hadn't wanted to be the least bit like Gavin Hawkins. Spending so much time on Meadowlark Lane—*Emily's house*—was going to test the man he'd tried to become.

Opening his eyes again, he found Emily watching him, her head cocked, as if trying to guess what he was thinking and feeling.

Fat chance.

No one in thirty-six years had managed it, and he was confident this flaky woman didn't have a prayer.

ONCE EDUARDO GAVE the all clear on the gas lines, Emily went into the dining room to assist with removing the old chandelier. She couldn't provide any serious help, but she handed tools up to Vince and took any small parts that came off, placing them carefully in a box. And when the entire unit came down, she helped lower it.

"I heard about someone who bought a house that had one of these that still worked," she said.

"It happens," Trent contributed. He'd been working nearby on the door frame, which had made Emily feel uncomfortable, though she wasn't sure why. "Last year a man inherited his grandmother's house and she'd been using her gaslights on a regular basis."

Emily shivered. "It doesn't sound safe." She patted a wall. "Don't worry, baby. We're going to make sure you have safe wiring." She glanced at Vince. "I guess it sounds silly, but I believe houses have personalities."

Vince laughed in a kindly way, but Trent seemed less sympathetic.

Well, too bad.

She was tired of arrogant men who passed judgment on her—men such as her ex-fiancé, who also happened to be Lauren's brother. Poor Lauren was the one who'd figured things out and spilled the truth about him cheating. Not that Dennis had been terribly upset when Emily confronted him. He'd seemed to think his sleeping with other women wasn't a big deal… She shook the thought away. She was in Montana now, with a whole new life.

Midmorning she remembered the crystal she'd brought home from the Emporium, so she went and hung it in the window that pulled the most sunshine.

"Hey, what's that?" Eduardo called, and came into the living room, with Trent following. "All of a sudden there are rainbows everywhere."

Emily laughed. "I hoped that would happen. I love crystals, and some people say they have healing power and create positive vibes."

Trent's eyebrows rose.

She smiled blandly at him. "You never know."

Eduardo nodded sagely. "I don't know about the mystical stuff, but something that pretty must send something good into a place."

Emily decided he'd just won her grateful-forever award.

The morning passed pleasantly, then during a coffee break she got a surprise from Mike.

"Emily, would you consider going out to dinner with me sometime?" he asked when they were sitting on the porch steps, enjoying the fresh air. The others had already gone back inside.

She blinked. Dating wasn't something she'd expected to do in Schuyler. After breaking off her engagement she had decided romance wasn't her thing. But Mike seemed nice and having dinner together didn't necessarily mean romance. More than anything, he probably felt sorry for someone whose kitchen he'd just knocked into oblivion.

"That would be nice," she replied.

"Would Saturday evening be good for you?"

"Sure."

He smiled, drained his coffee cup and headed indoors.

Emily pursed her lips, unsure what to think. While she wasn't the best judge, she hadn't sensed that Mike was especially attracted to her. He certainly hadn't acted the way guys did around her sister.

Oh, well. The evening out would be pleasant. Mike taught history to high school students during the school year. She enjoyed history, so they'd have plenty to talk about.

Inside the house, she glanced at Trent, who was pulling up the ancient carpet from the dining room floor. Dust was flying in a thick cloud, though she'd vacuumed the thing within an inch of its questionable life.

"Put on a dust mask if you're staying," he advised when she started coughing. "Though I won't be offended if you head downtown or something."

Once again she had the feeling he wanted her gone, but she only had his words to go by since his face was concealed by both a heavy dust mask and a pair of safety glasses. Anyhow, she probably should make an appearance at the shop.

"In that case, I'll see you in a couple of hours," she said.

He nodded and turned back to the carpet.

Emily walked down to the Emporium where she spoke to her manager, who reported everything was going well.

After going through the sales receipts to see if new stock needed to be ordered and chatting with a few customers, she strolled back to Meadowlark

Lane. Inside the house she stared in amazement. The wall between the living and dining rooms had been knocked down to floor level, with only the weight-bearing four-by-four posts left standing. Caveman, Vince, Mike and Eduardo were on the roof, so Trent must have abandoned the dining room carpet to take the thing apart.

"Wow," she said.

He must have worked like a man possessed to have gotten the wall demolished; most of the debris was even cleared away.

"We'll put in the low divider wall you want," he explained. "But the way it was built, it's cleaner to pull everything down and rebuild. The support beams will need to be faced, and we'll frame them at the top to echo the molding in both rooms. You've come up with a good plan. The change will create a more contemporary, open feeling without erasing the vintage appeal."

The long statement seemed uncharacteristic, especially since his face remained hard and stony, and his admission about it being a "good plan" held a grudging tone. But there was nothing actually wrong in what he'd said, so she nodded and collected a broom to sweep up the remaining bits of plaster and dust.

"I'VE GOT THE list you emailed," Alaina said into the phone on Thursday. "I'll take A through H, okay?"

"That's terrific," Janet Goodwell told her. "Most people hate recruiting bachelors and bachelorettes for the auction and I have to do most of it myself. Of course, my arm-twisting skills will probably deteriorate because of your willingness."

"If you prefer, I could just make cookies for Saturday's bake sale," Alaina suggested. It wasn't what *she* preferred, but she didn't want anyone to guess that she'd deliberately volunteered in order to be the one to recruit Mike.

"Don't you dare," Janet nearly screamed. "I've got cookies running out of my ears. I need recruiters."

Alaina put down the phone with a satisfied smile. Joining the Volunteer Firefighters Auxiliary was the least she could do, considering the work they accomplished all over town. And when they'd announced it was time to prep for the annual barbecue and auction, she'd broken a speed record volunteering for the planning committee.

The others had laughed and assumed she'd done it to avoid being tagged as a potential bachelorette—members were barred from participating that way. But she'd had something far more devious in mind, including taking the first part of the alphabetical list of potential auction volunteers... the section with Mike Carlisle's name.

Alaina glanced at the clock and picked up the receiver again to dial Emily.

"Hello, Alaina," Emily greeted her cheerily. "How are you today?"

"I'm good. I just wondered if you wanted to get lunch. The Roundup Café makes a mean fire-grilled burger."

"That would be great, except I ordered sandwiches for the guys. They're going to be delivered by 11:30."

"Oh."

"Why don't you come over and join the party? We'll have plenty of food."

Alaina's heart started rat-a-tat-tatting. She genuinely wanted to get acquainted with Emily, but she also wanted to run into Mike. Now she could end up eating lunch twice in one week with him. It wasn't a date, but more contact than she usually managed.

"It sounds like fun," she agreed. "But I want to bring something. What do you need?"

"How about chips? We have doughnuts left and I got a humongous container of fresh-made potato salad from the grocery deli."

"I'll be there in twenty minutes."

Hanging up the phone, Alaina jumped to her feet. When she'd decided to come back to Montana, she had been sure she'd see Mike often. After all, he was friends with her brothers and several cousins, and as Trent's office manager it had seemed a certainty Mike would cross her path frequently, at least during the summer. But he'd proven remarkably adept at treading a solitary path. She didn't think he was avoiding her in particular; it was more a serious case of lone wolf syndrome.

Well, it was time to change all of that.

CHAPTER FIVE

SOME OF THE tension eased from Trent as the crew broke for lunch. Emily's absence had left him free to take down one of the problem walls and dispose of the debris, and he'd done it in record time. His pockets were stuffed with the bits and pieces he'd recovered, while the rest had been thrown into the far end of the Dumpster.

"Alaina is joining us for lunch," Emily's voice said in the next room, where she'd gone to answer her cell.

His gaze raced around the area to double-check, but there was nothing that might prove suspicious. Imagine if Alaina saw one of his painfully written notes proclaiming *exactly* what he thought of Gavin Hawkins? And hidden in one of the still-standing walls was the paper he'd tried to make sound very legal, stating that Trent Hawkins no longer had a father because Gavin Hawkins was a son of a bitch. The language on some of the other messages was even worse, learned courtesy of Gavin's foul mouth.

The doorbell squawked and his stomach tightened. Emily hadn't asked them to replace it, but surely she didn't want to keep the atrocious-sounding bell. To never hear it again, he'd throw in a deluxe model and install it personally.

Emily stuck her head around one of the plastic curtains they'd hung to control dust from traveling as far. "Hey, the sandwiches are here. Are you hungry?"

Her smile was engaging and Trent was struck by surprise that she'd abandoned her previous life to move to Schuyler. Didn't she have a boyfriend or family who'd objected? The McGregors had hated it when Alaina had been working in New York.

"Sure," he answered truthfully. He'd skipped breakfast, something he couldn't admit since he encouraged his crews to show up at work with good meals in their stomachs.

"I moved the card table and chairs to the patio since it's so dusty in here," she explained. "Come and get it."

Come and get it.

A faint nostalgia went through him at hearing the expression his aunt Sarah…his mother often used. Mother or aunt… Even now he still mentally qualified his relationship with her, as he did with the whole family. Not that she'd ever insisted he call her Mom. Alaina said "Mom," but she couldn't remember any parents except Parker and Sarah McGregor.

Trent waited until Emily had disappeared

then did another visual search of the space. As he walked toward the back of the house, Alaina popped through the front door.

"Hey, big brother. Don't tell my boss, but I'm taking a long lunch today."

His lips twitched, and he was surprised to discover his sense of humor wasn't entirely absent, despite his self-imposed tenure on Meadowlark Lane.

"I won't mention it to him," he answered. "Emily says we're eating on the patio."

"Great. That's one of the places I didn't think about seeing the other day."

He led her through the dining room and kitchen into the long mud porch that served also as a utility room along the side of the house. Curiously, the original design had the door to the backyard on the opposite end of the porch, so getting there was basically a zigzag.

"This is interesting," Alaina murmured as they traversed the length of the porch away from the patio. "Isn't there a door that opens directly into the backyard?"

"Not right now, but one of Emily's renovations is to put a hallway along the dining room to a casual sitting room, with French doors onto the patio. She also wants us to cut another door on the mud porch and close off the existing one. That way food can be easily brought outside—she's got a thing about creating outdoor living space."

Reluctant as Trent was to admit it, Emily's plans for the house weren't bad. Montana wasn't Los Angeles, so there were fewer months where outdoor living was feasible, but everyone in Schuyler flocked outside when the weather was mild enough. And her plan for a well-equipped outdoor kitchen would be the envy of cooks all over town.

"Oooh," Alaina breathed as they followed the path around the side of the house. "This is lovely."

The rough brick patio was scented by a trellis covered by honeysuckle. The large yard was overgrown, but multicolored wildflowers provided a kaleidoscope background of hues.

"Hi," Emily greeted Alaina. "I should have warned you the seating is makeshift in this restaurant."

"The atmosphere makes up for it. I just wish I remembered living here," Alaina said, wistfully.

"You used to live here?" Eduardo asked.

"Before our folks were gone."

"Sure, sure, I remember now. It was before you moved out with the McGregors. So this is where Gavin and Fiona lived." Eduardo looked around. "I was real sorry about what happened to them. I remember Gavin saying he had the best kids and wanted to have a dozen before he and Fiona were through."

"Really?" Alaina asked, her face alight. "I never knew that."

"Your dad and me went to school together and I used to see him around town. We weren't exactly friends. He just made everyone feel like his best buddy. What a great guy."

Trent's jaw ached with renewed tension. Yeah, Gavin Hawkins had been popular and charming with everyone except his immediate family. Part of him wanted to shout the truth, to stop the pretty image Eduardo was painting for Alaina. But what good would it do? Gavin was dead and buried, and the past was best left that way.

Alaina would be crushed if she learned what her father had really been like. She might not even believe it. After all, it was essentially her brother's word against everyone else's.

Suddenly he felt a strange energy. He glanced around to see Emily staring at him with a puzzled expression.

"Is something wrong?" he asked.

"No," she answered in a low tone. "I was just wondering if something is bothering you."

"What do you mean?" Trent asked, though he should have kept his mouth shut. He didn't want Emily speculating about anything to his workers, or asking about his emotional state. But Alaina and Eduardo were chatting so they shouldn't overhear, and the others were still in the house.

Emily shrugged. "You seem uptight."

He managed a smile. "There's no mystery. I'm just hungry."

"In that case, relax. We ordered plenty."

Mike, Caveman and Vince came out a moment later.

"Hi, guys." Alaina handed a bag to Mike. "I got stuff to add to lunch."

"Nice of you."

"It's nice of Emily to have me. I called to see if she wanted to sample the Roundup Café and got invited here instead. Hope nobody minds."

"Hell, no," Vince said, grabbing the bag to check its contents. "You got tortilla chips and some of Sally's guacamole. I thought I smelled it."

"Yes, she'd just made a fresh batch and I couldn't resist."

In a few minutes, everyone was chowing down.

As he ate his sandwich, Trent watched Emily as unobtrusively as possible. She was discussing plumbing with Eduardo, giving the appearance of being fascinated by the subject. Clearly, it was making the middle-aged man feel important and knowledgeable.

Trent tried not to roll his eyes. Nobody was that fascinated by U-bends and closet augers.

Something about Emily raised a red flag. There was nothing outright that was questionable, but he was reluctant to trust her. Aside from anything else, she was a businesswoman from Southern California. It didn't mean she'd do anything underhanded, but he'd met some sharp operators from that part of the country. And her eager involvement was keeping up longer than it normally did with other clients. Along with her providing food and coffee for the crew…it made him wonder.

Still, Emily might actually *be* just a flaky odd-ball with an unfortunate streak of cheery optimism. Regardless, in fifteen years as a contractor he'd dealt with all sorts of people, including femme fatales using sex as a weapon, women using help-lessness as a ploy, and other greedy, crafty or manipulative customers. So he could deal with Emily George, whatever sort she turned out to be.

EMILY SNIFFED THE lovely scent of honeysuckle and hoped they'd be able to keep some of it alive when the patio was redone. She knew the vine could be invasive and needed to be kept tamed, but as long as she kept it on a trellis, surely it would be all right.

"This is such a huge yard," Alaina said. "Are you a gardener, Emily?"

"Sort of. I designed the garden for my house in Los Angeles and loved the way it turned out. But it was tiny, so now I've got plenty of space to go hog wild."

"A swimming pool might be nice."

"I've thought about that."

Every once in a while, Trent glanced at her and she had a feeling it wasn't just casual, more as if he was studying a bug under a magnifying glass. Good grief, the man was like a pressure cooker ready to blow.

The big mystery was why Trent hadn't explained that he and Alaina had lived in the house with his parents before their deaths. She would have understood if he'd wanted Wild Rose Cottage out of sentimentality, but it was too late to backtrack and sell to him now. In any case, he didn't seem to be the sentimental type. As a matter of fact, it was almost as if he hated the place.

A sudden thought struck her. What if the house symbolized losing his mother and father? Childhood traumas could influence people in odd ways. If that was the problem, wouldn't remaking it make him feel better? She hoped so, even if it wasn't any of her business.

It was so pleasant on the patio that no one seemed anxious to go back to work. But the guys from Big Sky were professionals, so after a suitable time, they thanked her for lunch and headed back inside…all except Trent, who went around the opposite side of the house.

She glanced at Alaina, whose expression seemed wistful.

"Something wrong?"

"What? Oh, no. Just thinking."

Emily grinned. "Be careful. I do that and lose track of what's going on around me."

"Doesn't everyone space out occasionally?"

"Yeah, but I've raised it to an art form."

"It's just that I was trying to remember this patio. I've always loved being outdoors. On the ranch I spent every possible minute in the garden or riding my horse, so it seems as if I ought to remember the yard at least."

"It might have changed a lot."

"True." Alaina was reflective. "I asked Trent to tell me stories about when we lived here, but he won't say much."

"Yeah, he probably just got that formal smile on his face."

"Formal?" Alaina repeated.

"You know, controlled. As if he has to think about doing it." Emily scooped more guacamole onto her plate, wishing she hadn't said anything. "This stuff is yummy," she said brightly.

"The grocery deli is tops, but this is the second lunch you've fed me this week. It's time I treated you to a meal. How about a girls' night out tomorrow?"

"Great, as long we go Dutch. After all, you brought half our lunch and I ordered too many sandwiches, anyway. It's a treat getting real food for people, instead of rabbit munchies, so I went overboard."

"Rabbit munchies?"

"Yeah. The sales associates in my Los Angeles

boutique don't approve of eating anything except lettuce, celery and carrots with the occasional stalk of broccoli."

Alaina laughed. "Let me guess, size zero working on skeletal proportions?"

"Yup. They thought it was absurd when I introduced larger sizes, only to discover that normal-size women have credit cards the same as anyone else. Their commissions doubled."

Alaina laughed again.

"Emily?" Trent had come back onto the patio. "You haven't said what you want done with the storm cellar."

Emily's jaw dropped. "You mean for tornadoes and stuff? Ohmigod, Montana doesn't have tornadoes, does it?"

"Montana isn't in tornado alley, but some folks still have storm cellars in case one goes through."

She jumped to her feet. "Show me."

"Me, too," Alaina added.

All at once Trent seemed uncomfortable, but he nodded and led the way to a badly overgrown area in the wide space between the house and the side fence. He had pushed enough of the overgrowth away to reveal rotted wood planks.

"I thought it would be under the house," Emily said.

"The idea was probably to have a spot away

from the structure, in case it collapses on top of the exit."

Alaina leaned forward with a puzzled look on her face. "Did we use to play down there, Trent?"

His face seemed to close down, then eased as his sister glanced back at him.

"We might have. It's been a long time and I don't remember everything."

"It seems familiar."

"You're probably thinking of that movie, *Twister*, or *The Wizard of Oz*."

"Yeah," Alaina agreed. "Well, I'd better get back to work or my slave driver boss will have my hide."

"Count on it."

She said goodbye and left as Trent pulled more vines from the storm cellar's entrance.

"Can I go down there?" Emily asked.

"Better not, the steps are rotted."

"What's the best thing to do with it? I mean… shouldn't I have a storm cellar?"

His eyebrow lifted. "Seriously? You come from a state famous for earthquakes, but you're afraid of tornados?"

Emily shivered. "You don't need to be sarcastic. Earthquakes don't worry me that much. I grew up with them. But tornadoes scare the heck out of me."

"I wasn't being sarcastic."

"Seriously?" she returned in the mocking tone he'd used.

He had the grace to appear embarrassed. "Whatever. We can repair the cellar if that's what you prefer."

"Give me an estimate and we'll go from there."

His eyebrow shifted again, but she didn't know why and didn't think he'd explain.

"I'm glad you knew about this," she said, determined to show there weren't any hard feelings. "I could have fallen in here, never to be seen again. Then they might have done a TV mystery movie about what happened to Emily George and I'd be famous. Not that I'd know anything about it."

She'd hoped Trent would crack a smile, but he simply nodded. "You mentioned wanting to work on the garden, so I thought I'd better check it out."

Jeez, the guy was impossible. She knew he didn't like her New Age ideas, but they weren't doing any harm to him, so what was the big deal?

Emily stuck out her chin. "Why didn't you tell me this was your house when you were a kid?"

His face froze into stiff lines. "As I mentioned before, it's personal."

Considering the way he'd acted the first time they'd met, she should have known better than to ask.

MIKE HAD DECIDED to clear out his classroom on Saturday and spent the afternoon at the school, ignoring broad hints from the principal about the coach's job still needing to be filled.

He'd *tried* coaching.

When it became apparent the final surgery on his knee had failed, he had gone to work for a Triple A ball team. He'd hated every minute, and his wounds were poked whenever one of the guys got called up to play in the majors. Just as bad, what did you say to a kid who wasn't good enough to ever *be* called up? Be honest, or let them keep hoping until they figured it out themselves? Either option stunk.

At his condo Mike showered and spent an hour on the internet, looking up Arts and Crafts architecture in case Emily wanted to discuss the renovations. Her house must have been one of the earliest Arts and Crafts homes built in Schuyler, and the design suggested a lingering Victorian influence. The place had plenty of potential, but it must be costing a fortune to fix up.

It was curious that Trent and Alaina had once lived there. He remembered when their parents had died, but Trent had never talked about it, and their teacher had warned everyone not to bring it up unless he did first.

Mike rang Emily's doorbell promptly at seven. She answered with a friendly smile and he was glad to see she hadn't dressed formally. It had belatedly occurred to him that he hadn't mentioned where they might be going. The choices were limited; taking her to a fine restaurant would have been nice, but Schuyler didn't have any.

Still, maybe he should switch gears from his original plan—Ryan's Roadhouse served decent food, but it wasn't ideal for a first date.

"I should have asked what kind of food you like," he said when they were in his Porsche, a leftover from his pro-ball days.

"Everything," she replied. "We traveled often when I was a kid, so I learned to eat different cuisines."

"I'm afraid there isn't much variety in Schuyler. How about the Lazy Y Surf and Turf? The seafood is average, but you can't beat their steaks and prime rib."

"That sounds fine."

Dinner was awkward at first—he was out of practice with casual social conversation. They chatted about a number of subjects, mostly feeling each other out for common interests.

She *did* have strong opinions about the way historical accounts were skewed depending on point of view. Apparently she was an avid reader of authors like David McCullough, along with anything relating to the American Civil War. As they lingered over coffee, they wrangled cordially over male versus female perspectives of the past.

"What do you most miss about California?" he asked as the waiter refilled their cups a third time.

"My family, though we don't have anything in common. We love each other, but they're all about fashion and appearance."

"I probably wouldn't have much in common with them, either, especially now that I'm back here teaching. Being in style is easy in Schuyler. You just wear jeans and a shirt, topped by a cowboy hat and boots."

"Back? You left?"

"Uh, yeah," he said, knowing he had to admit the truth, and hating it at the same time. "I played pro ball for a while."

She cocked her head. "Football?"

It pleased him that she didn't immediately know who he was…and dented his ego, as well.

"Baseball," Mike explained.

"That might be why you look familiar."

"You're a baseball fan?"

"Once in a while."

He didn't know what she meant by that and didn't ask, not wanting to discuss his years in the majors. At least he'd gotten his college degree before all of that, which had left more options open after the accident.

"Why did you stop—" Emily broke off the query and it wasn't hard to guess why. She'd been about to ask why he wasn't playing any longer, only to guess it had something to do with his bum leg.

"Anyway," he said, "I'm just a teacher now, nothing unusual."

"Good teachers are worth their weight in gold."

"I'm glad you think so. But I need a break from

it over the summer, so I work for Trent instead of teaching summer school. I hate being inactive."

"Yeah, I'm like that, too. I always want to stay busy."

By the time he'd brought Emily back to Meadowlark Lane, he'd decided there was potential for a future relationship. He wanted to get married someday and have children, and Emily was the kind of sweet, down-to-earth woman who fit his life now. Granted, she was a little unconventional, but not in a way that would concern parents or the school board. He'd already learned that people in Schuyler enjoyed prying into a teacher's private life…and some were more persistent than the paparazzi from his baseball days.

"Thanks for a great evening," Emily said.

He didn't try to kiss her. She had tried to pay for her own dinner, but seemed the old-fashioned type in other ways.

"Would you like to go out again next week?" he asked.

"I'm pretty crazy right now with the work going on in the house. Let's talk about it in a few days," she suggested.

It wasn't an eager reply, but he could hardly expect the kind of feminine response he'd received while playing ball. Hell, women had often suggested going straight back to his hotel room following dinner. And it was another reminder that he wasn't a star any longer, just a guy who taught school.

"Sounds like a plan," he agreed.

Emily let herself into the house and he returned to his condo. It was a small complex, the first condominiums in Schuyler, and had been built by Big Sky Construction. Trent was a terrific contractor, so Mike had known it was a sound investment to buy one of the units. It wasn't big enough to accommodate a family, but he'd cross that bridge if he came to it.

He got a can of beer from the fridge, but had barely popped the tab when there was a knock at the door.

It was Alaina Hawkins.

"Hey, Mike," she said, her gaze flicking to the beer he held then back to his face. "I was driving past and saw your Porsche outside, so I decided to drop by instead of phoning."

"Is there a change in next week's work schedule?"

"Nope, you're assigned to Emily's house. If everything goes as planned, we won't break up the crew until the renovations are finished."

"That's good." He wondered if he should offer Alaina a drink, but had a feeling she didn't care for beer and it was the only beverage readily available. "I prefer seeing a project through to the finish."

"Trent knows the guys feel that way."

Mike wondered for the hundredth time why a woman with a high-powered career in New York would leave to juggle work schedules for a construction company. While a skilled office manager was invaluable to Big Sky, office manager was as far as she could go in Montana. In New York she might have risen to become the head of a billion-dollar company, but she'd given it up to return to Schuyler. Nothing except blowing out his knee could have dragged him away from baseball.

"Actually, I have something nonwork-related to ask," Alaina said.

"Uh, okay," he said cautiously.

"I'm on the planning committee for the annual Volunteer Firefighters Auxiliary Barbecue, which is being combined this year with the bachelor and bachelorette auction. It works the same way it always has—people get to have dinner out with the person they 'win' in the auction. Anyway, we want you as one of our bachelors."

She had to be kidding.

"Sorry, I can't," Mike refused shortly. "I'll make a donation."

"But it's for a terrific cause. We're raising money for a new ladder truck."

"Forget it. I'm not Lightning Carlisle any longer."

Alaina planted her hands on her hips. "I don't like taking no for an answer. So the way I choose to see this is that you need time to think about it."

Mike ground his teeth. "Alaina, you must be out of your mind if you think—" he began saying, only to stop. He was talking to the back of her head as she walked toward the visitor parking area, her smooth dark hair swaying with each step.

Hell.

He couldn't believe she'd asked him to participate in the bachelor auction. Years ago he used to do it and his "sales" had brought in record bids, despite the proviso that the winner would have to wait until the end of baseball season before getting taken out to dinner. Most of the time he hadn't even been able to make it to the auction, so they'd bid on a picture of him. But there was no way he'd embarrass himself by doing it now.

Jeez, they must be desperate if they were asking him to volunteer. He could just hear the auctioneer: *Our next bachelor is former pro baseball player Michael Carlisle. Too bad his career tanked a few years ago.*

Well, maybe they wouldn't be that blunt, but he'd hate it, no matter what they said.

Mike dropped to the couch and put a heating pad on his knee.

He closed his eyes, trying to push Alaina's image from his head. She'd looked beautiful tonight, not to mention confident and thoroughly sexy. He knew she'd had a crush on him as a kid. Back then she was big-eyed string bean and it had been cute the way she tagged along when he was doing something with Trent. Then Alaina had grown up into a leggy beauty.

It was unlikely she remained interested, but it

didn't matter. He wanted to avoid messy relationships, and getting involved with the sister of a long-time buddy would be unbelievably messy. He liked Trent, but the guy was impossible to figure out, and had always been protective of his sister.

It was much better to pursue a pleasant, sensible woman like Emily, instead of a gorgeous idiot who'd voluntarily given up the success she could have had in the city.

ALAINA SAT IN her Audi sedan, tapping her fingers on the steering wheel as she regrouped.

She hadn't genuinely expected Mike to volunteer for the charity auction. He'd done it in the past, but only after becoming a well-known baseball player. It was guys like Billy Halloran who loved strutting and teasing women into outbidding each other for him.

Anyway, having Mike turn her down gave her an excuse to see him again about it, though she sometimes wondered why she bothered. At least tonight he hadn't made a snide comment about her quitting a lucrative job to work for peanuts, or sniped that she couldn't cut it in the city.

Alaina thought about the beer that Mike had been holding when he answered the door and a peculiar sensation went through her stomach.

It was probably guilt.

She shouldn't have stopped to see him, but she'd known about his date with Emily and had been elated to see he was home before 9:00 p.m. Then, when he'd answered the door, she'd been struck by a sudden fear that he wasn't alone. Of course, it was remotely possible Emily had been in the condo, only she didn't seem the type to hide in the bathroom to avoid being seen.

Alaina shuddered and started the car. The embarrassment of such an encounter could seriously damage a new friendship.

She drove past the Big Sky Construction yard and was surprised to see the office lights on and Trent's truck out front. Using the remote control to go through the gate, she parked and went inside.

"It's me," she called.

Trent was going through a pile of papers on his desk. "Why are you here so late?" he asked.

"Visiting my brother."

He glanced up and smiled.

Alaina blinked. A few days before Emily had commented that Trent's smile always seemed controlled, as if he had to think about doing it. She was right. Once in a while he would half grin if he found something amusing, but it rarely came naturally.

"Why the urge to visit your brother tonight?" he asked.

"I, uh, just dropped by after I... Never mind."

His eyes narrowed questioningly, but she ignored it and went to the coffeemaker. "How about a fresh pot?" she asked.

"Sure."

She put a handful of beans into the grinder, spun it a few times and tipped the contents into the filter. Soon the rich aroma of brewing coffee filled the air.

Before she'd begun working at Big Sky, Trent had bought ground coffee from the local grocer without paying attention to quality. Maybe he'd figured flavor didn't matter since he made the stuff so strong it threatened to eat holes in stomach linings, but Alaina *did* care about flavor, so she was now ordering her favorite blend over the internet.

When the pot had brewed she poured a cup for Trent and got one for herself. They drank silently; her brother wasn't one for light conversation, even with family.

She wanted to ask him for ideas on convincing Mike to volunteer for the auction, except he'd likely say it was none of his business. After all, Trent had also refused to volunteer himself…before she'd even asked. Huh. As far as she was concerned, it would be good for both of them to get involved in something outside of work.

Trent might be popular at the auction, particularly since a lot of women got off on that dark, silent thing he had going.

As for Mike?

He acted as if nobody would bid to have dinner out with him because he wasn't Lightning Carlisle any longer, but she disagreed. Besides, if a woman only cared whether he was a big-shot ballplayer, then she wasn't worth anything in the first place. And if the bids weren't as high as they'd been when he was in the major leagues, what difference did it make? Even the starting bid of fifty dollars would help the firehouse.

Perhaps it was stupid, but Alaina couldn't help thinking that if Mike got blasted out of his stubborn cocoon, he might start seeing other possibilities to life in Schuyler.

CHAPTER SIX

TRENT WALKED UP the creaky steps of Emily's house on Monday morning, hearing odd sounds drift through the open door. He listened and realized it was a weird combination of music and sounds from nature.

He might have known. She was a major flake and had really strange ideas. It was her success as a businesswoman that surprised him. She hadn't shown good sense about the house, but until a few months ago everyone had figured the Emporium was on its last legs, and now she'd completely turned it around.

"Hi, Trent," Emily said, stepping outside. "I saw you through the window. You're early."

"I hope it isn't inconvenient."

She wrinkled her nose, a gesture that seemed characteristic. "Only if you need to turn off the water before my clothes finish washing."

"I think we can refrain."

"In that case, it's fine. The coffee is on if you want a cup. I didn't know where you'd have everyone working today, so the pot is out on the patio."

"Well, if it isn't Trent Hawkins," an oily voice intruded.

Trent wheeled to see Bob Webber. Webber had been the landlord when the Hawkins family had moved into the house. There was an affable expression plastered on his round face, belying the snake underneath.

"You need something, Bob?" Trent asked.

"Not really. I'm just curious what's happening with this old place. I did own it for a long time."

"And it's finally getting fixed up, instead of being left to molder into a pile of splinters," Trent returned bluntly. The irony couldn't be escaped, because if he'd had his choice, he would have bulldozed the place.

Bob waved his right forefinger in a chiding gesture. "Surely you know I couldn't afford this kind of restoration and keep it affordable for folks to live here."

"As I recall, there were times you couldn't afford to fix a leaky pipe or broken furnace, either."

The genial smile on Webber's face flickered. "I tried to keep the rent down for tenants, even when it hurt me financially. But that's all water under the bridge. Perhaps I'll come back in a few days and check your progress."

"It isn't my call. The house belongs to Ms. George."

"Naturally." Webber tipped his hat to Emily and rolled down the front walk.

The renovation job was getting more and more bizarre. Trent didn't like Bob Webber any better now than when he was a kid, and the squint-eyed man undoubtedly wasn't fond of him in return. Life as his tenant hadn't been pleasant for the Hawkins family, particularly when the rent had fallen behind. There had been loud threats of eviction, followed by smarmy advances to Trent's mother, with the suggestion she could buy time by being extra "nice" to him.

"That coffee sounds good," Trent said tightly, turning back to Emily.

"Uh, sure."

The rest of the crew was arriving, so they waited for the men to come up the walk.

"Hi, Emily," Mike said with a smile.

Eduardo tweaked her hair, Vince winked and she and Caveman shoulder-bumped like old friends.

"Good grief," Vince exclaimed as they came into the entryway. "What is that?" At the moment the music was barely discernible over an especially loud clap of thunder and accompanying rainfall. He looked out at the early-morning sunshine, and back at Emily.

"Classical music with nature sounds," she explained. "Most of my collection is in storage, but I have CDs that are just ocean waves or mountain streams and some terrific New Age stuff from artists like Steven Halpern. Should I put something else on?"

"Naw. Guess we can stand it."

She laughed and told them to get coffee and Danish on the patio.

Trent knew about New Age music, but it was part of the counterculture garbage that few people in Schuyler cared about. Country and western was the music of choice, followed by gospel and blue-grass. Personally, he preferred silence.

As the others trooped out to the patio to get their morning pick-me-up, he glanced at the crystal hanging in the window and remembered Emily saying the house spoke to her. How soon would it be before she started talking about past-life regression and telepathic communication with animals and ghosts, or something equally ridiculous?

The idea sent a strange sensation down his back. He wasn't superstitious, but with what was hidden in the walls of the house, he was sure a few ghosts could speak volumes if they were able.

EMILY NIBBLED AN apricot Danish, trying to concentrate on something Vince was telling her, but the thought of Trent's terse exchange with Bob Webber kept intruding. What did it mean? Of course, it might not mean anything; Trent seemed to have a strained relationship with most people.

He certainly had a habit of annoying *her*.

She'd wanted to smack the disdainful expression from his face when she was explaining to Vince about the CDs she liked. She knew the other guys were amused by her ways, but that was okay; it was Trent's snooty attitude that got on her nerves.

Hell. She was just in a bad mood because of her evening with Mike. It had been pleasant at first, but slowly she'd gotten the impression he saw her as a "sensible" choice for a date, a woman too ordinary for high romantic aspirations.

So on Sunday she'd decided to research him on the internet. Before his career-ending injury, Michael "Lightning" Carlisle had been expected to eventually land a spot in the Baseball Hall of Fame. He was also described as a fan favorite, with an irresistible smile and a habit of winning on and off the field…especially with female fans.

Emily had seen his smile, but it was hardly irresistible, and he was undeniably moody. She didn't blame him for being disappointed about the way his baseball career had ended, but he acted as if he'd lowered his expectations about everything… and had asked her out because she met those lower expectations.

Jackass.

She might not be a supermodel like Nicole, but if she ever got involved with another guy, she wanted him to consider himself lucky to have her in his life. She would rather be alone than feel she was second-best ever again.

And on top of everything else, she'd figured out that Alaina had a yen for Mike. Unfortunately the realization had come after receiving his invitation to dinner, or she never would have accepted.

Following the morning "huddle" as Eduardo called the initial gathering around the coffeepot and pastry box, the crew went to work and Emily began beating back the overgrowth in the yard. But every twenty to thirty minutes she ran inside to see what was happening and take pictures to document the progress. Eduardo laughed when she even followed him into the basement and took photos of the tangled network of pipes.

Trent was the only one who seemed unhappy when she came into the room where he was removing some hideous fake paneling. She snapped a couple pictures and grabbed an armload of debris, musing on the fact that he often worked solo. It fit his general personality, but wasn't he lonely? Of course…maybe his crew preferred it that way.

"You're paying us to do this," he reminded her in a voice that was a little too patient for her taste.

"So?"

"Wouldn't you rather stay neat and clean at the Emporium?" he asked, reaching out to pluck a cobweb from the hair above her ear.

"Not really. Don't you have any women on your payroll who do this kind of work?"

"A few. I don't have a problem hiring women if they can do the job. Are you looking for other employment?"

Emily grinned. "Nope, I just want to be in on what happens here."

His smile had its usual measured quality. "That's your prerogative."

THAT EVENING, WHILE having dinner out with Alaina, Emily was tempted to ask if anyone ever got close to Trent. But she had the oddest feeling that Alaina didn't actually know her brother that well, either.

"By the way," Emily said cautiously as they waited for dessert. "I've, uh, noticed that you kind of like Mike Carlisle."

"That doesn't mean… That is, you shouldn't worry about…" Alaina's voice trailed off miserably.

"Don't worry," Emily assured her. "We went out, but I'm not interested. Regardless, the two of you are much better suited."

Alaina's shoulders slumped. "Not that it makes any difference. I've had a thing for Mike for most of my life. But before he left for college I was too young for him to notice me that way. Then later, when he was playing pro ball, he had scads of girlfriends. I know because the Schuyler newspaper used to pick up any story that mentioned him, whether it was for the sports page or a gossip column, and Mom mailed the papers to me."

Emily smiled sympathetically. It must have been hard for Alaina to know that the guy she cared about had been enjoying feminine companionship in every baseball city from Boston to San Diego.

"How about now?" she asked. "You both live in Schuyler and he obviously isn't committed to anyone."

"No luck so far," Alaina answered darkly. "Getting injured gave Mike a major attitude problem. I bet he's even angry at his parents because they insisted on college, which delayed his professional baseball career. Honestly, he acts as if everything in his life is bottom of the bucket because of that accident. The way he talks about teaching makes me want to scream. Teachers are important."

"That's what I told him, more or less."

"Bet he didn't pay any attention."

Emily's nose wrinkled. "Not so you'd notice."

"Kids deserve someone who really cares about what they learn. Heck, a single teacher can make a huge difference in a child's life, but he can't see it."

Alaina's ire was more and more evident, and it confirmed Emily's suspicion that Mike Carlisle's expectations were low for everything now, including women. "Just because he doesn't act interested doesn't mean he's indifferent," she suggested, trying to sound encouraging.

"Maybe, but let's refrain from discussing men

for the rest of the evening," Alaina said darkly. "Or even thinking about them. Instead, let's have fudge cake with ice cream and talk about your house. What about putting in a hot tub or gazebo?"

"I've played with those ideas, and I'm also considering built-in cabinets for a TV and other electronics."

"Vintage style would be fabulous."

Emily laughed. "I can just see your brother's face if I add anything to the list of stuff I want done. On the other hand, it is my house so I guess he'll have to lump it."

"Don't mention Trent. He's one of those men we aren't supposed to be thinking about."

After dinner they decided to check out the local bowling alley. The last time Emily had gone bowling had been in high school and she was surprised at how much fun it was. Alaina acted as if she was having a good time as well, but Emily suspected that deep down she remained despondent about how things were going with Mike. She wished there was a way to help, but matchmaking wasn't her forte.

It was late when they finished and went out to their cars.

"You're welcome to come over to Wild Rose Cottage anytime you want," Emily said before getting into her car. It was old in car years, but still ran great. "You don't need an invitation, whether it's just me at home…or when the guys are there, too."

"What do you mean?"

"Surely you've realized that it would put you and Mike in the same location." Issuing an open invitation to visit Wild Rose Cottage was the closest Emily could come to matchmaking.

"Are you sure you aren't interested in him?" Alaina asked. "I don't want to… Well, I never believed that stuff about all's fair in love and war, if you get my drift."

She was a nice person and Emily was glad she wanted to be friends.

"No, and he's not interested in me, not really, just in a woman he thinks will fit his new life, so I'm absolutely, positively, completely and totally sure I don't have the smallest interest in the guy. I can find additional adverbs if you need them."

Alaina drew a deep breath and visibly relaxed. "Okay. You're right that it's an opportunity to see Mike where he can't avoid me."

It surprised Emily that Alaina was having trouble getting Mike's attention. She was downright beautiful.

"You're looking at me funny," Alaina told her.

"Sorry, I was just thinking that you're as pretty as my sister. She's a supermodel, so I know pretty."

Alaina's eyebrows rose in a way that reminded Emily of Trent. "I don't get it."

Emily shrugged. "It's nothing." She yawned. "I'd better get to bed. The crew arrives before seven."

She got in her car and waited until Alaina was

in her Audi, then waved as they drove their separate ways.

The neighborhood was quiet when Emily let herself into Wild Rose Cottage. Most people in Schuyler were early-to-bed-early-to-rise types. For the most part it suited her, though she'd been known to enjoy a late movie at the theater. But the peace and quiet and friendliness of the small town were more than enough compensation for missing a midnight showing of the latest big-budget fantasy flick.

Yawning, she brushed her teeth and crawled into bed, pleasantly exhausted.

EMILY WOKE UP late and dashed to get the coffee started by the time Trent rang the front doorbell. The rest of the crew arrived a few minutes later and they went to the patio for the usual morning gathering.

It was disconcerting to have so many men in her home day after day. Her laundry and other chores had piled up because she'd been busy doing things for the Emporium after they left in the afternoons and on the weekends, and there was little time in the morning before they arrived. She could do it while they were working, but it felt strange to think about washing her personal items with them around.

Well, it mostly seemed strange because of Trent.

There was no denying she was attracted to him. Trent Hawkins was the kind of intense, driven guy that women often went nutty over, but she couldn't afford to join their ranks. With his looks he could have his choice of feminine companionship, and he certainly wasn't going to choose her.

Given their discussion the evening before, Emily wasn't surprised to see Alaina show up at lunchtime. Unfortunately Mike had left to meet with the principal at the high school and his departure had changed the rhythm of the day. Eduardo, Caveman and Vince had decided to go out for their meal, and Trent was running an errand of his own.

"Sorry, I should have called to let you know he wouldn't be here," Emily apologized.

"That's okay."

They scrounged leftovers from the refrigerator and sat on the patio to eat.

"This is nice," Alaina said when they were munching grapes for dessert.

"Yeah, just Mike-less."

"Another day. He is going to notice me," Alaina added darkly. Then she straightened. "We've got to find a nice guy for you, too."

Emily made a face. "I'm not interested in a romantic relationship—I just got out of a bad one. I should have realized he wasn't really in love with someone so ordinary."

As soon as the words left her mouth, Emily scolded herself. She was trying to avoid unfavorable comparisons to women such as Nicole, but sometimes it was hard not to feel inadequate.

"Don't put yourself down," Alaina ordered. "You're very attractive."

"It's just that I grew up with a gorgeous sister who became a supermodel and sometimes struggle with a small inferiority complex," Emily admitted. "On the other hand, I've always said that every well-adjusted woman needs at least one complex to keep her balanced. So this is mine."

Most people didn't get her sense of humor, but Alaina chuckled as she leaned back in her chair.

Alaina left and Emily went into the living room to eye the front windows. A bay window would look fantastic there.

When Trent came in, she wheeled enthusiastically toward him. "I have a terrific idea," she exclaimed. "A bay window in the living room would add so much."

A BAY WINDOW?

Trent stared at Emily, seriously annoyed. *Now* she wanted something like that? And she was making noises about other things she wanted, as well.

"That's a big job," he said, trying to keep his voice even.

"Yeah, but it would be great to have at Christmastime. I can see a huge decorated tree standing there. Can't we add it to the estimate?"

"I could work up some figures, but—"

"Great. I'll sketch out my idea for it. The room is just asking for that addition."

Trent regarded her narrowly. Emily knew perfectly well he'd been trying to head her off. "Rooms don't have minds of their own."

"How do you know?"

"Everyone knows it," he growled, regretting having said anything. She was a client, albeit one of the more irritating ones. Plenty of people added things midstream and a bay window was more doable than adding turrets or something.

On the other hand, with so much fanciful nonsense skidding through her brain, Emily was also less likely to listen to reason than other clients.

TRENT WENT INTO the Big Sky office on Tuesday morning before daybreak to sign off on a stack of paperwork. Acting as foreman five days a week was playing havoc with his responsibilities as owner of the company. Now he had to figure out how much a bay window in the living room would cost, and he had a doomed conviction this wasn't the last time she'd make such a request. Didn't the woman have any sense?

He wasn't obligated to tack anything onto the current contract, but he wanted the job finished so he'd never have to think about the blasted place again, which made her request for new work all the more annoying.

It was 6:00 a.m. when Trent signed the last document. He passed Alaina on the way in from her car as he headed for his truck.

"Morning," she said, seeming subdued, and he wondered if she wasn't feeling well.

"Are you all right?" he asked.

"Sure."

He wasn't convinced, but who was he to guess at a woman's moods?

After picking up doughnuts—the crew had announced they wanted to take turns because it wasn't fair to let Emily always provide morning treats—he headed for Meadowlark Lane. He knocked to avoid the jarring sound of the doorbell. Quick, light steps sounded and Emily peeked through the curtain on the glass side panel before opening the door.

She was wearing an oversize brown bathrobe and had her hair up in a towel.

"You're early," she announced, then grimaced. "Sorry, I didn't mean that was a problem. It's just that I was at the Emporium late and overslept, so I'm not quite put together this morning. But the coffee should be done brewing."

"You're not obligated to make us coffee every day," he pointed out. "It isn't part of the contract."

"Does it have to be?" she quipped, and Trent groaned to himself. Did that mean she wanted more things that weren't in the contract…side benefits she didn't have to pay to get?

"I'm making coffee for myself," she added, "so why not make enough for everyone? Go get a cup."

He started for the patio through the kitchen and

the combination mud porch and utility room. Emily must have been taking laundry from the front-load washing machine when he arrived, because the appliance's door stood open and the clothes were halfway between it and a basket, a red lace bra dangling over the side.

A sharp "oh" came from behind him and Emily rushed forward with a flushed face, hurriedly stuffing the damp clothing into the basket and hustling it away.

Trent shrugged. He hadn't seen anything he hadn't seen before. Emily's New Age-ish tendencies seemed out of step with something so provocative, but he'd heard that women who weren't geared for glamour often wished for it. And why shouldn't she dress the way she wanted? Still, he would have expected... Well, he wasn't sure what he would have expected. Nor was it any of his business.

While Emily had appeared embarrassed to have her lingerie on display, it could be because he was a man. Privacy was an issue that rose periodically on construction jobs when his crews worked on homes whose owners couldn't vacate during their renovations.

He put the doughnuts beside the coffeepot and poured a cup. The bold flavor rolled across his tongue and he savored it before selecting an apple fritter from the pastry box and sitting on the rickety patio bench. It was a pain to admit, but Emily made the best java in town—even better than his sister's.

Emily appeared around the corner of the house, her long wet hair pulled into a loose French braid.

"Sorry about the mess," she said. "I meant to get everything put away before you arrived."

"No need to apologize."

She poured herself a cup of coffee, adding plenty of cream and sugar.

"What's the point?" he surprised himself by asking. "I mean, if you're going to cover up the coffee taste, why bother?"

"Are you a purist?"

"No, but it's great the way it is."

"Glad I could do something right."

"I never said—"

She grinned. "Jeez, you have an easy chain to yank."

He settled back on the bench. "I'm out of practice knowing when I'm being targeted."

Trent pulled his face into emotionless lines as Emily cocked her head and studied him. Her perusal was unusually intent and she appeared ready to say something, then her mouth twitched and she concentrated on her coffee. He felt strangely disappointed, which was ridiculous; for years he'd worked to keep people from trying to get close to him. Light jokes and casual conversation were fine, but nothing else.

"What made you come to Montana?" he asked.

"I was here on vacation and fell in love with Schuyler," she enthused. "As soon as I saw the Emporium was up for sale I made an offer. It's weird because I don't make impulsive decisions."

Oh, really?

Trent gulped his coffee to keep from making a smart remark; she'd also purchased the house on Meadowlark Lane with impetuous speed.

Apparently Emily had read his mind, because she laughed. "It's true. I'm usually careful and businesslike, on the big stuff. People call me the smart George sister, so everyone back in Los Angeles thinks I've gone nuts."

The "smart" George sister? Seeing herself that way was vaguely arrogant, and Trent wondered if Emily's sister resented being considered less intelligent.

"Do you think you'll stay?" he asked. "We've had big-city folks who move to Montana for the fresh air, but it isn't long until they're desperate for their idea of civilization."

"They can have it." Emily's voice was definite. "Commuting for an hour on a smoggy freeway isn't civilized. Here it takes me just ten minutes to walk to my store, and that's at a strolling pace."

"There are other things that people enjoy about the city."

"Sure, but they don't mean much to me." She studied him again. "Don't you like it here? I mean, would you rather move somewhere larger?"

Trent frowned. "I never considered living any other place than Schuyler," he said.

"Is that because this is where your family is?"

Emily's questions bothered him. Why had he chosen to stay? Living in Montana made sense—the wide-open spaces appealed to him—but Schuyler held memories he'd rather forget. And in another town he wouldn't have to confront the ghost of his father on every corner, or deal with the comparisons between Gavin and himself.

"Actually, I didn't stay for any particular reason," Trent admitted. "I began working for a construction company while in high school, and started my business a few years later."

She still seemed puzzled, but the doorbell jangled, so she jumped up and went inside the house.

Trent was grateful for the reprieve. There was nothing unusual about Emily's inquiries—it was the kind of thing people discussed while chatting—but she was the first person who'd ever asked him how he felt about Schuyler, Montana.

MIKE'S NERVES TIGHTENED when Alaina appeared carrying bags from the deli.

It was annoying to see her so often. He couldn't get over her choosing to abandon a high-power career—perhaps because it reminded him of how his own career had ended.

The whole thing might be easier if he could blame someone else for what had happened that day, but he couldn't. After the accident, sportscasters and sports writers had lauded him for his dedication to the game, saying he always put out a thousand percent. But Mike knew the truth— showing off for a woman was a lousy way to play baseball.

"Hi, guys," Alaina said, barely flicking a look at him. "I've mooched meals here several times now, so it's my turn to provide the food."

"Hear that, Trent?" Vince called. "I like this gig more and more. We get Emily as a helper, and lunch shows up on our doorstep when we least expect it."

Trent walked into the bare kitchen. "Don't give me the credit," he replied, "and don't brag to the other crews, or they might go on strike."

"I heard that," Emily said. "If you've got labor problems, handle them yourself."

"I thought I just did."

Though the exchange sounded light, there was an underlying edge to the way they talked to each other and Mike figured it was his friend's fault. Emily had a friendly nature.

But why was he having trouble getting a second date with her? He thought they'd had a good time, but while she was friendly and appeared to like him, the subject always seemed to shift when he started to ask her out again. It was difficult to believe she was brushing him off, so it must be something else—maybe the craziness of having her house pulled apart.

"Is the patio still the dining hall?" Alaina asked Emily.

"Yep," Emily replied.

"Here." Alaina handed Mike the bags. "Take these out to the patio. I need to get the rest of our dinner from the car."

The way she'd said *dinner* instead of lunch made him think of the bachelor auction, and from the look in her eyes, he was pretty sure it had been deliberate. She hadn't given up, but neither had he. There wasn't a snowball's chance in hell that he'd become a bachelor for sale.

EMILY FINISHED HER sandwich and watched Alaina and Mike trade sharp retorts. Whether he realized it or not, Mike was as attracted to Alaina as she was to him. But they'd have to get past a boatload of hostility before anything could happen.

As for Trent… Emily was trying to ignore him. He was handsome, but she didn't actually like the guy, and it was depressing to be reminded that sexual attraction obviously had little to do with the meeting of like minds.

It didn't help that she'd seen him eyeing her bra in the laundry basket and had been hit by a sense of vulnerability…except *vulnerable* wasn't the right word. No guy had ever seen her lingerie except Dennis, and he'd claimed Victoria's Secret–style bras and panties didn't really suit her, which should have made her know he wasn't overly hot for his fiancée.

Alaina had left and the crew had settled back to work when the doorbell rang. Emily recognized Bob Webber, the previous owner…and the landlord when Trent had lived in Wild Rose Cottage.

"Howdy, Ms. George," Webber said. "How are the renovations going?"

"They're still deconstructing," she said, at the same time wondering about the "howdy." Was that something people actually said outside of a 1940s Western, or did it simply sound phony coming from him?

"Would you mind giving me a tour?" he asked. "I've been anxious to see what's being done with the old place."

Emily hesitated. In the city she would never let him into her home. Maybe she was just tuning into Trent's dislike for Webber, but the guy made her uncomfortable. Still, she wasn't used to small towns and it was probably the custom to be hospitable and let him satisfy his curiosity. Besides, the Big Sky crew was there, so she wasn't alone in the house.

"I guess," she said. Standing aside, she waited as he walked inside.

"I'm going for a more open concept," she explained in the dining room.

His sharp gaze examined the wall that had been stripped down to its support beams.

"Any other walls coming down?" he asked.

Emily shrugged and decided she didn't want Bob Webber to know her business. "I haven't decided."

He strode forward without letting her decide what to show him and she was hit with a wave of distaste, especially when he tried to enter her bedroom. She grabbed the door handle and held it.

"Not in there," she said. "That is private space and nothing's been done in there."

"Don't worry, I won't disturb anything. I just want to see everything."

Trent suddenly appeared and put himself between Webber and the door. "It's the lady's choice. This house no longer belongs to you."

An ugly expression crossed Webber's face, then his features became congenial once more. "My apologies, Ms. George. I wasn't thinking."

Trent scowled and returned to the living room.

Emily was caught between being grateful and aggravated.

Emily led Webber through the rest of the bottom floor, but stopped him from going upstairs.

"All the work is currently on the ground floor," she said firmly, "so there's nothing to see."

"Sure, sure. I appreciate your indulging my curiosity."

She was glad to see him go, though she figured

he'd probably be back. It was hard to believe that curiosity was his sole motivation. There was something off about Webber. Trent Hawkins was annoying and hard to get along with, but he wasn't creepy.

All the same, she didn't plan on answering the door if she was home alone and Webber showed up again.

FURIOUS WITH HIMSELF, Trent finished jerking out the rotten wood on the window frame. He'd wanted to plant a fist in Bob Webber's stomach, an impulse he despised. He knew that children who'd grown up with violence sometimes responded in kind when they became adults; it was one of the reasons he worked so hard to control his temper.

Suddenly aware that Emily had come back into the living room, he stopped and glanced at her.

"Um, I don't know the customs in Montana," she said, "but I kind of like handling things on my own. It was nice of you to try to head off Mr. Webber, but he needs to understand that I'm in charge of my house."

Humor rumbled in Trent's belly.

And amazement.

As a child he'd done his best to protect his mother, who'd been passive in the face of her husband's rages. Yet as time had gone by and the damage inflicted on both of them had gotten worse, a tiny corner of his brain had grown angry at her.

Fiona had never tried to change things, never tried to protect her children and never told Gavin Hawkins to go to hell. If she had, she might be alive today.

Through the years a few women had tried to capitalize on his instinctive urge to rush to the rescue, but however flaky Emily might be, she was telling him to back off. Of course, some people were independent for small stuff and ran for cover when things got serious, but he wouldn't be part of Emily's life, so it didn't matter.

"Understood," he told her.

"Great. I'm not the type for knights in shining armor." She gestured to the wall. "I'm going to start scraping wallpaper in here. It's hideous."

Trent let out a careful breath. "The first layer shouldn't be too bad. It's self-stick and already peeling, but the stuff underneath may have to be steamed off."

At least she'd be working on the walls while he was readily available. If any of his old patches failed, he'd rush to the "rescue," no matter what she said.

Cheerfully, Emily carried a ladder in and climbed to the top level. As she reached for the paper and pulled, he noted how gracefully she moved. Suddenly he had a vision of how she'd look wearing that sexy scrap of red lingerie.

The image kicked him in the gut.

He'd been trying not to pay attention, but there was no denying that Emily had an extremely nice figure under her haphazard clothing.

CHAPTER SEVEN

BY THE END of the week, Emily felt even worse for her new friend. Alaina had visited Wild Rose Cottage on both Wednesday and Thursday and Mike had ignored her both times. Now it was Friday, and Alaina was ignoring *him*.

"I just came by to ask you to a barbecue on Sunday," Alaina told her.

A barbecue?

Pleasant images rose in Emily's imagination. She'd never been to a real Western barbecue, just catered events in Los Angeles that pretended to be Western ho-downs. "That sounds fun. Where will it be?"

"At my folks' spread, the 'historic McGregor Family Ranch,'" Alaina intoned impressively and then laughed.

"Do they live in the original house?"

"No, the first McGregors decided they didn't like the original location and built a new place just nine years after settling in Montana. But part of the current house dates from the 1880s."

Emily was excited. She'd never been to a living breathing ranch.

"It's amazing to have that kind of history right at your fingertips," she said.

"Yeah, except when the teacher at school uses your family to illustrate a Montana State history lesson," Alaina returned wryly. "Anyhow, the barbecue is for Mom's birthday. But no gifts! I meant to invite you before and forgot."

Emily hesitated. "I shouldn't intrude on a family gathering."

"We'll also have lots of friends and neighbors and Mom will be thrilled if you come. She's crazy about you." Alaina winked. "She says you're an asset to the community. A real gem."

Warmth went through Emily. She'd never gotten unqualified support in her life, and it was lovely to encounter it unexpectedly.

"Okay, I'd love to attend."

Just then Trent came through the hallway with a load of lumber balanced on his shoulder. Along with the new bay window, it turned out that every downstairs window frame needed to be replaced due to rot and other damage. The ones on the second and third floors were probably just as bad, but she was trying not to think about it. Luckily Trent was considered tops in historic restoration, so it shouldn't be too much of a problem getting everything to look right.

If they ever finished. Admittedly, she'd come up with several extra projects. It was making things even tenser around Trent, even though she'd said she understood if they had to come back later to do them.

"Hey, Trent," Alaina said. "Emily is coming to Mom's party. Isn't that terrific?"

"Oh. Yes. Of course."

While he nodded politely, Emily suspected he wasn't pleased. He continued into the living room where he'd set up various pieces of woodworking equipment. The window frames had to be custom made and it was slow, tedious work. Still, she was impressed with how patient he could be...when it came to construction.

"Maybe I shouldn't go," she murmured, glancing into the other room and seeing how grim he looked.

"Don't be silly," Alaina whispered back. "Trent likes to keep work and social relationships separate, but you're my friend and I have the right to ask whoever I want. Besides, I work for him and *I'll* be there."

Quietly they moved out to the patio.

"Are you sure?" Emily said. "He seemed to tense up when you told him I was coming."

Alaina made a wry face. "That's just Trent being Trent. I love my brother, but he's hard to understand. Mom and Dad worry because he's so withdrawn and solitary. Do you suppose it's because our folks died and they adopted us? I mean, I think of my aunt and uncle as Mom and Dad, but I doubt he does."

"Well, he remembers your folks, and you don't, so maybe it feels disloyal to think of someone else as his parents," Emily said slowly. She was trying to envision Trent Hawkins as a child, without much luck.

"But Mom and Dad are terrific."

"I suppose experiences affect people in different ways."

"I guess." Alaina looked at her cell phone. "It's late. I'd better get back to the office."

She marched past Mike in the kitchen without a word and Emily decided if she ever got stupid enough to reconsider her stance on romance, she should remember what Alaina was going through. The woman was dazzling and still couldn't get Mike to notice her.

Sighing, Emily went back to work on the wallpaper. Once in a while she glanced at Trent, who was concentrating on the window frame he was crafting.

"The frames look great," she ventured when he'd stopped the table saw for a moment.

"I could still order modern, double-paned windows. They'd insulate better."

"Except they wouldn't look as good with wild roses climbing around them," she retorted.

"I suppose you think the house wouldn't 'like' modern windows…you know, the kind that save money and make everything more comfortable."

His mocking tone put Emily's teeth on edge. She

didn't mind the crew's gentle amusement about her ideas, but Trent's scorn was the same as pouring itching powder on her nerves. Besides, while installing double-paned windows with vinyl frames might be the "sensible" choice, it didn't fit the vintage appeal of Wild Rose Cottage. At any rate, it was her decision and she was paying for the privilege, so why was he so negative?

She almost snorted. People had described Trent as ornery, and they hadn't been exaggerating.

ON SUNDAY TRENT reluctantly headed for the McGregor ranch shortly before noon. His first choice would have been to ditch the birthday barbecue, but it would have hurt Aunt Sarah's feelings.

Sarah's father was the first guest he saw.

"Good afternoon," he said. Since his mother had been Uncle Parker's sister, he had no genetic relationship to Walt Nelson. Alaina called him Grandpa Walt, but Trent usually managed to avoid using a title of any kind.

"Afternoon, Trent. Your crew came out and fixed my chimney last week."

"That's good."

Walt narrowed his eyes at him. "I asked for a bill and they said to check with the office. Now Alaina tells me she can't find it."

"Guess you lucked out."

"I don't need any gifts."

"Walt, they were there for less than thirty minutes. Check with me when they're needed for over an hour."

Walt glared, and Trent went into the backyard to say hello to Aunt Sarah, who hugged him and scolded when he placed a gift in her hands.

"I have everything I need," she told him. "Well, almost everything, but what I really want can't be wrapped in paper."

He knew what she was referring to: grandchildren.

"I'll leave that to Jackson," Trent told her. His cousin's recent marriage to a former high school sweetheart had brought two grandchildren into the fold. Since Jackson already had a daughter, Morgan, it had tripled Sarah's blessings, as she called them.

"Humph," she grumbled. "You're all too stubborn."

Trent stayed with her until one of his great-aunts arrived, then headed to the barbecue grill. If he couldn't stay away, he'd stay busy. It didn't work; he got chased off by Uncle Parker. So he donned his swim trunks and dove into the pool.

EMILY SWUNG BY the market deli early in the afternoon and bought broccoli salad to contribute to Sarah McGregor's birthday celebration. When pressed, Alaina had admitted that the party was partly potluck, but insisted Emily shouldn't bring anything.

"Poppycock," Emily had retorted. "Bringing something is part of the fun."

It had been a relief to shed jeans and T-shirts for the day and wear a soft blouse and skirt with sandals. Since there was a pool, Alaina had told her to bring a swimsuit, so it had gone into the trunk with an outrageously colored beach towel.

Parking in front of the large ranch house, Emily saw a bunch of vehicles were already under the trees. Alaina must have been watching, because she met her halfway to the house.

"Come on, I'll introduce you around."

Leaving the salad with the housekeeper, Emily followed Alaina into the backyard.

Sarah McGregor hurried over and hugged her. "I'm so glad you came," the older woman enthused.

"Happy birthday."

"Thank you. I didn't realize what house you'd bought until Alaina told me, and now Trent is fixing it up. That makes you one of the family."

Emily was sure that Trent wouldn't agree, but decided not to worry about him. And she succeeded until she saw him bare-chested, wearing his swim trunks.

Whoa.

He was trim, muscled and thoroughly male.

She ordered herself to look away—she refused to turn into one of those unwanted women who leered at sexy men.

Alaina seemed determined to introduce her to

everyone and the names and faces began to blur. Luckily she'd already met some of them around town.

Madison, Alaina's sister, had recently moved to Seattle and hadn't been able to make it back. But another sibling had arrived unexpectedly and he jumped up to give Alaina a hug. Josh was the foreman at a ranch down in Texas.

"Texas?" Emily asked when they were alone again. Considering the McGregor and Nelson ranching tradition in the Schuyler area, it seemed odd that he was working so far away.

"It's complicated. Josh is waiting for Mom's father to retire and give him the ranch," Alaina explained. "It was decided a long time ago that he's to get the Nelson spread, but Grandpa Walt can't seem to let go. Grandma and Grandpa Nelson are over there." She motioned toward an older couple.

"I met Mrs. Nelson when she came into my store a few weeks ago, but I didn't realize she was Sarah's mother."

"Yup. I'm sure there are too many McGregors here for Grandpa Walt's taste," Alaina whispered mischievously. "Not me, of course. I don't have any Nelson blood, but he's forgiven me for that shortcoming."

"I understand the Parkers and Nelsons used to be ranching rivals."

"That's right. Then Mom and Dad got married and it all had to end. Now they compete by playing horseshoes. I think Grandpa Walt is up by two games."

It sounded fun, but Emily didn't have a chance to ask for details before she was introduced to Alaina's brother Jackson and his wife, Kayla. They were the son and daughter-in-law Sarah had shopped for at the Emporium. It was almost depressing to see the attractive couple. Was everyone in Montana that happy and good-looking? Well, all except Mike Carlisle—he didn't seem happy, though he got more than his share of points in the looks department.

The gathering was exactly what Emily had imagined a Western barbecue would be. Someone had even brought a banjo, and someone else played a harmonica. Everyone was warm and cordial…with the exception of Trent. He only nodded politely at her, but she also noticed he didn't appear cozy with anyone.

Too bad. They were a great bunch of folks.

TRENT HAD PLANNED to avoid Emily at the party, but she and Alaina ended up at the same table with him.

"How on earth did I get so much food on my plate?" his sister demanded as she sat down.

"Beats me," Emily replied. "I asked for a small steak and got half a cow."

"Mmm," Alaina said after munching down a

mouthful. "The broccoli salad you brought is divine. The deli just added it to their lineup."

"I would have made something, but I'm lacking some equipment at the moment. You know, sink, kitchen counters...a stove."

Trent forked a bite of the same salad into his mouth. Odd combo of flavors—broccoli with bacon, onions and raisins—but it wasn't bad. He finished his meal quickly and relieved Uncle Parker at the grill so he could sit with his wife.

Although everybody ate heartily, there was a pile of leftovers. He moved the meat into pans and put them into the large refrigerator that he'd installed when building the outdoor kitchen three years before. It had been a gift for his aunt and uncle's thirty-fifth wedding anniversary, chosen because they entertained so much.

With the grill cleaned and the housekeeper hustling the remaining food into containers, Trent was once again left without a task. Casual conversation wasn't something he did well, so he returned to the pool, pulled off his T-shirt and dove into the water.

Hmm. Perhaps he should build a pool at the Balderdash. The house was just a place to sleep, but swimming was healthy exercise.

Upon opening his eyes, his gaze was caught immediately by Emily. She stood poolside in a sleek white suit that confirmed his speculations about her physical endowments. Her figure was extremely nice, something he'd rather not think about while still working on her house. Not that he was going to do anything about it, either before or after the renovation was completed, since Emily didn't seem the sort for casual affairs and she wasn't his type of woman in the first place.

Unfortunately his body didn't care if she was off-limits, and he was grateful that the water in the pool was cool.

WHEN ALAINA WAS ready to leave the barbecue, she wrapped a steak and several chicken hindquarters in heavy foil, and drove to Mike's condo.

"Hi," she said when he answered the door, handing over the package of food. "We had tons left, so I brought you a bribe. You don't have to give me an answer right now about the auction, but—"

"I've already given you an answer."

She waved a hand in the air. "Certain answers just fly past my ears without being heard. I'll see you Monday."

Wheeling, she started for her car, almost expecting to see the meat she'd brought him go sailing past her; Mike still had a great throwing arm. But she got to her Audi without having to deal with flying meat.

Alaina drove away, controlling the trembling in her hands with an effort. She needed to focus. Her firm in New York had sent a stack of work and needed it back by Monday morning. That was okay; at least it would keep her from thinking what an idiot she was to hang around Schuyler, hoping to catch Mike's attention.

Emily had pointed out a couple of times that Mike wasn't necessarily indifferent, no matter how he behaved. That was some comfort, but it didn't mean he was in love with her, either.

Yeah, she was an idiot, working on moron status.

EMILY HUMMED AS she drove home. The harmonica and banjo players had put together an impromptu band, getting her to beat some bongo drums that Jackson McGregor had unearthed from his childhood. She'd played drums in the high school marching band and had forgotten how much fun it was to help make music.

Most of the partygoers had joined in the singing. Not Trent, but she hadn't expected him to relax his stiff exterior.

It was interesting. Sarah and Parker McGregor clearly loved their niece and nephew just as much as their biological children, but while Alaina returned the affection, it was harder to tell about Trent. There wasn't anything contentious or negative in how he interacted with his family. He just didn't seem comfortable with them.

Emily sighed with exasperation. She was spending too much time thinking about the guy. Of course, he was in her house almost every day, so naturally he was part of her mental landscape.

Unfortunately, she was used to guys seeing her

as ordinary. And maybe she was supersensitive because of her ex-fiancé, who'd thought she should have been grateful he wanted to marry her, despite his cheating. At least she'd dented his monumental ego when telling him where to go…and giving him directions.

Back at Wild Rose Cottage, Emily reminded herself that she'd had a wonderful time at the barbecue, despite Trent. And in a month or two the house would be remade and he'd be out of her hair.

That was a cheerful thought.

But an odd sensation hit her as she opened the front door. Nervous chills ran down her spine and she was certain that the house felt nervous, as well. Walking from room to room, she found nothing had been disturbed, but she couldn't shake the conviction that somebody had been inside while she'd been gone. Could they still be there? Upstairs, perhaps?

She reached for the phone, drew back, then grabbed the receiver and called the sheriff's office. While waiting she parked herself next to the front door, ready to open it and run like hell if necessary.

Five minutes later there was a firm knock. Emily peeked out and saw a tall man in a sheriff's uniform.

"Good evening," he said as she opened the door. "I'm Carl Stanfield."

Emily heaved a sigh. "I'm Emily George. It probably sounds silly, but I can't help feeling someone has been in the house. It's ridiculous because there's nothing worth stealing. Big Sky Construction is remodeling, so there's hardly anything here."

"Don't worry, I'll check everything. Wait on the porch."

Twenty minutes later he came back. "I've gone over the entire house, basement to attic, including the closets and showers. No one is here, now at least."

Her tension eased. "You must think I'm a terrible goose," she told him.

"Nope. I've known men and women both who can imagine an intruder out of a stray piece of lint. But you don't seem the type. In any case, here's my card. Promise you'll call if something doesn't feel right."

She smiled. "Okay," she agreed and tucked the business card into her smartphone sleeve.

Jeez, the people in Schuyler were nice.

TRENT PREPARED TO leave the family barbecue, grateful the ordeal was concluded.

"Thank you for the lovely paperweight," Sarah said as she hugged him good-night. "Where did you find it?"

"Over the internet," he explained. "It's made with a little ash from Mount St. Helens."

They'd visited the national monument in Washington State a month before the formal adoption had been finalized. He still remembered standing at Windy Ridge, looking out at the devastated mountain as they asked if he minded…with a quick assurance his last name would remain Hawkins. He could have told them that he wasn't proud to be a Hawkins, but his mouth had remained stubbornly shut.

Aunt Sarah plainly recalled the same moment, because her face became even more emotional. "That makes it extra special, but you didn't need to get me anything."

"I wanted to. Happy birthday, Mom," he managed to say, in almost natural tones. The glow in her eyes made him feel guilty—calling her Mom was what meant the most to her. She rose on her toes and kissed him on the cheek.

"Good night, dear."

He drove home and dialed into the message center when he saw he had voice mail.

"Trent, this is Carl Stanfield," said the voice. "Emily George mentioned that you're remodeling her house. She called this evening, concerned about a possible intruder. I checked it out and made sure the doors and windows were locked, but wanted you to know. The place isn't that secure and she's there on her own."

Trent cursed silently.

If Emily had moved into an apartment while the work was being done, there wouldn't be any questions about her safety. Even better, if she'd let him have the property, there wouldn't have been any concerns at all.

Trent stopped at Big Sky Construction the next morning to pick up the locks he'd ordered for Emily's house. He quietly circled the property when he arrived. There was more than one sign of forced entry, but he couldn't tell if any were fresh. Aside from that, there was no way to know how many people had a key. It was unlikely Bob Webber had changed the locks for new tenants, and Emily might not have considered it worth the trouble with the planned remodeling.

All at once Trent frowned, recalling Webber's eagerness to get inside, supposedly to see the renovations. Was he anxious enough to break in? A vision of Bob Webber going to prison was immensely appealing, but Trent promptly dismissed the possibility; he was prejudiced against the guy. Besides, why would Bob care so much?

Eduardo was the first member of the crew to arrive and Trent took him aside. "Change the locks on the doors and fix the windows so they can't be jimmied easily. Don't make a big deal out of it." The windows he'd already reframed shouldn't be an issue—so far the ones he'd finished were all decorative, rather than functional.

"Has there been a problem?"

"Possible intruder."

"We'll get it done. Can't leave our Em unprotected."

Fortunately, Emily was so busy trying to remove

layers of wallpaper, she didn't seem to notice the crew working to secure her windows and doors.

At noon Trent handed her a new set of keys. "The hardware has been sticking," he explained. "Replacing the locks is in the contract, so I decided to take care of it now, rather than waiting."

Her head cocked and her eyes narrowed.

"Liar," she accused. "The sheriff called you, didn't he?"

"Yes," he admitted, "but it isn't a big deal." Trent didn't know which way she would jump—anger that he'd done something to help, or anxiety because he'd felt it safer to fix the locks.

A grin lit up Emily's face and she laughed. "I'm not used to such wonderful small-town unity. It's amazing."

Her enthusiasm was confusing and Trent could only chalk it up to her previous life in an impersonal city. He might cultivate his reputation as an ornery polecat, but he believed in taking care of his neighbors. Most folks in Schuyler felt the same, so it didn't mean he was behaving like the hapless prince in a fairy tale, rescuing maidens right and left.

Doing the right thing was important—he just didn't want to be a chump.

"Thanks," Emily said.

It was hard to evaluate what was in her mind. One minute she told him off for trying to help her against Bob Webber, the next she was celebrating small-town unity in looking after neighbors. Perhaps it was just another example of her flakiness.

CHAPTER EIGHT

"EMILY?" TRENT SAID. She was so deep into reading a letter that she hadn't heard him the first time he'd said her name.

She looked up and set the letter aside. "Is something wrong?"

"Vince wants me to tell you that the mantelpiece in the living room can't be saved. He's done his best, but the wood is too far gone."

Her face fell and Trent understood why Vince had bailed on the task of breaking the news. The crew had become absurdly fond of Emily in the weeks they'd been working on her house and hated disappointing her about anything. Not that Trent was surprised she'd wanted to save the fireplace mantel. It was intricately carved, with inlaid pillars on each side, but it had suffered too many years of neglect.

"Can it be reproduced?" she asked finally. "I've taken pictures."

"Possibly, but the cost would be sky-high since it's mostly an art piece. Finding an artist skilled enough would be difficult, and then they'd have to be willing to accept the commission. I doubt you'd be happy with anything that wasn't made by a master craftsman."

Visibly dejected, Emily stared out the window.

He put a sketchpad on the card table and sat on the chair across from her. "There are several options. The first is creating something out of brick." Quickly he sketched how it would appear.

She nodded without enthusiasm.

"A broad wood mantel could be added." He applied that to the sketch.

"I'm sure it will be very nice," she said politely.

Trent continued adding various embellishments, but it was clear that a modern substitute couldn't match what she'd envisioned for the living room.

"I'm sorry," Emily apologized. "It's just that I've been seeing it a certain way and now I have to adjust."

"Pine boughs at Christmas, right?" he asked, recalling what she'd said to Vince on the day they'd started work.

A hint of a smile tugged at her mouth. "Yes, and maybe Victorian-style bows or something. I shouldn't have gotten my hopes up since I knew it was chancy."

The wistfulness in her eyes got to Trent, and he uneasily recalled an email he'd recently received from a real estate office near Helena. A 1890s-era farmhouse was being torn down in September and the broker had offered to let Big Sky salvage items from it.

They had done this sort of thing often, but his company was so busy that summer Trent hadn't expected to take advantage of the offer. However, the list from the broker had indicated three fireplace mantelpieces were in the house. If he kept his mouth shut, Emily would never know. It was good business to make his clients happy, but it was irritating at the same time, because he wondered if she was trying to manipulate him with her visible disappointment.

"There's one other possibility," he said. "I've been told about a Victorian farmhouse near Helena that's being torn down. It has three fireplaces with vintage mantelpieces. I don't know what they look like, only what was on the broker's inventory."

Her eyes lit up. "Could one of them be used here?"

"There's no way to know for sure without going there," he replied quickly. "And remember the house is Victorian, not Arts and Crafts, so the style would be different."

"Uh… I don't think the damaged fireplace mantel is true Arts and Crafts anyway."

Trent didn't have an answer to the obvious, so he chose another tactic. "It would still be expensive. On top of that, even if a suitable one is available, it would mean more delays while it's being salvaged. I shouldn't have brought it up. The whole idea is impractical."

Now that he'd introduced the idea, Trent decided he'd been a sap. Satisfying a client didn't mean going this far, did it?

EMILY LEANED FORWARD. "Haven't you realized by now that practical isn't my strong suit? At least when it comes to Wild Rose Cottage," she added hastily.

"No kidding," he said. "Look, it would take a full day, maybe even two, just to go see if one of the mantels could be used, and then to pull it out. I've checked out enough places like this to know people can be unrealistic about the value of anything on the inventory, or else they're handing me a line. This particular broker has exaggerated before, so I'm not optimistic."

Emily's feet danced at the vision of visiting another old house, particularly one that might contain material useful for restoring Wild Rose Cottage.

"I still want to see it," she said.

"You want to go?" he asked. Clearly the possibility hadn't occurred to him.

"Of course. That way it wouldn't take time from the crew. Just tell me what to look for and what measurements to use. Who knows, there might be other neat stuff, too."

Trent appeared torn, but he finally sighed. "I'll drive over myself and check it out for you."

"No way. You might be able to tell if something is useable, but I'm the only one who'd know if it's something I want."

"I can email pictures," he offered.

"That wouldn't be the same."

Frustration filled his face. "Fine. I was going to pass on salvaging this particular house, but since you're determined to have the place checked, we'll go together and I'll see if there are a few items I can use for Big Sky's inventory."

He didn't seem particularly happy over having made the offer, but she decided not to worry about that. After all, this way he could add items to his company's inventory.

"Okay," she said, "tell me when to meet you there."

"Er...your car is pretty old to travel that far."

He was plainly trying to be diplomatic—something that was out of character for him—but Emily knew exactly how many miles were on the odometer.

When she'd decided to move to Montana, she had parked her Jaguar in the garage of her house in Southern California and would likely sell both the house and Jag before long. The Jag didn't seem to fit Schuyler, so she'd brought the sedan she'd owned since high school. However aged, she took good care of it and trusted her little baby to get her places.

"My car is reliable and I want to make double use of the trip," she insisted. "This way I can meet with my Helena-based suppliers for the Emporium and straighten out a few things."

Another odd expression flashed across his face, but as usual, Emily couldn't decipher it. The guy was a puzzle. Her sister could probably wrap Trent around her little finger, except Nicole was dating an Italian businessman and probably wouldn't be caught dead in a town without a Neiman Marcus store.

The thought sent a flash of guilty gratitude through Emily. Nothing was going to happen between her and Trent, but it would have been miserable to see yet *another* guy she found attractive go loopy over her sister. That was one of the nice things about Schuyler—nobody had met Nicole, so there weren't any comparisons, conscious or otherwise, between them.

"All right," he agreed. "I'll contact the broker to find out when we can get inside the house."

"Great. Let's go eat."

Relieved, Emily jumped up and headed for the patio, glad to get away from him. Trent was overwhelming, even when he wasn't being a pain in the ass. The other day he'd practically exploded when she stopped the crew from tearing up the damaged floor in the old parlor. It was beautiful, with an intricate design created from ribbons of bent wood. Unfortunately, several sections had buckled from a water leak.

"It can't be repaired," he'd snarled after sending Eduardo and Caveman to do something else.

"I read about a similar floor being repaired at

the Pittock Mansion in Portland," Emily had insisted. "They soaked it again, then laid out planks and weighed them down with barrels of water to gradually ease them back in place."

"This isn't the Pittock Mansion."

"I don't care."

"It isn't in—"

"I know, it isn't in the contract," she'd interrupted. Loudly. "Or at least, I wasn't *specific* enough about the repairs I wanted. Just give me a new estimate."

They'd glared at each other a couple of minutes before he'd stomped out and told the others to leave the floor alone...for the time being.

Sometimes it was exhausting to deal with Trent, which was why she hadn't wanted to drive with him to Helena.

"Emily, come have some pizza," Caveman called, distracting her from the memory.

Emily fixed a smile on her face. The crew had asked her to join them for lunch and she didn't want them to think anything was wrong.

On the days she provided lunch, Emily always invited Alaina, who still wasn't making any headway with Mike. The guy was a stone wall. He continued making noises to Emily about taking her out and she'd needed to do some quick thinking to head him off. She didn't want to say anything outright—not wanting to spoil the camaraderie that was making the construction project so enjoyable—but when was he going to get the message? He'd even hinted about them going out in front of Alaina.

Emily winced at the memory.

Afterward, to keep her friend from feeling worse, she'd privately revealed her conviction that Mike was only interested because he saw her as a sensible choice to date. She didn't have any proof, but the little things he'd let drop made her sure it was the reason.

"Really? I can't understand why I'm hung up on him," Alaina had grumbled. "He can be such a jerk and he's blind if he doesn't see how terrific you are."

Alaina's staunch support had soothed Emily's ego, bruised from confessing something so embarrassing. That was the great thing about a genuine friend—she could support you, even when her heart was breaking over some man.

"That's nice of you to say, but I'm used to guys seeing me a certain way," Emily had admitted. "My ex-fiancé wanted a practical kind of woman as a wife, yet expected to sleep around with women as glamorous as my sister. Unlike Dennis, however, I'm sure Mike doesn't have visions of cheating with someone before he goes home to his nice, sensible choice."

Alaina had stared at her in amazement. "If that's what your ex-fiancé expected, you're better off without him. I hope you drop-kicked him into the Pacific Ocean."

"Almost."

Right then Eduardo had come around the corner of the house to get a cup of coffee, so they'd changed the subject.

THE FOLLOWING MONDAY Trent assigned the Meadowlark Lane crew to work on the roof and storm cellar while he and Emily were out of town. Eduardo endorsed the plan, saying, "It's best to leave the interior work for when Emily is home. We have more fun when she's here."

Huh. It might be the first time one of his crews had thought a restoration job was this much fun. They were having a grand time working with Emily and treated her like a favorite kid sister. They happily asked her to help with tasks they considered safe and gave lessons in anything requiring specific knowledge, though she was so flighty, Trent couldn't imagine her truly mastering any of the skills. It still amazed him that she managed two successful businesses—luck maybe?

The most vexing part about the situation was that he could have scheduled someone else to go to Helena in his place. With Emily out of town, it would have been a great opportunity to retrieve everything he'd hidden in the walls as a boy. She'd even suggested again that she could go on her own, but sending her to explore a deserted house in the country hadn't seemed right.

So he was stuck. Really bad planning. He didn't need to spend more time with Emily. At the thought, an image flashed through his head of what one of her lacy bras must look like while cupping her round curves.

He cursed.

Despite his best efforts he hadn't been able to suppress the desire he felt around her. At first he'd refused to acknowledge his reaction. Now he was just doing his best to master it.

Emily had said she could meet him whenever he suggested; she was spending the night in Helena after a late-afternoon meeting with her suppliers. He'd told her to arrive at the farmhouse midmorning, figuring that if he left Schuyler early enough, he would have time to check the building first. That way he could determine if any of the fireplace mantels were suitable before she saw them and got her hopes raised…another action he didn't care to examine too closely. Not that it meant anything. He was just getting sucked into his crew's devotion to their client, which irritated him all over again.

Shortly before 8:00 a.m. he pulled into the farmhouse drive and found Emily's ancient sedan already parked nearby. She wasn't anywhere in sight and alarm shot through him.

Deserted houses could attract vagrants; it wasn't safe for a woman to head into the place by herself, particularly since the broker had planned to unlock it the night before. Trent hadn't thought to warn Emily since he'd expected to be there a couple of hours in advance. He slid from the truck and sprinted to the front porch.

"Emily," he called, taking the front steps two at a time.

The door opened and she stepped outside, a paper cup in her right hand. "Wow, you're early, too. I've been exploring. It's a shame they're tearing this place down. I wish I had a billion bucks to fix up old houses that no one cares about any longer."

Trent's alarm vanished, leaving him annoyed.

"You shouldn't go into deserted buildings by yourself," he told her sharply. "It isn't safe."

Considering her previous anger at him for trying to be protective, he half expected a royal scolding. Once again she surprised him as she cocked her head and studied him for a moment.

"You haven't had your morning coffee, have you?" she asked. "And you probably skipped breakfast. That's why you're such a grump. Not that you're a spoonful of sunshine any day, but it's more pronounced this morning."

"You…" Trent didn't know what to say and couldn't admit that concern for her safety had been the real motivation. Besides, he hadn't made coffee, or even eaten the protein bars he kept stashed in the glove compartment. He'd just climbed into the truck and left.

"It's okay," she assured. "I've got a big thermos I brewed at the motel and picked up provisions at the supermarket."

She led the way into the house. A rickety chair held a large stainless steel thermos and the cup she poured smelled ambrosial. Still, Trent hesitated to take it.

Her eyes twinkled. "Don't let pride stand in your way."

With a sigh he accepted the cup and took a swallow. It was the same brew she made every day and his nerves began to settle.

"There's other stuff in the bag if you want it," she advised.

Trent ate a slice of cheese and a handful of crackers as he glanced around the large living room. The oversize fireplace was ornately framed and crowned by an attractive mantelpiece, but it wasn't the right dimensions for Emily's house.

As they walked through the house, there were other good architectural features he immediately wanted to salvage. It *was* a shame the farmhouse was being torn down; the Victorian must have been a showplace in its day. But at least he could preserve pieces of it.

"Ooh," Emily exclaimed as she walked into the kitchen. "I didn't see this before. Could I have the farm sink for my kitchen?"

Trent gazed at it with a practiced eye. "We'll have to do some redesigning, but it's possible."

In a room that may have functioned as a formal parlor, Emily sighed ecstatically at the row of five stained-glass windows.

"How about those?"

"Uh, yeah, but keep in mind this is a big house. I'm not sure there's space for everything at Wild Rose Cottage." He paused a moment and realized he'd used Emily's name for the place. He cocked his head, thinking back. The day they'd moved in had actually been very happy; his parents had danced in the living room and his mother had seen the wild roses afterward, instantly deciding what the house should be called. Gavin had enthusiastically agreed.

There had been so few good memories, but something about Emily's joy in exploring the farmhouse brought this one back. At the same time, sorrow went through him because Fiona's hopes when they had moved into the house had been quickly dashed. That had been part of the problem…she'd always thought things would change.

Emily shook her head. "I don't care if everything fits, I still want it…just in case of…oh, I don't know. I can't bear the thought of such a glorious old place going unappreciated. It's as if the house is saying, 'Please save part of me.'"

"Maybe it is," Trent said before doing another mental double take. He *didn't* believe houses talked.

Emily went to the parlor fireplace and ran her fingers over the framing before looking up with a hopeful expression. "I like this one. Will it fit?"

"I'll find out."

Taking out his measuring tape, he checked the dimensions. "We can make it work."

With a cry of delight, she gave him a quick hug. "I guess this is too big, isn't it?" she asked, leading him into the dining room and pointing to the enormous built-in china closet. It was a magnificent piece and had miraculously escaped being painted and repainted over the years.

Trent sucked in a breath, trying to banish the memory of Emily's body against his. "Sorry," he managed to say, "it's too big for any room in your house."

"I guess, but what a shame it's going to be demolished."

Initially Trent had planned to just take a few things out of the house in addition to what Emily wanted, but now he decided to schedule a crew to do a thorough salvage job. While the house was in sad structural condition, many of its features were so beautifully made, it *did* seem wrong not to save them.

If he was building his own home, the china closet and several… He cut off his thoughts. He had no need of houses with china closets and mahogany door frames. Unless the ranch house on the Balderdash fell down, he was fine.

"There's obviously more than we can get in a day, so I'll send a crew back to get the items you want, and others for me," he said, directing his thoughts in a less ridiculous direction.

"It seems silly not to make use of the trip here. Can't we get some of them today?" she asked. "After all, you brought a truck. Wasn't that the point, to take stuff back with you?"

"I can try," he said. He had hoped to make it entirely a one-day trip, with no need to send anyone back, but that was when he'd anticipated the place being a bust, with nothing worth salvaging.

"Not just you. I'll help."

He agreed reluctantly. In his experience inept help could be worse than none at all. While the renovation crew seemed to appreciate her assistance, they were also able to pick and choose which tasks to give her. Still, he could probably find something for Emily to do that wouldn't be too much of a problem.

ALAINA'S PHONE BUZZED midafternoon on Monday and she read the text message Trent had sent her.

Pull 3 for salvage crew to come to Helena.

They must have found some good stuff in the farmhouse.

He'd left it up to her to choose who would go, which was good. The intestinal flu going around had hit the company and it was hard keeping crews adequately filled. Still, they could send a team to Helena between jobs.

Alaina looked at the schedule. Honestly, Mike didn't have a clue how much work it required to juggle everything for six construction yards.

Irritation hit her at the thought.

Would she spend the rest of her life with his voice in her head? Leaving New York City had been her decision, and she didn't regret it…other than him proving to be a stubborn jackass.

She drummed her fingers on the desk. Mike was one of their employees out with the flu. It usually lasted the better part of a week and he'd only come down with it over the weekend. Perhaps she should bring him some chicken soup tomorrow, a nice, friendly half gallon in one of her good pots, a pot he'd have to return when he got better. And if he didn't return the pot, she'd go to his condo to get it.

The question was whether she should tackle him again about the bachelor auction. He'd probably be in a foul temper, but that was nothing new. Folks in Schuyler tried to be understanding about Mike's moods—actually, they bent over backward to be understanding—but maybe that was part of the problem. He just kept getting away with bad manners.

It could be time to practice tough love and be completely frank with him.

EMILY CHEWED HER lip as Trent used a crowbar on the wall around the edge of the fireplace setting. She knew it was necessary, but it seemed such an indignity to the house.

He ripped out a chunk of the more modern drywall, applied long after the place was built, exposing a darker surface beneath.

"Holy cow," Trent murmured. "That's cherrywood."

"Who would cover cherry paneling?" she asked.

"Someone who didn't appreciate what they had. You'd be amazed at the stuff people cover up with drywall or paint."

She liked the way he crouched and examined the wood more closely.

"It must have been brought in from a distance," she said. "The people who built this place couldn't have been like a lot of the small farmers I've read about. I mean, they make a living, but I understand it can be a marginal business for the average family farm. And Helena doesn't seem to be a major agrarian capital, either."

Trent nodded. "Farming is a lot like ranching, at least since the beef market has become more unstable. It's a way of life that nobody wants to give up. The McGregors and Nelsons love it."

"But you didn't want to be a rancher?"

"I always preferred the idea of building and construction. Did you always want to own a store?"

"Not really. A boutique fit since I know something about fashion, even if I'm not the best representative for it."

As he loosened the mantel, Emily helped lift it down. She wanted to start carrying it to the truck, but he stopped and brought in a dolly to help.

"You're right, we should let Archimedes give us some help," she said. "Isn't a dolly based on the principle of a lever and fulcrum?"

"Yes, and we don't need to move the world, just a mantel."

"When I was a kid, I used to imagine him trying to do it, then just as he lifted it, the whole planet rolled away on him and all the people got dizzy."

Trent chuckled. "Believe it or not, I pictured the same thing, except I kept seeing multistoried buildings tipping over like dominoes."

They deposited the parlor mantel next to the truck and then brought out the side pieces.

"What do we do next?" Emily asked. "Load them first, or wait to see how everything we're getting today can be jigsawed into the truck bed?"

"Let's do jigsaw."

The muscles in Trent's arms flexed as he carried the dolly up the steps. Emily gulped, feeling an involuntary flash of warmth, though it was rather like being attracted to a mountain lion—exciting, dangerous and impossible, all at the same moment.

As the hours passed Trent was reluctantly impressed by Emily's willingness to keep working through dirty tasks in the mice-infested house, and her ability to be of genuine assistance. She'd clearly paid attention to what the crew had been teaching her and swiftly caught on to anything new.

Beyond that, she was a lively conversationalist. From ancient Egypt to Picasso, she had an opinion on everything and they had several good-natured debates.

He did notice a faint hint of self-deprecation whenever she referenced anything personal. In his experience some women used that as a tactic to elicit compliments, so he'd learned to say nothing.

Regardless, her enthusiasm was infectious. After asking what pieces he was interested in for his own inventory, she insisted on helping to remove the smaller ones that could be transported that day.

"I suppose Archimedes isn't the only one we should thank," he said as they stacked the cherrywood paneling they'd recovered so far from the parlor. His instructions to the salvage crew would include checking under every shred of drywall to be sure other treasures weren't missed.

"What do you mean?" she asked.

"The guy who invented the wheel was pretty important."

"You're assuming it was a guy? Maybe it was a woman who got tired of lugging rocks from the field while her husband plowed."

"Uh…yeah," Trent muttered.

He'd lost track of his place in the conversation.

A trickle of perspiration was rolling down Emily's neck, into the deep V of her shirt. It was a warm day and she'd opened the top buttons, revealing the taut upper swell of her breasts. He'd tried to ignore the sight of her in a swimsuit at the family barbecue, but it was getting harder to pretend he didn't see her peekaboo curves.

A short time later Trent noticed the rays of sunlight coming through the window were growing long.

"Damn." He pulled out his smartphone to check the time. "I should have paid more attention. It's after seven. We don't have enough time to load everything and get back before dark. We'd better stay at a motel in town and finish in the morning."

"Can't we drive back after sunset?" Emily asked. "If we load fast we might still catch some light— it's amazing how much longer the summer days are in Montana."

"I'd rather travel in full daylight," he returned, casting a dubious look at Emily's old car. "Schuyler is off the beaten track and if we have mechanical trouble, it could be a problem."

She lifted an eyebrow. "You mean if my car has trouble."

"I didn't say that."

"Right."

"Any vehicle can have a breakdown," he said firmly. "How about taking the truck into Helena and leaving yours here?"

"I can't leave my baby alone in the country."

"Fine. Whatever. You mentioned liking the motel where you stayed last night, so lead the way."

Trent waited until Emily was behind the wheel of her car before climbing into his truck and turning the key in the ignition.

The engine made a strangled sound and died.

CHAPTER NINE

EMILY WONDERED WHAT was wrong. Trent's truck had squealed and suddenly quit. She jumped from her own car and hurried over as he got out and slammed the door.

The look on his face as he started cursing at his late-model pickup was hilarious.

"You stupid fuel-sucking jerk of a truck," he snarled. "Your company has some nerve putting their logo on your hood." He started to kick one of the tires, then apparently thought better of it.

Emily laughed and he swung around, looking chagrinned.

"Do you think there's a garage still open in town?" she asked politely.

"Unlikely." He glanced at her car. "I'll have to accept a ride to the motel from you."

"Sure. On the other hand…" What she was considering seemed ridiculous and he'd probably think she was nuts, but she decided to throw caution to the winds. "Why don't we clear the tools from your truck and sleep under the stars? I suppose we could also sleep in the house, but it's pretty stuffy and the mouse population will be even more active after dark."

Trent stared, eyes narrowed in an expression she couldn't quite interpret. "I'm not sure staying is a good idea."

"It isn't a good idea to leave a late-model truck sitting here, either," Emily retorted. "It's a target."

"Unlikely. Especially since the damn thing isn't running."

"Hey, you're the one who claimed it wasn't safe for me to be in the house alone. Besides, you brought a bunch of those padded moving blankets. They look clean."

"They're a long way from a mattress and pillows."

"I haven't slept under the stars for years, and then it was only once, when I was a kid and my folks let my friend and me sleep in the backyard."

"Your folks didn't go camping?"

She laughed. "My parents aren't the roughing-it type. And they'd have worried that sleeping on the ground would give my sister bad posture. She's been a model practically since she was born. Come on, it might be fun, and even if it isn't, it's an adventure."

TRENT HESITATED. SLEEPING IN the truck struck him as entirely screwball and probably a mistake, considering his attraction to Emily. Still, there was a childlike appeal to the idea and it did have the air of an adventure.

"All right," he agreed. "But don't complain in the morning if *you* have bad posture."

"It's a deal."

Together they made up bedrolls. Emily had a couple of cloth bags in her car and stuffed them to form rough pillows, while he called and arranged for his hired hand to bed down the animals at the Balderdash.

"See?" she said when he got off the phone. "All the comforts of home."

"Except a kitchen." The appliances inside the house had been removed, though a half bath in the back was still minimally functional.

"True, but I've got provisions from my trip to the grocery store this morning."

They spread their meal out on the tailgate and there was more than enough fruit, cheese, crackers, protein bars and nuts to eat. Trent found it an enjoyable dinner as they watched a spectacular sunset, though he was more accustomed to eating a steak or burger. From what he'd seen of Emily's choice of cuisine, she leaned heavily toward fruit and veggies, which seemed appropriate for someone coming from the land of alfalfa sprouts and surfboards.

"The restaurant may lack waiters, table service and hot food," Emily said, "but the view is first-rate. No wonder they call Montana Big Sky Country. A person could get dizzy trying to take it in."

The scarlet-and-gold glow above slowly faded into inky blue and a faint star finally glimmered into sight.

"Starlight, star bright, first star I see tonight. Wish I may, wish I might, have the wish I wish tonight," Emily chanted.

The softly spoken words made Trent ache. Life had been a little happier before his father's drinking had gotten worse. They'd traveled occasionally and his mother had seemed more cheerful. Wherever they might have been, she'd gazed into the sky each evening, chanting the same old rhyme with a soft smile. Then as her husband began staying out later, drinking and carousing and refusing to leave Schuyler, her wishing had grown desperate.

"Wishes are for victims," he couldn't keep from saying.

Emily cocked her head. "You sound as bad as Cleveland Amory. From what I've read, he wanted to send Virginia a note saying to forget about Santa Claus and get on with her life…or something of the sort."

Trent recalled reading the piece and heartily agreeing with the philosophy behind it. "You'd rather wish for things than work for them?" he asked.

"Nope. When I was a kid, I wished for lots of stuff I was pretty sure couldn't come true. So I worked for other things. I just don't think anyone should give up having dreams."

Trent's gut tightened. Emily had made a drastic change in her life so maybe she wasn't totally like his mother, but she still seemed to have a fairy-tale view of the world. Some might be able to survive in a mental fantasy, but the people around them generally took a beating.

"You don't believe in dreams, do you?" she asked.

"I built a company from scratch to what Big Sky Construction is today."

"That was an ambition, not a dream."

"Is there a difference?"

She shrugged.

Trent didn't know what to say; he was getting distracted by more primal needs. The faint light remaining in the western sky fell on the curves of Emily's face. The top buttons on her shirt remained unfastened in the warm evening air, the breeze caressing her collarbone and the top swell of her breasts.

It was making Trent wish he was a normal guy who didn't have so many hang-ups about life and relationships.

Wish?

Crap. Being around Emily was corrupting him, and an old nursery rhyme popped into his head. If wishes were horses, beggars would ride. That was his philosophy, action over wishing, and it worked for the moment, as well as any other. Besides, he'd given into the whimsy of spending the night under the stars; Why not this, as well?

So, surrendering to temptation, he tugged her close.

THE UNEXPECTED EMBRACE startled Emily, but her pulse surged for another reason as Trent's lips moved over hers. Heavens, he was good at kissing.

Breathing faster, she opened her mouth and he pressed harder, his tongue gently exploring. His fingers gripped her rib cage and she shivered with pleasure. More than anything she wanted him to delve under her silk bra and...

Sitting up, she eased away.

Trent stared at her with raised eyebrows. She hoped he didn't realize how hard her heart was pounding, or recognize how reluctantly she'd put a stop to the moment. Right now she'd love to get naked and crazy with him, but she wasn't eager to deal with the inevitable morning-after awkwardness.

She reached up and patted his cheek. "You're an excellent kisser, but you'll be sorry if we go any further."

With a determined smile, Emily crawled to where their "pillows" lay and slid under the light blanket she'd planned for a coverlet. She didn't need it yet, but by morning it would be cooler and dew might fall.

Lying on her back, she watched the rest of the stars come out. Since the electricity in the farmhouse was off and there were no earthbound lights for over a quarter mile, the stars burned in a massive display she could hardly believe was real.

Still, it was difficult to enjoy the view as thoroughly as she'd planned when Trent had agreed to spend the night in the truck. Their kiss had complicated everything, making her ache with need. Damn it. He probably would have had sex with her if she'd shown any willingness—after all, despite his antisocial tendencies, he was a virile guy.

But she didn't want to just be a convenient woman; she wanted to be chosen. It might be different if she shared some of the stunning beauty possessed by her Los Angeles boutique clients. If she looked at all like them she could believe Trent had some genuine interest in her. Not that she was into casual sex, but tonight she might have succumbed. If only…

Emily closed her eyes, fighting the insecurities she'd tried to defeat. Some of her earliest memories were of people's surprise when they saw her and Nicole together.

Emily rolled onto her side, away from Trent. She ought to be glad that they'd had an enjoyable day gathering treasures from the old house. He'd proved capable of having a normal discussion on a variety of subjects. Maybe it was hard for him to relax when his employees were around. When they got back to Schuyler, he'd likely turn back into the gruff man of few words she was accustomed to having around.

But not if they'd ended up in the sack together. She shivered, envisioning the embarrassment and stiffness that would have followed.

The way things had turned out was for the best. It had nothing to do with her being the not-so-gorgeous George sister. She'd simply exercised good sense.

Trent woke slowly to the lilting song of a meadowlark. It was one of the most beautiful sounds in nature and a far better alarm clock than the one he usually employed. He'd slept soundly, something he hadn't expected given the hard bed and strange surroundings…not to mention how he'd needed a cold shower after kissing Emily.

Coming more fully aware, he realized that she was curled close in the chill of the morning. Trent craned his head to look down at her.

How had he missed how sexy she was?

Carefully restraining his response, he eased away, edging down and off the tailgate to find a spot out of earshot. His insurance provided emergency road service and they promised to have a tow truck out within the hour. With any luck, he'd be mobile again before long.

The sooner he and Emily returned to a proper client-contractor relationship, the better. After all, the only reason he was so deeply involved in renovating her house was to make sure there weren't any revelations about Gavin Hawkins that would embarrass his family.

It was an odd reality to know that he might be the only person alive who knew that his father had been an abusive louse. Trent was convinced his father would have ended up in prison if he'd lived. Then Gavin had died and life had seemed relatively safe again.

AFTER ONLY TWO days of the flu, Mike felt considerably better than most other folks who'd gotten it. His immune system had served him well while he'd worn a major-league uniform.

Nonetheless, in terms of getting back on the job, feeling pretty good didn't carry any weight. Trent was one of those rare employers who actually gave sick time and expected employees to use it, both to prevent the spread of germs and to minimize work-related accidents.

Sitting in his recliner, Mike dozed and only woke when the doorbell rang.

He went to the door.

It was Alaina.

"Aren't you going to invite me in?" she asked.

"Better not," he told her. "You don't want to catch the flu."

"I had it weeks ago."

"This could be a different strain."

"I'll take my chances," she returned calmly. "I brought some of my aunt's chicken soup—she swears by the recipe. She says it cures everything from the common cold to a lack of common sense."

"Take it to someone who's really sick."

"Everyone else in the company has a wife, girlfriend or family to take care of them. You're the only one who lives alone."

"My parents live in Schuyler," he reminded her. "Mom would bring me anything if I needed it, but I don't. If it wasn't for Trent's rules, I could be back on the job."

"Yeah, the Iron Man of Schuyler, Montana," Alaina said in a mocking tone.

Mike flinched. The Iron Man had been Cal Ripken's nickname—the Orioles' ballplayer had even broken legendary Lou Gehrig's record for consecutive games, and once upon a time Mike had envisioned beating both records in turn.

"I'm not an Iron Man," he snapped back.

"No, just trying to be. Let me in, Mike. This pot is getting heavier by the second."

Reluctantly he stepped back and she marched past him toward the kitchen and set her pan on the stove.

She seemed to hesitate at the sight of a carton of pale ale he'd left on the counter, then shoved it away. "I'll heat some up," she said, opening cupboards until she found a small pan, "and put the rest in the fridge for later."

"I'm not hungry."

She ignored him.

Who could have guessed that Alaina Hawkins could be as stubborn as her brother?

She ladled soup into the pan, put the remainder into the refrigerator and turned with a smile. "Where are your bowls?"

"Upper cabinet, left of the stove," he admitted grudgingly. Maybe she'd leave him alone once she'd served him.

"Since you don't feel that bad," she said, "we can talk about that other matter... You know, the bachelor auction. We're getting close to the deadline for putting out names to promote the event, so I need an answer."

"I gave you an answer, you just didn't like it."

Alaina's eyes narrowed. "You're right, and I'm sick of you acting this way. Think of other people for once. The firehouse helps everyone."

"I know that," Mike muttered.

"Do you? Those volunteers run toward fires when everyone else is running away. So get off your duff and give them a hand. It isn't as if you have to do that much. Just be there for the auction and then take some lady out to dinner. We're all sorry about your knee, but stop feeling sorry for yourself."

Shock slapped him in the face. "I don't feel sorry for myself."

Alaina rolled her eyes. "Sure you do. But be

bitter and pity yourself on your own time, not everyone else's."

"I'm not bitter, either."

"Really? You're doing a grand imitation. The way you've acted about me and New York has been downright nasty. Get over it. Coming back to Schuyler was my choice and I don't intend to defend it any longer."

At least she'd had a choice. Alaina just didn't understand what it was like to go from being the toast of the baseball world to being "almost one of the greats."

"I mean it," she continued hotly. "Schuyler made sure that both professional and college scouts saw you play ball in high school and cheered you for years in the majors. Now you need to give something back to the community—something more active than simply writing out a check."

"I've done the auction plenty of times," he said defensively.

"And you can do it again. You've been a prickly sourpuss since moving back and you owe the town for putting up with you."

"Fine." Mike gritted out the word. "I'll be one of your bachelors."

"Good." She poured the now steaming soup into a bowl and set it on the kitchen table with a spoon. "Feel better soon," she said sunnily and headed out the front door.

Despite himself, the scent of chicken and vegetables made Mike's stomach growl. Since his nausea was almost gone he felt safe eating; he slumped into a chair and started spooning it into his mouth, but even the rich flavor couldn't wash away the taste of regret.

He'd been goaded by Alaina's taunts. He should have held out. No one would want to pay to have dinner with a broken-down ballplayer, and recognizing it didn't mean he was guilty of self-pity.

But he couldn't back out now without feeling like a coward. And it was only a minor consolation to know that Alaina would see what a disaster his participation would be…because unfortunately, everyone else would see it, too.

TRENT WAS PLEASED when the truck repairs didn't take long and they quickly returned to the farmhouse to load everything up. By noon he was leading the way back to Schuyler, only to lift his foot from the accelerator when he saw the sign reading Livestock Auction Today. It was the same small auction yard where he'd found Speakeasy, and the memory of the stallion's poor condition was hard to forget. With a resigned sigh, he put on his signal and turned into the parking area.

Emily pulled in nearby. "What's up?" she asked, getting out.

"It's all right if you want to go on ahead. I just want to take a look."

She glanced around. "That's okay. I've never been to a livestock auction. It might be interesting."

"Not if it's the same as the last one I went to," Trent muttered.

"Oh?"

"Sometimes you see animals being sold that haven't been treated properly. My cousins could tell you some horror stories—they've done a fair number of rescues."

He deliberately made it sound as if Jackson and Josh were the only ones who took in abused animals, and not him.

They walked past the tired bleachers that overlooked the primary auction area, to the animal pens beyond. For the most part the livestock appeared healthy enough, though an Appaloosa mare in a rear paddock seemed underweight, minimally groomed and quite nervous.

"Trent Hawkins, isn't it?" called a gruff voice.

Trent saw Harold Burrows, a former rancher who now ran several auction yards in the region. He turned to introduce Emily, but she was trying to coax the Appaloosa forward with an apple.

"What's the mare's story?" he asked quietly.

"She's mine," Harold murmured. "Couldn't figure out why she was so high-strung, then my barn caught fire and I found out my grandson had been sneaking in every Friday night with his friends, drinking, smoking and whooping it up."

Trent nodded. Horses recovered fairly well from

single traumatic events, but it was more difficult when the trauma occurred over an extended period. That was Speakeasy's problem—he'd been abused for most of his young life.

Harold's weathered face was troubled as he gazed at the mare. He was a decent guy and kept his operation as clean as possible, so it must have been tough revealing what had happened to the horse he'd raised. They'd both been appalled by Speakeasy's condition and had turned the owner into the authorities for cruelty.

"I've been tryin' to work with her," Harold said, "but she won't let anyone… Say, will you look at that."

The mare had sidled over to the paddock fence, but instead of taking the apple, had pushed her head into Emily's shoulder. Her trembling eased as Emily gently stroked her silvery-gray neck and whispered a long string of words…nonsense words, as far as Trent could tell, but that didn't matter. What mattered was how the tension had visibly drained from the animal.

"Is she one of them horse whisperers?" Harold asked, looking awed.

"I wouldn't know," Trent replied. He was rather startled himself. Supposedly there were people with a rare, uncanny ability to communicate with animals, though he'd always believed the stories were exaggerations.

Harold stepped closer to Emily. "Ma'am, are you

a horsewoman? Cuz you got a real way with Stella Luna. That's her name."

She shook her head. "I've never even touched a horse. Is something wrong with her?"

Harold explained and tears began running down Emily's cheeks.

Hell. Trent had a dismal feeling that Stella Luna was about to become part of his life. Yet he didn't have to get involved, though there was something eerie about the way the mare had responded to Emily. But surely it was just a fluke.

"You can buy her if you got somebody to help with horse care," Harold offered. "Maybe Trent will do it. He's workin' with a problem stallion right now. Real sad case."

Trent tried not to glare. Stopping at the auction yard had been a lapse in judgment. Except…there was no doubt that Stella Luna had worried herself into an unhealthy condition, and his stubborn urge to jump to the rescue wasn't limited to the human race.

"I've got my hands full with Big Sky Construction," he said, "but if you're interested, Emily, I'll call Jackson and see if he's willing to board her." No way was he going to have Emily coming out to the Balderdash every day.

"That would be great," she said eagerly. "I could go see her in the late afternoon or evenings."

Daytime would be even better, Trent thought,

thinking about the privacy he needed to retrieve his father's gun.

He called Jackson, who was amenable to boarding the skittish mare on the Crazy Horse Ranch. Harold said he would deliver her in a few days when he was bringing another horse to a ranch near Schuyler.

"It was a pleasure, ma'am," Harold answered her thanks. "I been worried about Stella Luna and never seen somethin' like the way she came to you." Harold tipped his hat as they walked out to the parking area, then closed the sedan door for her with old-fashioned courtesy.

"Are you crazy?" Trent growled to the auctioneer before getting into his own truck. "Emily is a New Age city woman who thinks houses talk and have feelings. She doesn't ride, probably won't stay in Schuyler and doesn't have a clue how much work is involved in caring for a horse."

Harold shrugged. "My gut says she can do more for Stella Luna than I ever could. Jackson will handle everything else and I don't mind if he ends up owning her."

"Whatever."

Trent drove out of the auction yard, Emily following. His cousin had been happy to provide a home for the traumatized animal, even offering to buy the Appaloosa, being particularly fond of the breed.

So there wasn't any real need to be concerned, either about Stella Luna or his solitude on the Balderdash.

WHEN EMILY PULLED up in front of Wild Rose Cottage she saw part of the roof had been removed and the front yard was full of loose shingles. It was something to think about instead of the enormity of what she'd done at the auction yard.

Trent didn't realize it, but she'd heard part of what he'd said to Harold Burrows. She *was* crazy. What had happened to her normally sharp business brain that thought things through and made better decisions?

Of course, buying the Emporium had turned out all right. And things were looking pretty good for Wild Rose Cottage. But a horse, especially a horse with problems? Maybe her brain had gotten scrambled by kissing Trent, followed by trying to pretend it didn't matter. Well…it *didn't*. She just had to keep reminding herself of that.

She got out of her car and smiled bravely at Trent, who'd parked closest to the door.

"The shingles and other debris will be cleaned up, though it may take a few extra days," he explained. "The guys I usually hire for cleanup jobs have been scarce because of that bug going around. By the way, Alaina texted that Mike and the rest of the crew have it, too, so I doubt they'll be back until next week."

"They have my sympathy. I got it before the renovations started."

"At least it's behind you. If I have any spare men I'll send them over tomorrow to get the shingles into the Dumpster."

"Thanks."

Smiling again with casual friendliness, Emily unlocked the door so they could carry everything inside. "This has been fun," she said as they took the stained-glass windows into one of the side rooms for storage. "Any time you want clumsy help while salvaging a house, give me a call."

"You weren't clumsy," he shocked her by saying. "You catch on quickly."

"Yeah, well, I'm the smart Geor—" She cut the words off. Repeating the things she'd heard all her life wouldn't help her overcome those blasted insecurities. "Thanks for the night under the stars. I wouldn't feel comfortable doing it by myself."

He glanced around. "You're welcome, but if you don't mind, I'll do more work on the window frames before I leave."

"You don't want to go home?"

"I'm used to a very full workday. Just go do whatever you need to do."

What Emily wanted most was a shower—the downside to sleeping in the truck had been the primitive bathroom facilities. And why shouldn't she take a quick one? Trent would respect her privacy.

The hot running water felt wonderful. The bathrooms in Wild Rose Cottage had suffered from lack of attention over the years, but at least they provided more than a trickle of rusty water, which was all the faucet at the Helena farmhouse had emitted. However much she loved old houses, the twenty-first century was a vast improvement when it came to plumbing.

Waking up that morning, she'd decided to act as if nothing had happened. All that had occurred was a kiss…a really hot kiss, but just a kiss, and a brief one at that. So she'd said good morning and shared the coffee left in her thermos.

Before the tow truck arrived they'd organized everything they had removed from the house. She was delighted that Trent was sending a crew to do a full salvage job, and thought the farmhouse was happy, too, that its treasures wouldn't be completely lost.

As for Wild Rose Cottage…it felt as if it was waiting for something, and the sensation was even stronger now that she'd returned.

WHILE TRENT REGRETTED his employees being ill, he relished the possibility of private work time on Emily's house. In fact… He pulled out his smartphone and texted Alaina, telling her that when Mike returned to work, he should be assigned to another crew for the rest of the week.

He tucked the cell back in his pocket and examined the window frame he was finishing. It had been a while since he'd done such detailed work. The economy was improving, but until it was strong again, few people wanted to spend the kind of money required for historic restoration.

In the rear of the house he heard the shower running and tried to ignore the sound. It was too tempting to envision what Emily looked like, sleek and bare under the stream of water.

Hell. What was it about her that was eroding his self-control? And he reminded himself of how flaky and unrealistic she was about everything. That kind of woman was pure trouble.

He began working and Emily soon came in to strip more wallpaper using the steamer he'd brought a few days ago.

"This gadget is great," she enthused, "much better than brute force or trying to soak the stuff off. It's dumb, I should have realized there'd be something to make the job easier."

The comment, along the one made earlier, reminded him of the way she'd once described herself…as the "smart George sister." At the time he'd thought it was rather egotistical, but she didn't seem egotistical. Not that it was any of his business, and the less attention he paid to her quirks and idiosyncrasies, the better.

TRENT RELISHED BEING able to work on the house alone the next day and it would have been a perfect opportunity to retrieve everything if only Emily would stop trying to pitch in. It was partly his own fault since he had admitted that she'd provided genuine assistance at the old farmhouse. Her persistent helpfulness was inconvenient and he still wondered about her motives. But maybe she was just trying to make up for all the changes she wanted to the contract.

And she was damned cute with plaster powdering on her cheeks, as if she'd been sprinkled with pixie dust.

The fanciful image was enough to promote heartburn. Trent excused himself on the pretext of going outside to call the office. He wouldn't allow himself to savor Emily's charms. Mean polecats didn't need charming. Instead they climbed trees and spat at the world.

CHAPTER TEN

EMILY BOUNCED OFF her bed on Thursday morning, determined to make it better than Wednesday had been. Trent had gone stiff and uncommunicative the previous day, similar to when he'd first begun the renovations. After their work together at the farmhouse, she'd hoped he'd warm up from frigid to merely cool.

Of course, maybe he didn't want to be friendly.

He could have decided he'd come too close to making a mistake that night in the truck and was trying to keep his distance so she wouldn't get the wrong idea. That was fine.

Curiously, 7:00 a.m. came and went without Trent knocking on her door, then the phone rang shortly before 8:00. Caller ID showed it was Big Sky Construction.

"Trent?" she answered.

"Sorry, Em, it's Alaina. Trent came down with that flu as well, so I'm afraid no one will be there today. Mike is back and I could send him—"

"You'd better not," Emily cut in swiftly. "He might try to…well, you know." Mike kept trying to get a second date and she was still trying to head him off.

Alaina was silent for a moment. "You're a good friend. Trent wants Mike to fill in holes on other crews this week unless you can't live with the debris in your yard any longer."

"Nope, it's fine. Did you hear about me buying a horse?"

"Lord, yes. Jackson wants to drive over and get her himself. His personal riding stallion is an Appaloosa—he loves the breed. So if you want to sell the mare to him, I'm sure he'll be delighted to have her."

Emily wondered if Trent had suggested the possibility to his sister. It would probably be for the best, but she remembered the way Stella Luna had pushed into her shoulder, as if seeking a safe place. Harold Burrows had entrusted his mare to her and she couldn't see surrendering her without giving the whole thing a fair chance.

"I'll think about it. It must be pretty hard taking care of a horse."

"You get used to it," Alaina said casually. "Of course, I was just three when Mom and Dad brought us out to their ranch to live, so I grew up with horses. Why don't we meet for lunch at the Roundup Café?"

"Sure."

Emily spent a couple of hours tossing shingles from her front yard into the Dumpster, then showered and headed for the Emporium to touch base with her manager. Business was brisk, though it would undoubtedly slow down once the tourist season ended.

The Emporium *had* been in trouble when she'd bought it, but mostly it had needed a facelift and a better selection of merchandise. So she'd changed the inventory, advertised in key tourist publications, painted, and the place had become surprisingly profitable in a short period of time…but she wasn't really needed now, except to pick out stock.

Maybe she should buy another business.

Or maybe not.

She didn't want to be one of those people who flitted from place to place and project to project. Besides, she had lots to do in Schuyler…including getting to know a horse.

Feeling better, Emily left to meet Alaina. The restaurant food in Schuyler was good, but didn't have the international variety she'd enjoyed in Los Angeles. Perhaps cooking new cuisines was a hobby she could explore in her new kitchen.

Alaina was waiting for her and they chose a table near the window.

"I'm glad you suggested getting together," Emily said after they'd given the server their order. "The quiet at the house felt weird."

"Wish I could say the same about the office. I'm juggling crews to get the priority jobs done.

You can't leave a ninety-year-old woman without plumbing."

"That's for sure."

Emily wondered if the ninety-year-old woman was one of Big Sky's "special" jobs. She'd overheard comments the crew had made and figured out that Trent sometimes worked free for certain people. It was an interesting insight into his character.

When she'd asked Eduardo about it, he'd been embarrassed and asked her not to say anything.

The boss wants to keep that kind of thing under the radar, Eduardo had told her. *We shouldn't have been talking about it.*

No worries, she'd assured him. Emily knew how to keep secrets. And it was Trent's concern if he wanted to keep a softer side of his personality private. But *why* keep it private? Despite his reputation for honesty, most folks thought he was as tough as old rawhide, which wasn't a reputation she'd cultivate.

"You look pale," Emily commented. "Is everything all right?"

Alaina yawned and rubbed the back of her neck. "I've been having nightmares lately. I think it's the same one I used to have as a kid, with lots of yelling. I remember feeling scared, but no real details."

"That's too bad. A friend of mine says dreams can tell us what's going on in our lives and how we feel about stuff."

Alaina snorted. "I know exactly how frustrated I am with Mike. I don't need a dream to tell me that."

Emily knew how she felt. She was frustrated with Trent, though for entirely different reasons. Or maybe she was just annoyed with herself for thinking about him so much. He wasn't her business and he never would be. Nor was she interested; he was too cynical. Even friendship with someone like that would be a challenge.

ALAINA SIPPED HER iced tea and relaxed for the first time since the worst of the flu epidemic had begun.

For days she'd been bursting with the news that she'd convinced Mike to be in the auction. Well... had badgered him into it. Part of her felt guilty, but she also knew she'd told him the plain truth. Yet however much she wanted to tell Emily, the committee kept the list private until they were ready to advertise.

When Trent had come home from his trip to Helena she'd even felt bold enough to see if he'd reconsider volunteering, as well. The committee hadn't dared put him on the list of potentials. But she'd decided it couldn't hurt to ask.

He'd stared as if she was from another planet. *Don't be ridiculous. I told you it wasn't going to happen. I'll make my usual donation and that's it.*

Alaina hadn't pressed the point. Trent did plenty of hush-hush stuff to help people, so she couldn't argue that he needed to support Schuyler with more than his money, the way she had with Mike. *You're still going to the barbecue, aren't you?*

Yes.

As with family gatherings, he generally attended community affairs, though she knew he didn't enjoy them. Trent simply felt he *should* go, so that's what he did.

Alaina had never understood her brother. He was protective and had faithfully shown up for her special days, including flying to California for her college graduation. He listened if she had a problem. But that strange distance between them remained.

"I'm afraid I had an ulterior motive in asking you to lunch," Alaina admitted while they ate the Roundup's special of the day—bacon burgers with a heap of fresh coleslaw.

"Oh?"

"Yeah. I'm on the Firefighters Auxiliary. We raise money to support our volunteer firefighters."

Emily wiped a drip of barbecue sauce from her chin. "I think all firefighters are terrific, but it's even more incredible when someone is doing it without being paid. How can I help?"

"Every summer we have a bachelor and bachelorette auction—the winner gets taken out to dinner by the person they bid on. This year we're combining our annual barbecue with the auction. You're on my list to recruit as a bachelorette."

From Emily's panicked expression, Alaina realized she'd hit a nerve.

Before she could say anything, Emily let out a forced laugh. "Sorry, it wouldn't work. I'm not the right type to pull it off."

"I wouldn't dream of pushing, but I can't help wondering why?" Then Alaina remembered Emily's engagement had ended only earlier that year. "Ohmigosh, I should have remembered your stupid fiancé and realized you wouldn't be interested."

Emily made a face. "It's more than that. Dennis and I were engaged for five years. His sister was the one who finally told me what was happening. I felt like an idiot. I mean, unless there's a special reason, who waits that long to get married or at least move in together? But there was always an excuse and I just accepted it."

"Um…it sounds as if he was never faithful."

"Dennis doesn't know the meaning of the word. He even thought I should be grateful he wanted to marry me, no matter how many times he'd cheated."

A flash of anger went through Alaina on behalf of her friend. "You've mentioned that he's hung up on glamour, but most guys get past that stage. It's childish for them to expect to marry someone like Cindy Crawford or Gisele Bündchen. Besides, I bet some supermodels aren't that glamorous when they don't have a makeup artist in their skinny-jeans back pocket."

Emily's nose wrinkled. "Actually, Dennis doesn't want to marry a glamour princess—she might expect too much from him. He enjoys the idea of being married and having someone to keep everything running smoothly in his life, but he gets bored easily and thinks fidelity is for other people. Basically, he wants a bread-and-butter wife who won't object if he samples jam from lots of pretty jars."

Alaina frowned. "I understand how having a supermodel sister must have been hard on the ego, but why are you still letting anyone else influence how you see yourself?"

"You didn't grow up being compared to someone like Nicole. There's nothing wrong with how I look, but there's nothing particularly special about me, either. I'm used to it."

"I may not be a guy, but I think you're special. And just so you know, the committee was thrilled to put you on the list of potential recruits."

"That's nice, but I'd hate getting up on a platform and waiting for guys to bid on me. All my insecurities would attack."

"I understand." Alaina winced, remembering how she'd goaded Mike into volunteering. But surely it wasn't the same with him. He'd always been supremely confident, practically to the point of arrogance, and now was acting like a bad-tempered hermit. She felt bad about his accident, but he'd played in the majors for a decade, which was a whole lot more than most people got. She ought to point that out the next time he was being an ass.

"I'd be glad to do something else," Emily said. "Have you thought of having a silent auction for donated items? It would be fun, particularly for people who aren't bidding on a date."

"We've talked about it, but nobody has time to solicit donations."

Brightening, Emily leaned forward. "I'll do it if you don't mind that I'm not on the committee."

"You're just as busy as everyone else and now you've got a horse."

Emily laughed. "Stella Luna won't be at Jackson's ranch until next week. I'll make some calls and twist arms if that's what you want."

"Just a minute." Grabbing her cell, Alaina phoned the chair of the steering committee, who was delighted with the turn of events. Punching the off button, she beamed across the table. "Congratulations, you're now an honorary member and can start twisting arms."

"Great. Just this morning I was thinking I needed a new project."

Alaina gave her friend a droll look. "Right, as if a skittish horse, two businesses, major house renovations and dealing with my cantankerous brother weren't enough of a challenge."

For some reason Emily's face suddenly looked strained, but Alaina decided not to question it.

INSTEAD OF GOING straight home, Emily began visiting local businesses. Within three hours she'd gotten donation pledges for everything from a cowboy hat to a free haircut. Then she dropped into several restaurants who donated gift certificates for meals. In particular, the unmarried business owners and managers seemed so relieved she wasn't trying to recruit them for the auction, they were eager to be generous.

It was a good beginning and she finally headed back to Wild Rose Cottage. Yet her adrenaline ebbed when she walked through the front door.

After the conversation with Alaina, she'd tried not to think about what Dennis had done and how it was tied up with how Trent made her feel. Now it returned.

Emily was sick of her ex-fiancé's memory hanging around like a ghost. He didn't deserve it.

She eyed the left side of the living room. At some point a flimsy wall had been erected to make an extra bedroom, or maybe an office. But it was awkward because it blocked the windows on that side and simply didn't fit. Removing it was in the contract, but it wasn't a weight-bearing wall, so maybe she could knock the thing out herself.

Of course, she ought to be contacting more of the folks she'd gotten to know through the Chamber of Commerce. The donation pledges she'd already received were nice, but they were only a start.

Nonetheless, the temptation to hit something with a sledgehammer was too much to resist.

Mindful of Trent's insistence about safety, Emily put on a hard hat and safety glasses from the cache of tools the guys left at the end of each workday. The sledgehammer weighed a ton, but she hefted it over her shoulder and started whacking.

With each blow she shoved out some of her lingering rage at Dennis and how he'd treated her. His tone had been so patronizing when he'd said that of course he cared for her, but it was unreasonable to expect him to resist genuine beauty.

Pieces of wood and plaster flew.

After a couple of hours, the wall lay in pieces.

Sticking her chin up, she smiled. Okay, so she wasn't a raving beauty, but she deserved better. A lot better.

Trent was probably going to throw a fit about the wall, but he'd have to lump it.

THE WORST OF the stomach flu had passed by Friday evening, leaving Trent exasperated. Getting sick had forced him to miss one of his best opportunities to search for his father's handgun.

But maybe he could still make it work.

He dialed Emily's number and was glad when she answered instead of getting voice mail.

"It's Trent," he said.

"Hey, are you doing better?"

"Much better, that's why I'm calling. I'm concerned we didn't make any progress this week. If it won't interfere with your schedule, I want to put in some time tomorrow."

"It won't bother me, but surely you want the weekend to recuperate."

As if he could relax with Wild Rose Cottage looming over his head like an ax hanging on a thread.

"If I'm not working there, I'll be doing other work at Big Sky, and I'd rather get something accomplished on your house."

"In that case, I'll see you in the morning. The usual time?"

Trent agreed and at 7:00 a.m. sharp, he was at her door. He stepped into the living room and dropped his toolbox with a bang. The wall behind the door was gone. Emily must have knocked the damn thing out—she'd even removed the debris. It didn't matter since it postdated his childhood, but what if she'd dismantled the walls upstairs? He instinctively turned to go up and check, only to see Emily staring at him with a rebellious expression.

She stuck her chin in the air. "Yeah, I took it down."

"You shouldn't have," he said tightly. "It's our job and we know how to do it safely."

"It was therapy. I got to thinking about the way my fiancé treated me and how we broke up. It made me angry so I took it out on the wall."

Trent bit back an ironic laugh. He could have

told her that he'd been trying to work off anger for years, without noticeable success.

"All the same," he returned carefully, "I'll be more comfortable if you don't do this sort of thing again. You could have got hurt and no one would have been here to help."

"I wore a hard hat and safety glasses."

Frustrated, he spun and headed for the kitchen. It would make her suspicious if he lunged upstairs the way he wanted to. Anyway, she surely would have mentioned finding a gun. So now his problem was finagling a way to go after it himself before she did any more personal demolition.

Thinking furiously, he worked on the glass-and-stone-tile backsplash Emily had chosen, wondering if he could ask her to pick up supplies or something. Simply going upstairs wouldn't do any good; she'd just follow to help or watch.

Then in the midst of his turmoil, the specifics of what she'd said suddenly hit his consciousness... that she'd had a fiancé who had treated her badly. Generally there were two sides to any story, but curiously, Trent didn't question whether she was accurately remembering past events. As a rule he figured women were skewed in the way they saw things.

In the background he heard the old landline phone ring. A minute later Emily came into the kitchen.

"I need to go down to the Emporium," she explained. "The flu has hit my staff, as well."

Trent couldn't believe his luck. It was unfortunate someone was ill, but now he'd get the time alone that he needed.

"That's too bad," he told her. "I'll take care of things here."

She paused and he hoped she wouldn't suggest he leave as well, then shrugged and smiled. "See you later, then."

As soon as Trent saw her car drive out of sight, he dropped everything and headed upstairs.

NORMALLY EMILY WOULDN'T have driven to the Emporium, but Trudy had been terribly upset about getting sick.

"I'm sorry," the teenager wailed as she came through the door. "I felt great an hour ago."

Emily smiled reassuringly. "Don't worry about it."

Trudy gagged and ran for the stockroom where there was a small bathroom for the staff.

The bell on the door tinkled as a couple came inside.

"Hi," Emily said. "Before you come any farther, let me warn you that one of my staff just came down with the flu. You might not want to get exposed."

"Stomach?" the man asked. When Emily nodded, he and his wife exchanged glances. "We just got over it. Imagine having intestinal flu while camping in a tent and having to use a campground restroom."

Emily groaned in sympathy. "That sounds terrible."

"It was hideous," the woman agreed. "As soon as we got better, we tossed everything in the SUV and went to a motel.

Is it okay if we look around? We heard about your store and want to salvage something from our vacation."

"Be my guest."

Back in the stockroom Trudy was sitting on a chair, tears rolling down her cheeks.

"Jimmy will be here soon," Emily told her. "He's thrilled to get extra work hours. Is your mom coming to pick you up?"

"She got sick last night. I'll walk."

"Nonsense, I'll take you."

Jim Jenkins arrived a few minutes later, so Emily got the teenager home as quickly as possible before heading back to Meadowlark Lane. She'd hated leaving. There was something so odd about the way Trent had acted…or maybe it was the lingering weirdness in the house. The sense of waiting or anticipation was still present, no matter how hard she'd tried to dismiss it.

Parking in the driveway, she hurried inside, but Trent wasn't in the kitchen. Instead, loud bangs were coming from the second floor.

What?

She climbed the front staircase and peeked through the door of the room she'd decided to expand into a master bedroom. Trent was pounding on the wall with a ferocity that easily outstripped the energy she'd put into the one in the living room.

The air whooshed from her lungs.

It was the wall that had always given her an odd feeling. Honestly, if she'd known it wasn't load bearing, she would have already taken a sledgehammer to it. Why was he doing it in her absence? Weeks ago she'd told him she wanted to be there when it was removed.

He seemed angry and in a terrible hurry, pausing to grope through the debris after each crash brought chunks down. Finally a piece of wall came off in a large section. He seized something from the ground. For a moment he stared at the object before wrapping it in a cloth and shoving it into his pocket.

Shaken, Emily turned and tiptoed down the stairs and out of the house. Needing time to think, she drove to the county park on the edge of town.

She was certain the mysterious object had been a handgun, even though it had been wrapped in plastic. The shape was distinctive and she'd gotten a clear look. Moreover, Trent had been looking for it. There was no doubt about that.

What the hell was going on?

AN ENORMOUS WEIGHT had rolled from Trent when he'd tucked his father's gun out of sight. There were probably other troublesome items still hidden in the house, but the worst of his worries had been addressed.

Glancing at the rubble on the floor, he wasn't sure what he'd say if Emily asked about it. She had been clear about wanting to be there when the wall was demolished—something to do with her feelings about the place and how it "spoke to her."

It was ridiculous, yet he couldn't deny that something *had* been different about this particular wall.

He went to one of the front windows and checked for Emily's car. It was unlikely she'd be back soon; she was probably covering the Emporium for her sick sales clerk. If she asked, he would have to say he'd forgotten that she wanted to be there. Lying was distasteful, but the truth was ugly, as well.

After locking the gun in his office safe, he went home for the first good night's sleep he'd had since the work on Meadowlark Lane had started.

ON MONDAY MORNING, Trent waited for Emily to tackle him about the wall, but she seemed normal, offering him a cup of coffee and pointing at a box of pastries on the rickety card table in the living room. Maybe she hadn't been upstairs to see it. When the crew finished their coffee, Emily went to help Eduardo work on the pipes under the laundry room.

Caveman came to him an hour later. "Hey, boss," he said. "I've been thinking about the hallway chandelier that broke apart when we took it down. It might be possible to find a vintage light online."

"We already installed a new one."

"I know, but Em is awful nice and she's helped out so much, it seems as if we could find something she'd like better."

"I'll think about it."

"Okay, boss, just a thought. She said something the other day and I know she's disappointed. We're willing to install it on our own time."

As soon as he had an opportunity, Trent took Emily into the yard where they couldn't be overheard.

"I need to discuss something with you," he said stiffly.

"Yeah?"

"If you want extra work or items that aren't in the contract, you need to check with me, not my crew."

Her eyes opened wide. "What do mean?"

"Caveman told me you want a different chandelier in the hallway."

Emily crossed her arms over her stomach in a gesture that was becoming all too familiar. "I mentioned the modern light fixture doesn't fit the vintage atmosphere, that's all. Exactly *what* are you accusing me of?"

Trent took a deep breath. "In my experience customers act nice, expecting a little extra to come out of it."

Her eyes sparked angrily. "*That's* your problem? Being nice is suspicious?"

"You aren't that naive. People do it all the time."

"Maybe some people do, but that doesn't mean it's what *I* was doing, or most other folks, either. You're an ass, Trent. By your reasoning, the only reason someone is nice is because they have ulterior motives."

She raked him with a scornful expression, spun and marched away. Trent closed his eyes, trying not to think of how amazing she'd looked as she'd lectured him.

He couldn't make up his mind about Emily. Was she trying to work the situation for what she could get? Or was she as naive as his mother had been, needing rescue when the world had fallen apart around her? Maybe she was simply a flake who left havoc behind wherever she went.

EMILY STOMPED DOWNTOWN, not wanting to go into the house and risk the crew seeing her anger. Trent's words made her feel soiled, even though she wasn't guilty of what he'd accused. What was wrong with him? Every time she'd asked for something differing from the contract, she'd told him to give her an estimate. Never *once* had she implied she wanted something free or for a reduced cost.

What sort of person was so suspicious of every-

body? She might feel sorry for him if he wasn't
so awful.

As Emily neared the Emporium, her steps fal-
tered. She shouldn't go in there, either. In fact, she
didn't want to see anyone she knew well until she'd
had a chance to cool down.

Heading across the street, she went into the
Schuyler clothing shop and asked to try on the
dress displayed in the window.

As she tried on dress after dress, Emily fumed.
There was something wrong with being nice? Trent
did his best to create a good working environment,
but she'd never accused him of manipulating his
employees by treating them fairly. After all, that
would be ridiculous.

Sighing, she finally made a selection and signed
a credit card slip, walking out with a sundress
that she probably wouldn't have considered if
she'd been entirely rational. She'd heard that you
should never drive angry. Maybe you shouldn't
shop angry, either.

CHAPTER ELEVEN

ON THE DAY of the big firehouse fund-raiser, Emily nervously checked herself out in the mirror. It was the blue sundress she'd bought the day that she and Trent had argued about the hallway chandelier. It showed her figure more than the tailored business suits she'd once worn, or the loose flowing blouses and skirts she'd favored since moving to Montana.

Despite having been angry when she'd bought the outfit, it didn't look bad, and it wasn't as if they had fashion police in Schuyler.

She hurried into the kitchen to collect the cookies she'd baked the night before…and gave a sigh of pleasure over the way the room had turned out. Except for the bedroom she was using, the past few weeks had seen a transformation of the ground floor; Wild Rose Cottage was going to be as beautiful as she'd dreamed it could be. Even the wood floor that had buckled looked nice. Right after they'd "discussed" it, Emily had done some research and then tried one of the methods suggested. It had taken a while, but the hard work was worth every minute…including the chagrin on Trent's face when she'd unveiled her success.

Emily still didn't know what to do about Trent. She wasn't mad at him anymore—she wasn't good at holding a grudge—but that didn't mean she trusted him. Besides, he was just the construction foreman on her house, not someone whose accusations mattered.

But no longer being angry didn't tell her what to think about the handgun Trent had removed from the upstairs wall.

She'd had long conversations with Stella Luna about it when no one else was around. As it turned out, horses were excellent company—they didn't talk back and never offered annoying opinions.

It was her good fortune that the horse-loving McGregors were willing to board the mare, especially for the nominal fee she'd finally gotten them to accept. But the best part was seeing Stella Luna eating better and becoming less nervous. It was nice that Harold Burrow's faith in her was justified, and having a distraction each evening had been a godsend.

Emily frowned as her thoughts inevitably circled back to Trent and the gun.

He couldn't be a criminal. However grim and solitary, with edges galore, she was sure he was honest. It had even appeared as though he was wrapping the weapon to preserve fingerprints. Nevertheless, she'd endured more than her share of sleepless nights trying to sort it out.

Should she at least talk to him?

So far, she'd just...waited.

Trent certainly hadn't said anything about the wall, and as far as he knew, she hadn't gone upstairs to see it. But she was running out of time to make a decision since the crew was scheduled to start working on the second floor the next week.

Criminy. There was no point in fussing, and she didn't want to miss a minute of the barbecue and auction.

Amazingly, the fund-raiser was taking place on a Friday afternoon and evening. The town actually declared its own holiday for the event and most of the businesses would be closed. Alaina had laughed, claiming it was because everyone needed the weekend to recuperate. Emily didn't mind closing the Emporium or having work halt on Wild Rose Cottage for the day.

Of course, in her case the crew was planning to come in on Saturday because so much time had been lost due to the flu. She'd felt bad about it, but the guys had assured her no one was being required to work. Trent had an odd expression on his face when the men had talked about it, and she'd been frustrated. How could a guy leave so much distrust in his wake?

Shaking her head, she walked briskly toward the downtown park.

She'd gotten stacks of donations for the silent auction and was proud of the results. At the same time she was nervous, in case it didn't turn out well. But it *should* be all right. Despite the short lead time, the committee had done a fair amount of advertising. The committee had even shifted some of the donated goods to the live auction, so more people could get in on the fun.

At the park, Emily left her cookies with the dessert coordinator and started exploring. Despite the carnival rides operating a hundred feet away, crowds were milling in and out of the large tent dedicated to the silent auction. She peeked inside. The bidding lists were already filling with names and there were friendly scuffles as people raced back and forth to outdo each other.

"Emily." Janet Goodwell rushed over and gave her a hug. "This is great. I knew it would be a success, but I didn't realize how many people would participate."

"I'm glad it's working out."

Emily wandered over to where the barbecue was being held and presented her ticket. She sat down with Alaina, a daunting amount of food heaped on her plate.

"Wow," she said, looking at the pile of sliced tri-tip. "I won't be hungry for a week."

Alaina nodded. "I always have to go on a diet after the barbecue—or at least I *should* go on a diet."

The meat was savory, the potato salad had been made by the premiere potato-salad maker in town and there were baskets of French bread on every table. Emily was stuffed by the time she was finished.

"I'd better walk around awhile," she said, pressing a hand to her tummy and hoping she didn't look pregnant after eating so much. It would have been a neat trick since she hadn't had sex in ages.

"I'd go with you, but I need to do some final checks for the live auction," Alaina explained. "See you later."

Emily wandered around. A band was playing in one area and there were activity booths for the kids along with the carnival rides. A happy-faced clown insisted she sit down while he painted a sunflower on her cheek.

She also saw Trent. He was carrying supplies, his muscles flexing as he delivered ice and other heavy goods to the kitchen area. Suddenly the day seemed a whole lot warmer.

"Afternoon," he said as he passed near the booth where she was trying to knock metal bowling pins over for a prize. His gaze barely flicked over her and she restrained a sigh. After all, despite everything, she was merely a client. And that was a good thing. Who wanted a man suspicious of everyone?

MIKE TRIED NOT to limp as he carried his plate from the serving area to the closest table—it was possible if he concentrated and ignored the pain.

The doctors had said he would slowly improve and his knee *was* better; they just couldn't give him back his career.

"Hi, Mike," Candy McCoy said, sitting across the table. "I understand you're one of our bachelors at the auction."

"That's right." He decided not to mention that he'd rather slam his hand in a car door.

She smiled coyly. "I wasn't going to bid on anyone, but now I've changed my mind."

"That's nice," he returned, unsure of what else to say. How had he gotten so lame around women? He couldn't even manufacture the right moment to ask Emily out a second time. "The firefighters will appreciate your support."

"I won't be doing it for them. I've been trying to get your attention again for years."

"Don't make me blush."

She let out a high-pitched giggle and Mike worked to keep his face neutral.

Great. Candy McCoy. The town nympho. He'd made the mistake of spending a night with her years ago. He was fine with women being assertive, but Candy was just tacky.

Mike wanted to remind her that the auction was for dinner and nothing more, but a family was sitting next to them, so he kept his mouth shut.

One thing was for sure though, if Candy won the auction, he'd wring Alaina's neck.

TRENT WAS ABOUT to leave the barbecue when he heard Emily's voice over the loudspeaker calling everyone to attention.

He found himself heading toward the bandstand.

"Hi, everyone," she said into the microphone. "The regular auctioneer had to go home. The flu strikes again. He wasn't able to eat, so tell the guys at the barbecue pit to stick a plate in the fridge. By the way, that's my way of saying that if you haven't eaten yet, you're missing out on a good thing."

Trent moved closer. Emily stood smiling on the platform. Earlier he'd tried not to look too closely at her. Now he stared hungrily at her slender figure hugged by sky blue fabric. The sundress was a surprising switch from her usual clothes.

He sucked in a breath.

Emily had very nice curves, belying the sunflower painted on her left cheek that made her look like a kid. He didn't know how she could be so cute and alluring at the same time.

Hell, he ought to leave before anyone guessed how aroused he was at the sight of her, but he couldn't make his feet move.

"I've been drafted to fill in for Pete," she announced. "As some of you already know, my name is Emily George and I'm pretty new in town. The only explanation for me agreeing to do this is temporary insanity, which confirms the suspicions you had when you saw my taste in real estate. Don't think I didn't hear the whispered suggestions of a straitjacket."

A general chuckle rippled through the crowd. The house on Meadowlark Lane had long been a sore spot for the town. No one would have cared if he'd bulldozed it.

"Listen carefully, folks," Emily continued. "Among the items up for your interest are bachelors, bachelorettes, a riding lawn mower and deep-dish apple pie. They're all terrific, but not interchangeable, so think before you bid. And remember, this supports those dedicated folks at the Schuyler Fire Station. I hear that if they don't finish earning enough for a new ladder truck, they're threatening to do one of those stud calendars, and I don't mean Appaloosa stallions."

"Are you crazy?" a feminine voice sang out from the crowd. "If we bid too much, we'll miss out on the calendar."

"You're right," Emily agreed, "so put your wallets away. Oh, wait a minute." She whipped out her cell phone and acted as if she was listening before sticking it back in her pocket. "Okay, folks," she announced, "I'm from California and it seems I got studs and steers mixed up. If we don't earn enough on the auction, it's going to be photos of longhorn bulls...from Texas."

A smile twitched on Trent's lips as a mix of laughter and groans went through the crowd.

"We're starting with some of the generous contributions from local businesses," Emily told the crowd. "After that we'll get to Schuyler's traditional bachelor and bachelorette auction."

Bidding was brisk, with items going for generous prices.

"Hey, Trent," Alaina murmured, coming up beside him. "Isn't Em doing a fantastic job?"

"Uh…yeah," he said.

He was reluctantly impressed. Emily had thrown herself into the moment, gently hamming it up, but not getting too corny as she encouraged everyone to have fun.

"She also got the local merchants to donate all this stuff," Alaina murmured.

"I know."

Pique traveled through Trent. Emily hadn't asked Big Sky Construction to donate anything. Not that he should be surprised, given how many times they'd argued. Still, she'd apparently contacted just about every other business in town. He'd finally given Alaina a gift certificate for a low-flow toilet, including installation.

Though Trent didn't usually care for public events, it was entertaining to watch Emily, and when the certificates for the pie-a-month came up, he offered an opening bid of a hundred dollars.

"Anyone else? These pies are really delicious," Emily urged.

"One fifty," called Uncle Parker. The mayor raised him ten dollars.

"Two hundred," Trent offered, only to be promptly outbid by someone he couldn't see at the back of the crowd.

The closing bid was for two seventy-five.

"Congratulations," Emily sang out to the lanky rancher.

Twenty minutes later a painting by a local artist was brought out on the platform. Emily started taking bids and showed no hint that she'd hoped to win it herself. The only reason Trent knew was because he'd overheard her talking to Alaina about it.

"Fourteen hundred," he called, outbidding the last offer by three hundred dollars.

No one else raised him.

"Great taste, Trent," Emily called out. "This is something you can hang on your wall with pride."

Making his way to the cashier's booth he paid for the painting. It was a beautiful piece depicting a vista of hills and prairie land near Schuyler. The artist was becoming well-known in Montana and Trent already had one of his paintings displayed at Big Sky Construction. It made sense to buy it as an investment…except he wasn't sure that was his real reason, and he had to remember his determination not to do any rescuing.

Trent had planned to take the painting and leave, except it was too enjoyable listening as Emily charmed the crowd. She was breathtaking with her face lit up and he fought another surge of desire. He had never taken a client to bed and he couldn't believe how close he'd come that night in the truck. Worse, she was the one who'd pulled back.

He didn't think it was a lack of desire, yet she'd ended their brief, searing kiss with a kind, almost philosophical air. Beyond complimenting him on being a good kisser, she hadn't shown any sign it was difficult to stop.

Trent had never imagined that women found him irresistible. A few had claimed he was good in bed, and he'd run across others who would have happily shared his financial success, but most women said he was too hard and insensitive. So he could be wrong about Emily's response to him.

ALAINA TENSED AS number thirty-six on the auction list approached. Some members of the committee had wanted to assign Mike to the same number he'd had on his uniform when he still played baseball, and she'd quickly squashed the idea, arguing that it might remind him of the day his career had ended.

Come to think of it, there was something to admire about Mike's refusal to trade on his former fame. He didn't spin endless tales about ball games or seek the adoring attention he'd once received from fans and sportscasters alike. But surely there was a balance between becoming sourpuss lone wolf and a glory hound.

"Here we've got Mike Carlisle, ladies," Emily finally announced. "Mike is intelligent, teaches at the local high school and does a great job remodeling kitchens, but you don't get him for that long. However, if you win this bid, the two of you will enjoy a nice dinner out together."

Triumph surged through Alaina as the bidding began. Mike had acted as if no one would want him at any price, yet voice after voice pushed the number higher. At the same moment it was a bittersweet achievement—by getting him to volunteer for the auction, she'd set him up to go on a date with another woman…unless she bid on him herself, which he might not like.

The last straw came when Candy McCoy offered nine hundred dollars and it looked as if it might be the final bid.

Alaina straightened. She wasn't taking that lying down. Candy was a bloodsucker; she'd tried to steal every boyfriend that Alaina or her sister had ever had, and would do her best to eat Mike alive.

"One thousand," Alaina sang out. Candy gave her an ugly scowl and offered eleven hundred.

The bids went up by increments.

"Fifteen hundred," Alaina called, topping Candy's last bid.

Candy scowled harder, clenched and unclenched her fists a couple of times, then subsided.

"Fifteen hundred dollars," Emily intoned, "going once, going twice, sold to the lady from Big Sky Construction."

No other dinner date sold for half that much,

and except for Mike, no real heat had gone into the competition.

When the auction concluded, everyone applauded Emily.

"See?" Alaina told her when they met up again. "I knew you'd be terrific."

Emily grinned. "It was fun. Everyone was nice and they didn't mind my screwy sense of humor."

"They liked it. Pete Grasse is a great guy, but he's awfully serious when he does the auction."

"I'll bet we made more this year than ever," Janet ran over to say ecstatically. "With the funds we've already raised, I'm sure we'll have enough for the new ladder truck."

Alaina smiled at the woman, who was a powerhouse at the Firefighters Auxiliary. Janet's husband and brothers were all volunteer firefighters, so ensuring the department had the best equipment was very personal to her.

When things quieted down, she and Emily collected a piece of pie from the bakery tent and found a place on the grass to sit and eat in the late-afternoon sunshine.

"I didn't know you were going to bid for Mike," Emily commented.

"I wasn't," Alaina said darkly. "But I couldn't stand the thought of Candy McCoy winning."

Emily wiped her fingers with a napkin and leaned against a tree. "Candy McCoy? I don't think I've met her."

"Believe me, it's an experience you'll never forget. We were in the same grade all through school and she never could keep her hands off other people's stuff, whether it was their lunch money or their guys."

"She sounds horrid." Straightening abruptly, Emily leaned forward and whispered, "Your bachelor is headed this way."

Alaina twisted and saw Mike.

"Could I have a word with you?" he asked.

"Sure, go ahead."

"Privately. Emily doesn't need to hear this."

Emily jumped to her feet. "I should head home in any case."

MIKE FELT BAD as Emily hurried away. It wasn't her fault that Alaina had pulled a fast one.

"That was rude," Alaina told him, getting up and dumping her dessert plate in the trash.

"Ruder than setting me up?"

"What are you talking about?"

"I'm talking about getting a bunch of women to bid on me by promising to top the final price. Was it so important to prove you were right that I'd be a success in the auction? It must have been a shock when they pushed the price so high."

Mike knew he was probably being unreasonable. Plenty of men wouldn't have minded, but this was a special circumstance.

Unreasonable or not, he was startled by the fury

Alaina turned on him. "I never asked anyone to bid on you, and if you think I'd collude with that slut Candy McCoy, then you're off your rocker."

That brought Mike up short, but he soon recovered. "One of the other women could have told her about it."

"I know every single woman who bid for you, Mr. Lightning Carlisle, and not one of them would give Candy the time of day."

Ouch. He should have remembered the general feminine distrust for Candy McCoy before accusing Alaina of anything. In fact, he should have considered the possibility that she'd been rescuing him and thanked her instead of going on the attack.

"I'm sorry," he said stiffly. "That's how it looked to me."

Alaina planted her hands on her hips and leaned toward him with a glare that could have melted steel. He was distracted by the way her breasts heaved against her T-shirt. She wasn't wearing a bra and all memory of her being a skinny little tagalong was erased by a surge of pure lust.

Damn it.

"Silly me, I've thought you were special my entire life," she said slowly and distinctly. "I never gave a hang whether you were a ballplayer or not. In fact, that was the part I liked the least."

"Don't bad-mouth something I loved doing," he snapped back. "Something I'd still be doing if I could."

"I'm not bad-mouthing baseball. I have my own reasons for how I feel. Right now I'm just hoping that you're a better teacher than a ballplayer, because teachers are important and kids deserve the best. But until you get rid of that poor-me syndrome, you won't be able to help anybody, much less yourself."

His jaw clenched. "That's the second time you've accused me of self-pity and it isn't true."

"Maybe, maybe not. All I know is what I can see from the cheap seats. This is the last straw. For that matter, I'm beginning to wonder why I ever bothered with you in the first place."

The scorn in her voice was clear before she wheeled and marched away.

Mike frowned, a prickling sensation going through him. His instincts had once been outstanding. He'd always seemed to know where a long ball was headed or whether he had time to steal a base. Or exactly where a floating fly ball might drop.

And right now he was getting the distinct feeling that he'd just lost something…something he was going to regret.

EMILY WISHED SHE could be a ladybug on a blade of grass, listening to Alaina and Mike. Would they manage to get past the awkward stage they were in? She sure hoped so—the strain was beginning to wear on everyone.

She hadn't gone far before she encountered Sarah and Parker McGregor.

"Emily, what a wonderful day," Sarah exclaimed. "I understand you had a big part in it, even beyond filling in for Pete Grasse."

"I just made a few calls," she said. "It was other people who pitched in so generously."

"You're too modest. Schuyler is fortunate to have you."

Parker smiled his agreement. "I heard they've got enough to order that new ladder truck. The town has been raising money to buy one for over two years—they're very expensive and we wanted the best."

"That's great."

"So, how is the house renovation going?" Sarah asked.

"Terrific. You were right, Big Sky Construction does a fabulous job." Emily smiled brightly, though she wondered how the McGregors would react if she told them about the handgun. Would they know what it was all about? But she dismissed the thought. Obviously Trent hadn't wanted anyone to learn about the weapon.

She sighed, wishing she was able to forget about it for the day. Tomorrow was Saturday and she could have contemplated it then, instead of while she was having so much fun.

"I'm glad," Sarah was saying, "but not surprised.

I'm totally biased when it comes to my boys and I'm sure your folks are the same way about you."

"No doubt," Emily agreed, though it wasn't true. Her sister had practically walked on water for the Georges, while they'd struggled to understand their older daughter.

"How much longer before the renovations are done?" Parker wanted to know.

"Uh…" Emily's train of thought went sideways when she caught sight of Trent leaning against the flagpole, looking in their direction. "It'll be a while, but at least I've got a kitchen now."

"I suppose you've heard that my sister and brother-in-law used to live there."

"Alaina mentioned it."

Once again Emily was bursting with a question…whether Trent might hate Wild Rose Cottage because it reminded him of his parents' fatal accident. But she kept silent. After all, it was Parker McGregor's sister who'd died in that accident, and they'd adopted Trent and Alaina. Their own emotions about the place were bound to be complicated. Besides, it didn't seem fair to ask them about Trent.

Emily said goodbye to the McGregors and continued through the park. Her progress was slow because everyone kept stopping her to chat. With so many people who seemed to like her, seemed to be glad she was in Schuyler, she forgot everything else and floated home on a wave of pleasure.

Outside Wild Rose Cottage, she stood and gazed at the house. She had a clear vision of how it would look when finished. A wide porch would stretch around the front and side, where comfortable chairs and tables could be scattered. On warm evenings she'd sit and wave at the neighbors, or invite them over for iced tea and cookies. There'd be flowers in the yard, lace curtains at the windows, and...

The windows?

An odd feeling abruptly shot through Emily and alarm replaced everything else. A window at the side of the house didn't look right. She ran to the side of the house opposite the driveway, pushed the undergrowth away and found one of Trent's newly restored windows had been smashed. Muddy footprints led across the living room, empty except for Big Sky's equipment.

Why did someone have to be so stinking on such a great day? Not that she wanted to be robbed at any time, but it seemed worse having it done during the fund-raiser. And now she'd have to drag someone away from the fun.

She called the sheriff's office.

"Sheriff Stanfield." In the background she heard the music from the barbecue and realized she must have entered the cell number off Carl's business card.

"Carl, this is Emily," she said, proud her voice wasn't trembling. "Someone has broken a window at my house and I can tell they went inside."

"You didn't go in, did you?"

"No."

"Good, stay out. I'll get there as fast as I can."

Not wanting to sit on the rickety front steps, Emily perched on the trunk of her car, thinking darkly about anyone who could hurt Wild Rose Cottage. She was certain the house was offended. A good home wanted to be a place of peace and safety for the people who lived there. Violating that was a revolting thing to do.

A few minutes later the sheriff's cruiser pulled up with a jerk and Carl jumped out, followed by a deputy.

"Stay there," he ordered again.

After what seemed forever, Carl came to the door and waved her inside.

"No one is here now," he said. "I want you to check for anything missing."

"There's hardly anything in the house. You can tell by looking through the window he broke. The curtain was open and shows the house is practically empty except for Big Sky's tools."

"Perhaps he thought you had something valuable in another room," Carl suggested. "But I... uh, also have to ask if there's anyone who might have something personal against you, from either Schuyler or California?"

The inquiry sent a jolt through Emily. "I ended an engagement before moving here, but Dennis wasn't that upset about it."

The sheriff's eyebrows shot up. "Dennis?"

"Dennis Spencer. He's a roving consultant with Trifab Chemical Engineering International, which is based in Los Angeles. But he couldn't have anything to do with this. He isn't the type."

Nevertheless, Carl wrote down the information.

The deputy was busily dusting for fingerprints around the window and Emily waited, unhappy thoughts going through her head. According to Alaina, property crimes were practically nonexistent in Schuyler—most people didn't even lock their doors at night. The authorities largely dealt with traffic violations and rowdy cowboys, along with a few domestic disputes. Since this was the second time she'd called about a break-in, they'd probably decide she was the Typhoid Mary of criminal activity.

When the deputy finished working, he consulted with Carl, pointing to a couple of spots on the windowsill.

"We'll cross-check the latent prints against the Big Sky Construction crew," Carl told her, "but I'm not hopeful we'll find any that don't match. We've found overlying smudges that are likely from a glove."

Frustrated, Emily did her own walk-through of the house, but with the renovations in progress, she couldn't tell if anything had been disturbed.

"Nothing seems to be missing," she told Carl. "I

can't tell you about Big Sky's equipment. The crew will be here tomorrow and I'll have them check."

Just then heavy footsteps sounded on the porch and the door opened. It was Trent carrying a large sheet of plywood. "I brought this to secure the window."

Emily felt worse than ever. "I don't want to spoil everyone's evening. I can nail something over it myself."

"It's no problem," Trent said in a neutral tone, his face equally neutral.

The day was not ending the way it was supposed to. Somebody was going to pay for this, or her name wasn't Emily George.

CHAPTER TWELVE

DESPITE HIS INTENTION to leave the fund-raiser as soon as possible, Trent had still been there when Carl called about the break-in at Emily's house.

Soon after the auction ended he had seen Alaina angrily roaming the site, grabbing bits of trash and hurling them into a trash can. When asked what was wrong, she'd grumbled something about bone-headed men and wasting too much time on a jerk.

"Who are you talking about?" he'd demanded.

"None of your business," she had muttered, adding, "Men," in a disgusted tone.

That was when his phone had rung. Alaina had immediately stalked away to help in the kitchen.

Trent rigged a covering for the broken window, thinking that if he hadn't given in to the temptation of watching Emily at the auction, he wouldn't be wondering now what she'd said to his folks or about what had upset his sister.

Emily was still talking to Carl, so Trent decided to check the house himself.

It was puzzling. The culprit must have been searching for something, and it was even more obvious on the second floor than on the first.

Loose floorboards had been lifted and fitted back in place—he could tell by the dust that had been disturbed. Heat vents had received the same treatment. He instantly recalled Bob Webber's curiosity about the renovations, but Webber had owned the house for over thirty years. There wasn't any reason for him to search it now...however much Trent remained thoroughly in favor of the asshole going to jail for any reason, including being butt-ugly and offensive.

He went down and explained to Carl what he'd found.

The sheriff made a couple of notes. "Thanks. Let me know if you spot anything else. I have a lead from Ms. George I'm going to look into—someone from California—though she seems quite certain the individual isn't involved."

Carl drove away with his deputy and Trent stood on the curb, debating. He should have told Alaina what had happened. She could have come with him—the other volunteers would have filled in for her at the park—and Emily might appreciate having a friend there. Yet even as the thought formed, he heard a muffled shriek and hurried inside the house.

Emily was stalking back and forth across the floor and she cast him a single searing glance.

"That no-good sniveling creep," she hissed, shaking a fist at the plywood clamped over the window. "How dare he break into Wild Rose Cottage? The universe has a suitable punishment waiting and I hope it includes a garbage truck filled with rotted fish."

Trent watched in bemused awe as she paced the length of the living room.

"Who does he think I am?" she fumed. "A patsy who'll roll over and play an extinct T. rex while he sneaks into my house and does God knows what?" She threw a fulminating glare at Trent. "You think I'm faking being nice, while *he* thinks I'm a patsy. I don't know what's worse, but just let him come back while I'm here. He'll learn his lesson from the woman who got top marks in every self-defense class she's ever taken. I'll tie his legs to his ears and make a pretzel out of him. He'll wish he'd gone to Tibet and become a hermit."

Not once did she curse or swear.

"I know what I'll do," Emily declared. "One of those tricks the kid used in the *Home Alone* movies. He'll wish he was Daniel Stern or Joe Pesci when I get finished. And I'm not the only one. Wild Rose Cottage won't put up with it, either. The guy will think a gang of Klingons got hold of him and swept him off his feet and severed his manhood with a silver bullet."

Trent watched the show with increasing enjoyment. Her choice of Klingon weapons was a little off—he didn't think they used silver bullets—but she continued verbally dissecting the intruder's innards with an excellent understanding of human anatomy. He was grateful that her anger was no longer directed at him, at least for the moment.

"You believe I can do it, don't you?" she demanded, coming up to Trent and shaking her fist once more.

"Absolutely," he breathed.

Unable to resist, he snatched her into his arms for a long, scorching kiss.

EMILY'S BLOOD WAS boiling and now her temperature surged even higher. Trent's embrace was so tight that it should have been uncomfortable, but instead felt more erotic than anything she could remember.

She strained closer, running her hands over the taut muscles of his back.

The kiss deepened and they shared breaths as his tongue delved between her teeth. A minute later he nibbled a string of kisses down her throat and she felt his lips exploring the skin left bare by her sundress.

His hands had been busy unfastening the buttons on her shoulder straps and now he pulled back, his eyes fastened on her bustline as he eased the fabric downward.

She hadn't found the nerve to go natural and was wearing a strapless bra. Trent grinned when he saw it, and teasingly eased a finger beneath the lacy fabric, slowly pulling it forward until stopped by her nipple, already puckered in excitement.

"I wonder what's obstructing traffic," he whispered, brushing his finger back and forth against the sensitive nub.

With her knees buckling and afraid she'd move too much and end the delicious torture, Emily grasped his shoulders and held on for dear life. Breathing harder, Trent slipped his other hand in on the other side and Emily thought she'd die of pleasure as both her breasts received the same treatment.

Then he pulled the fabric down, leaving her bare to his gaze.

"That's a beautiful sight," he said hoarsely.

Her bra dropped to the ground while she unbuckled his belt. At the back of her mind she knew this was a bad idea, but decided to ignore the annoying voice of caution. After tugging the belt free, she quickly dealt with his jeans.

"You're good at that," he gasped.

"I own a fashion boutique. That makes me an expert at buttons and zips," she managed to say.

As she tugged his jeans down, he grasped her hands to stop her, reached back and pulled his wallet from a rear pocket, fumbling until he found a condom.

"A man who's always prepared?" she asked as she busily undid the buttons on his black shirt.

"Find me a single man with good sense who *isn't* prepared."

"True," she said, baring his muscular chest. It

was mostly smooth with only a narrow wedge of dark hair that she carefully ran her fingers through, before drawing them across a jagged scar along his rib cage.

"What happened?"

"Stupidity on the job site," he groaned, seeming to be aroused by her fingers exploring the ridge of white scar tissue.

His erection jutted out, hard and ready under his boxers.

Bra, shirt, sundress, jeans…a trail of clothing was scattered across the floor to the door of her bedroom. Emily fumbled with the knob, managed to open it, and they succeeded in getting inside to tumble onto the mattress she used for a bed.

She gasped as she bounced.

"Nice-quality mattress," Trent told her, fastening his mouth upon her right breast, licking, teasing, sucking.

"Local supplier," she gasped. "I couldn't take the air bed any longer."

"Good choice," he said with a grin, lifting his hips, his hands moving in a way where she knew he was donning the condom. Then he nudged her legs apart and lay hard and satisfying against her.

Yeah…quality all the way.

EMILY DROWSILY LISTENED to the sound of kids playing and the drone of a lawn mower in the distance.

Her neighbors didn't sleep in on Saturday mornings; they got right down to the business of living.

She and Trent lay on their sides, her back against his chest, and his arm curved over her waist. The prior evening had brought the kind of pleasure she'd only imagined in the past. Trent was very, *very* good in bed, and he'd made sure she was completely satisfied. Maybe it was the contrast between him and Dennis that… She stopped herself. No comparisons or thinking of unimportant things.

Part of her believed she was still asleep and had enjoyed a mind-blowing dream. Surely it wasn't possible that they'd spent the night together. He was still the prickly, *impossible* man who thought she'd been trying to manipulate free stuff out of his men.

A cold chill ran down her back. Would he accuse her of sleeping with him in order to get some new folderol on the house?

If he said even one word to that effect he'd find out she could be incredibly *not* nice.

Regardless, now she had to return to reality. Someone had broken into her home and she was convinced it was for the second time. Fortunately, the culprit seemed more interested in Wild Rose Cottage than her. But what about the handgun Trent had taken from the upstairs wall? It seemed unlikely there was a connection, but she couldn't avoid talking to him about it any longer.

She shivered as Trent's body showed hints of

waking energy. His muscles tautened, tension gathering in knots. Asleep he was calm and relaxed. Awake he was…Trent Hawkins, the formidable owner of Big Sky Construction—a man people treated as if he was a live grenade, ready to go off if they accidentally pulled the pin.

But a different primal energy seemed to be building as well… The arm around her waist shifted as Trent's hand went traveling. Interesting, her almost rational mind observed, he explored the curve of her hip first before sliding down to delve into the curls at the apex of her legs.

Well, maybe explanations could wait for a few minutes.

TRENT LIFTED HIMSELF on his elbows and stared down at Emily. Her light brown hair tumbled across the pillow and her pretty brown eyes were fringed with dark lashes. He was still inside of her and hated to leave, despite being fully sated. But he eased away.

"Can we talk?" she asked.

He could have guessed that was coming. It was why he normally stuck with women whose sole interest was a good time. This was the payment for breaking all of his rules about sex and business relationships.

He sat up, pulling the blanket over his lap, hiding the evidence that he was rapidly becoming aroused again, while Emily found a short silk robe and pulled it on. He found it easier to breathe once her breasts were covered.

"Trent," she said firmly, "something happened a few weeks ago that we need to discuss."

He blinked. This wasn't the typical opening to the what-is-our-relationship-and-where-are-we-going-from-here discussion.

"Yes?"

"On the Saturday you worked at the house alone, I came back and you were upstairs, knocking the wall apart for the master bedroom."

All desire vanished.

"Yeah, I..." He couldn't voice the lie he'd planned—that he'd forgotten she wanted to be there when it was demolished.

"I saw you take a handgun out of the wall. You must have a good reason, but I haven't known if I should say something. Now with the break-in, we have to deal with it. The two probably have nothing to do with each other, but they're both creepy."

Trent's brain reeled. He'd figured the whole thing was behind him...except for the gun hidden in his private safe.

He'd planned to drop it in several tons of concrete—Big Sky was always pouring a foundation at one site or another—yet something had held him back.

"I'm sure there's no connection," he said.

"Perhaps not, but I need to know what it's about."

"It's about the past, which is much better left that way."

"It might be about the past, but the gun was in *my* house."

He didn't want to acknowledge she had a point, didn't want to think about the whole mess.

"I don't want to talk about it."

"Sorry, I don't care what you want. And I have to point out that since the gun was in my house, technically, you stole it from me."

Her words were a goad. "Then call the police," he dared.

"Maybe I will, if I don't get the truth."

He didn't think she meant it, but couldn't be completely sure.

"It's about a crap-load of unpleasantness, so can't we just leave it?" he demanded.

Her gaze was unwavering. "No. I've never thought you'd done anything bad with it, but the gun was in my house and I have a right to know what it's about. And if you don't explain, I'm going to start asking other people."

"Damnation," he swore. "I've never met such a stubborn, obnoxious woman in my life."

"You can drop the compliments. They won't distract me," she said, the ironic expression in her eyes telling him she was thinking of his accusations that she'd acted "nice" for a purpose. He didn't know where he stood on that question at the moment, but it was obvious Emily had no intention of moving an inch until he'd explained.

"All right," he said through gritted teeth. "I never used that gun to do something illegal, but my father may have."

"Your father?" she repeated, looking confused. "Everyone says he was a great guy."

"Everyone is wrong. The truth is… I've always wondered if he was involved in several armed robberies the year before he died."

Emily's eyes opened wide. "Did he have a split personality?"

"In a way. In public he was charming and charismatic, but no one knew what kind of man he was inside this house. To me he was a drunk who'd beat his wife and son for any reason."

"Oh, my God," Emily murmured.

Trent gulped a lungful of air, curiously grateful that he'd been forced into revealing the truth. "I told you it wasn't pleasant. Mom pretended everything was fine, as if we were the perfect family. How could she just let it happen and not try to stop him?"

Emily traced a pattern on the blanket before looking up at him. "Some women can't get out of abusive relationships. There's guilt and fear and shame involved, and probably stuff that's unique to each situation."

Thinking back, Trent remembered asking his mother why she didn't leave and she'd stuttered something about loving Gavin and how she was sure it would get better.

"I tried to protect her," he said. "Dad would break things or punch holes in the plaster walls. She was afraid someone in the family would find out or that we'd be evicted, so I learned how to do repairs."

Emily nodded.

Trent grinned savagely. "I used to drop things inside the wall, stuff he wanted, and I wrote notes about how much I hated him and threw them in, as well."

"And the gun," Emily added softly.

"Right, the gun," Trent agreed. "I was afraid that sooner or later he'd shoot my mom. In fact, I was afraid *I'd* grab it and shoot *him* one night. Gavin Hawkins was a mean drunk. It's why I don't drink much. Hell, I just don't want to end up like him. Alaina isn't much of a drinker, either. She hates beer and only has a little dry wine now and then. Maybe she subconsciously knows it's a bad idea."

Now that the dam had broken, it was easier to talk with Emily than Trent had expected. He wasn't sure how he would have expected her to react, but her rational ability to discuss it was a relief.

Her brow creased as if she was thinking deeply. "He never hit Alaina?"

"No," Trent returned harshly. "I promised if he ever laid a finger on her, I'd kill him. He knew I

meant it, because drunk as he was, it was the one time he backed off."

A sad smile curved Emily's lips. "So you were a tough guy, even then."

"Survival required a steep learning curve."

A buzzing from the alarm clock interrupted them and she pivoted to her knees. "Ohmigosh, the crew will be here in half an hour." She grabbed clothes from the plastic boxes sitting next to the mattress. "We'll talk more tonight," she called over her shoulder as she ran for the bathroom.

So she wasn't going to drop it.

But he couldn't spend time trying to convince her otherwise; he didn't want his employees to learn where he'd spent the night and hastily gathered the trail of clothing they'd left through the house. He sorted them out, dropping Emily's inside her door, and was buckling his belt when she flew past with a hurried "I'll get the coffee started."

As he closed the door, he couldn't stop a lingering gaze at the mattress where they'd spent the night. It had been an extremely enjoyable interlude, with a highly unexpected ending.

Tonight would tell him more.

ALAINA WAS STILL furious when she stormed into the office on Saturday morning. Trent hadn't asked her to work that day, but she was so angry, she figured she might as well get boring paperwork done while she had a headful of steam driving her.

What a nerve Mike had, to suggest she'd set him up—as if she didn't have better things to do.

It was time to see Mike for what he really was.

When the office door opened ten minutes later she put on her calmest, most professional expression. Customers and staff didn't care whether the office manager was having a bad weekend; they simply wanted their issues efficiently resolved.

She kept the expression firmly fixed when she saw it was Mike who'd arrived.

"Can I help you?" she asked crisply.

"I was hoping we could talk."

She glanced at the wall clock. "You're already late for work."

Mike's jaw hardened. "Dock my pay. Please, Alaina, I want to apologize for yesterday. It was rude and ungracious."

"You forgot stupid."

"And stupid," he agreed. "I didn't think before opening my big mouth and made a fool of myself."

Alaina closed her desk drawer with a snap. "Apology accepted. You can go to work now."

"I was also wondering when we could go out to dinner."

Alaina raised her eyebrow. "You're off the hook. I'm treating my winning bid as a no-strings-attached donation toward the ladder truck."

"This has nothing to do with the auction. It would mean a lot to me if you'd agree."

Pursing her lips, Alaina considered how to respond. She was so angry and frustrated with Mike that she could hardly see straight, but if she didn't get to know him better, how could she answer the hard question she kept asking herself?

Was she really in love with Mike Carlisle, or had she mistaken a girlhood fantasy for the real thing?

He was no longer the ambitious boy who'd dazzled Schuyler with his talent and easygoing friendliness. Instead, he was a complicated man with a whole lot of problems. She didn't mind sharing problems with someone she loved, but she no longer knew how she felt about him.

Of course, that could mean she was a fool, that she'd left her life in New York for nothing more than a lingering crush. But she'd be a bigger fool if she didn't figure out whether she loved Mike, or if he'd just been a childish fantasy.

"I'll consider it," she answered at length.

Mike seemed disappointed not to get an immediate agreement, but that was too bad. She wasn't playing games or trying to dangle him on a hook. Just because he'd finally asked her out was no reason to fall at his feet, even if it turned out that she really loved him. It was time for some equality in their relationship, whether he liked it or not.

"I'll call you later," Mike said as he stood at the door, watching her intently.

"Fine."

Strangely, it was almost as if he was seeing her in a new way, but her imagination was probably just working overtime.

CHAPTER THIRTEEN

SOON AFTER EMILY started the coffee, Trent left to pick up pastries. She had planned to bake something the night before, but other things had pushed that idea out the window.

Trent probably thought being absent when the crew arrived would prevent gossip. Not likely. Someone in the neighborhood was bound to have noticed his truck parked in front of the house all night. She'd already learned that rumor-sharing was a staple entertainment in Schuyler, though people who learned about the break-in might think he'd stayed to keep an eye on the place.

Well…maybe.

Trent worked so hard keeping everyone from knowing a decent guy lurked beneath his tough exterior, people might question him having an altruistic impulse.

"Hell, Em," Vince yelped when he saw plywood over the window he'd helped glaze three days earlier. "What happened?"

"Someone broke in," she explained.

A sad-faced Caveman went to get a broom to

clean up the glass while Eduardo gave her a comforting hug.

"What a horrid thing to happen," Eduardo said.

"Yeah, and if I ever lay my hands on the guy who did it, he'll have thorny wild rose canes up his nose...or another part of his anatomy," she promised.

The men chuckled.

Mike wasn't there yet, which seemed strange. He was always on time—the Big Sky crews were known for their reliability. He hustled in twenty minutes later and gave her a sheepish smile.

"Hi," he said. "Sorry I'm late. I, uh, went by the office to discuss something with Alaina."

"That's okay." Emily hoped the discussion was more than dutifully checking when Alaina wanted to have dinner with the bachelor she'd won at the auction.

Mike glanced around. "Where's Trent?"

"He was here earlier, but decided to get doughnuts." Pretending she hadn't seen him would just raise more questions.

After finishing their coffee, the men launched into work. Emily was putting the cups into her new dishwasher when the phone rang. It was Alaina asking if she'd be able to have lunch. Emily hoped she had good news to share, but the tight, weary sound in her friend's voice didn't sound promising.

"Sure, how about getting something from Simpson's Deli?"

"Sounds good. I'll meet you there at noon."

When Trent walked in a short time later, she smiled nonchalantly.

"I explained that you were here early and decided to go out for pastries," she said, in case there might be listening ears.

"I picked up an assortment."

Nodding as if nothing unusual had happened, she went to see if she could help Eduardo dismantle the upstairs bathroom.

A few hours later she left to meet Alaina at the deli. They got sandwiches and went to the park to eat at one of the picnic tables. Aside from trampled places in the grass, there were no signs of the huge event that had taken place the day before.

"Wow, everything is cleaned up already," Emily marveled.

"We've got a good crew with lots of practice. The barbecue has been held here for over thirty years."

"Impressive." Emily unwrapped her veggie sandwich, thinking about Trent's revelations. She wanted to act naturally, but it was uncomfortable knowing intimate details about her friend's childhood that Alaina didn't remember. He'd been right about the load of unpleasantness.

Most of all Emily felt bad for Trent. It must have been lonely growing up with all those secrets, keeping them hidden from the rest of his family.

No wonder he was so solitary, putting up barriers to keep everyone away.

The problem was that understanding Trent's cynicism didn't make him any easier to be with.

"What happened with Mike yesterday?" she asked Alaina.

"The jackass accused me of setting him up... saying I promised to outbid everyone, just to make him look good. I was tempted to turn him into a soprano."

Emily couldn't help thinking how often people blithely said something like *I could have killed him,* or *I wanted to strangle the guy.* Or *I was tempted to turn him into a soprano.* Most people didn't mean anything by it, but it was a curious reminder of the violence Trent had known as a child.

Alaina continued, "Now I'm wondering how I really feel about him." Alaina gazed across the park, her eyes troubled.

Whoa. They'd both had significant revelations over the past twenty-four hours.

"Mike mentioned going by the Big Sky office this morning. Was it to continue the argument?" asked Emily.

"Actually, he apologized and asked me to dinner, but not because of the auction. Supposedly it's to get to know me better. I'm thinking about it."

Emily grinned. "Tell him it has to be a whole lot of dates, because that's the only way to really know each other."

"He may not want to do that." Alaina tossed a crust from her sandwich to a blue jay perched on the end of the table. "Everything came easily for Mike before the accident. Maybe he thinks relationships should be the same."

"You can't make a go of it if he isn't willing to do the work needed to be a couple."

"Yeah, except now I'm wondering if I gambled everything on a childhood fantasy."

"At least this way you'll know for sure." Emily had never found anything she wanted badly enough that she'd gamble everything to get it, but she admired people willing to take those chances.

Alaina sighed. "Maybe. I'm going to tell him to meet me tonight—not as a date, just to talk. Tomorrow is out because there's always a big family meal at the ranch on Sundays."

"Then why don't we eat at the Roundup Café on Monday so I can hear the grisly details?" Emily suggested.

"Sounds good. I'll come over after work."

On her walk home Emily pondered how strangely things had turned out. She'd never expected to know so much about Trent—between his reputation and stony face she would have said it would take a ball and crane to get anything out of the guy. In a way, it had been a wrecking ball that had done it—an emotional one.

Everyone had childhood wounds. Heck, she had

her own scars, though Trent's were far uglier than a few lacerations to the ego.

Emily glanced down at the trim pair of shorts she was wearing, another recent clothing purchase. For most of her life she'd hidden behind stiff suits, or clothes that were loose and comfortable, and neither were becoming on her. After all, why bother trying to look attractive when she couldn't possibly compete with women like Nicole?

Nonetheless, Trent had seemed eager to take her to bed. Really eager. And while the old movie line she'd once heard might be true—men don't need a reason for sex, just a place—she was sure that he'd genuinely wanted her in that moment, and no one else.

The insecure part of Emily's brain whispered that he'd been thrown off balance by having to confront his childhood memories. And to a certain extent it must have played a role—she just didn't know how much of one.

Tiredly, she told herself to stop borrowing trouble. She wasn't great at figuring men out, anyway. Dennis was the only other guy she'd slept with, and they hadn't gotten together very often. At the time she'd assumed the demands of his business travel were keeping them apart, but in all honesty, she hadn't regretted it. Of course, now that she knew how good it could be between the sheets, she was going to miss sex a whole lot more.

EMILY GREW INCREASINGLY nervous as she waited for Trent that evening.

Would he come?

That morning when she'd said they would talk later, she hadn't meant another tumble into bed. It wasn't that she'd mind, but she didn't want to come off as a desperate woman grabbing whatever she could. Besides, men being men, she would never assume that a night together constituted the start of a relationship.

After the crew had left for the day she'd hurried out to the Crazy Horse Ranch to visit Stella Luna, not wanting to disappoint her. Jackson McGregor had claimed the mare pricked her ears at the sound of every car engine and would watch eagerly to see if it was Emily arriving. He'd offered to buy Stella Luna, but the horse was so firmly fixed in Emily's heart, giving her up would be impossible.

Back at the house Emily was determined not to act as if she was expecting a social evening, so she made a chef salad and set out a single plate on the card table she'd brought in from the patio. The table didn't do justice to the new breakfast nook, but it would have to do until she'd moved her furniture from Los Angeles, or bought new items. She was just sitting down when a knock sounded on the front door.

Trent?

Generally he knocked rather than ringing. Still, she checked to be sure it was him before answering.

"I was just going to eat, but there's extra if you're hungry," she offered. "Fair warning though, it's girlie food."

"That would be nice," he said, obviously distracted. She wanted to believe it wasn't because he regretted their night together. After all, he had his father's handgun to think about, which was considerably more important than having broken a rule about keeping one's work and personal life separate.

TRENT FOLLOWED EMILY to the kitchen, noticing she hadn't dressed up or worn anything date-like or provocative. Not that she needed it, particularly now that he'd seen the beauty beneath her casual clothing. With any other woman he would have wondered why she hadn't put on something special, but the feminine motivations behind Emily's elfin face were still a mystery.

He hadn't expected to be fed, but he sat down with the plate of salad she'd made up for him. It was tasty and hearty, despite her calling it a girlie offering.

"I wanted to ask something about the break-in," he said, unwilling to abruptly leap back into the stressful discussion from that morning. "Carl mentioned he had a lead to follow up, checking out someone from California?"

Emily shook her head. "He's just being care-ful, but my ex-fiancé can't be responsible. Dennis wasn't very upset about the breakup."

Trent frowned. "He may have changed his mind."

"Dennis is an ass, but he isn't the type to smash windows."

"There's nobody else who might have a grudge against you, even for a stupid reason?"

"Nobody except Santa Claus—I stopped believ-ing in him a long time before I figured out the tooth fairy was really our housekeeper."

The temptation to laugh caught Trent by sur-prise. "Your housekeeper played tooth fairy?"

"Well, yeah. My parents didn't have time for that stuff, and they sure wouldn't have given me chocolate the way she did. I doubt they even knew what Zelda was doing."

The matter-of-fact statement made Trent think about the way Aunt Sarah and Uncle Parker had always found time for their children, including the niece and nephew they'd adopted. They were won-derful parents, even if he hadn't properly appre-ciated them.

"Zelda sounds interesting," he said.

"She was great. On top of everything else, she was the only one who didn't call me the smart George sister. I loved it."

"Didn't you enjoy being called smart?"

Emily gave him an incredulous look. "It was a

pitying comment, not a compliment. My sister is a gorgeous bombshell that everyone adores. She's been a top model since before she could walk and I just didn't measure up."

Whoa. He'd gotten that one wrong. Here he'd thought Emily was patting herself on the back for being intelligent—instead, it was a negative label stuck on her as a kid.

"Then the people you grew up with were focused on appearance."

"It isn't that unusual," Emily said wryly. "After all, you don't hear anyone saying, 'What a smart little girl you have in that stroller.' They tell you how pretty she is, or they don't say anything."

"I suppose."

"Basically, my parents' livelihood is based on how people look. They're clothing buyers for a high-end department store and most of their friends are in the fashion industry. That's why opening a boutique seemed a natural choice for me. I grew up learning what the beautiful people want."

She pushed her plate away. "It's wonderful living in a place where nobody knows my family. It gets old when people can't believe we're from the same gene pool. I've even been asked if I was adopted."

Trent was lousy at empathy, but he suspected Emily had revealed a lot about herself. "Not everyone thinks beauty has to come in a single shape."

She rolled her eyes. "Thanks, but while I don't frighten children, I grew up with a stiff standard.

Even my ex-fiancé finally admitted I was just plain bread and butter, so he wanted cake on the side."

Emily shrugged as if it didn't matter, but Trent knew she was pretending. Then he did a double take. Her fiancé had actually built infidelity into his marriage plan? While Trent didn't want to get married himself, that sort of behavior was repulsive.

"I don't think you're plain anything," he told her awkwardly, giving compliments being a talent he'd refused to cultivate.

"That's nice of you to say," she said, clearly disbelieving him. "Would you like more salad?"

"No, thanks. It was delicious."

"I'm glad you liked it. I also brought some to the neighbor across the street, though it probably isn't the meat-and-potatoes type of dish she usually eats."

For most of his life, Trent had tried to send the message "stay away from me," thinking little about the wounds suffered by others. Now he looked at Emily loading the dishwasher and wondered how self-centered he'd become. She wasn't a saint, but perhaps she genuinely cared about people.

"I'm sure your neighbor appreciated it," he said.

"She's a shut-in, which means there's absolutely nothing she can do for me, so you'll have to look for another ulterior motive."

"Give me a break," he muttered.

Emily confused him. When it came to most people outside his family he could figure out where they were coming from; you either gave or denied them what they wanted and that was it. But Emily defied his attempt to understand her. He'd always looked for underlying motives in women, either conscious or subconscious. It was the unwitting pleas for rescue that he tried hardest to avoid. That kind of woman could suck you under.

He didn't want to get lost with Emily. Something about her seemed dangerous. She reminded him of the time he'd been on the highway, watching a tornado, not knowing in which direction he'd find safety.

EMILY OPENED THE freezer and took out the ice cream she'd bought to celebrate the kitchen being finished.

"How about a sundae?" she asked.

"Sounds good. I hope you have peanuts to put on top."

"Um…sure." She'd almost said, *You're a man after my own heart.* She wouldn't have meant anything by it, only that she also liked peanuts on her sundaes, but he might have misunderstood.

She served two bowls of vanilla and set out a selection of toppings.

"Sorry, no fruit sauce," she apologized.

"I prefer it this way."

Emily noticed that Trent selected caramel, chocolate and peanuts, her favorite combo, but she didn't say anything about that, either.

"Mmm," she murmured as the chocolate rolled over her tongue. "I once read that the taste of chocolate makes you feel the same way falling in love does." She laughed. "Sorry, that's the sort of thing women say at a chick-fest."

His smile seemed strained. "No problem. Do you agree about chocolate?"

"I'm not sure. It isn't how I felt with Dennis, so either the researchers are wrong or I wasn't really in love. And in the end, maybe it was my fault he couldn't commit. Would a guy feel different with a woman who truly loved him?"

"It wasn't your fault that he's a jerk," Trent surprised her by saying. "But tell me more about growing up in LA."

Emily ate a bite of ice cream. She didn't like talking about her childhood, and considering how terrible things had been for Trent, her issues seemed trivial.

"We traveled a lot," she said slowly. "I loved it more than Nicole did, which is ironic because she's still on the road all the time."

She debated for a moment, then retrieved a photo of her sister on her phone. Nicole gazed seductively at the camera, wearing a sarong and a hibiscus blossom in her hair. Once Trent saw it, he'd understand why the contrast between them had struck people so strongly.

"This is my sister at a photo shoot in Bali," she explained, handing him the phone.

He gazed at the picture with no reaction. It was a first; men generally came close to drooling.

Trent handed the phone back. "She's pretty, but only by a single standard of evaluation."

"By every standard," Emily protested, instantly springing to Nicole's defense—her sister wasn't just beautiful, she was a darned nice person.

"I disagree."

Emily waited for the usual consoling comment—*beauty isn't all on the outside*—but he didn't say it.

"What did you do when she was modeling?" Trent asked.

"Mostly I did my own thing. I loved to explore when we were traveling, at least when I got old enough to go on my own. For a while I knew the Louvre inside and out—the Mona Lisa became one of my closest friends."

"You may have gotten the best of the deal."

"True." In a way, she even felt sorry for her sister. "Nicole was stuck with fittings and makeup sessions, along with practicing poses and getting critiqued on walking the right way, while I got to see all sorts of amazing things."

"What about school during all that travel?"

"We had a tutor." She cocked her head at his oddly quizzical expression. "What is it?"

"I was wondering how you turned out so flaky and avant-garde."

Sourness twisted her stomach. She knew people considered her flaky, but Trent didn't make it sound like an acceptable eccentricity. At least the men she'd known in the past had enjoyed her personality. Depression nibbled and she wondered if that was why Trent hadn't talked about beauty being on the inside…because he didn't especially like her inside.

"That's enough about me," Emily declared firmly, resisting the temptation of self-pity. "We got interrupted this morning when you were telling me about Wild Rose Cottage."

Trent turned to stare out the window. His face had the hard, stern expression he often wore and she wondered how much he'd been hiding over the years. The problem with barricades to keep something from escaping was that no one could get in, either.

"Haven't you been lonely," she asked, "keeping it shut inside yourself?"

TRENT FLINCHED AT Emily's question; it hit too close to the bone. He *had* been lonely. With a loving family surrounding him, he'd still been alone.

"It wasn't so bad," he asserted. "I wanted people to stay away."

"I kind of understand. You needed to keep a secret and it's easier to keep secrets if no one gets close. But why didn't you want them to know?"

"How could I tell Uncle Parker that his sister's husband knocked her around?" Trent growled. "Would you want to know?"

"Yes, so I could talk her into leaving him."

"And if she was gone and you couldn't help her any longer, wouldn't you rather think she'd been happy?"

Emily was silent for a long minute, her brow creased in thought. "I wouldn't want my nephew dealing with it alone," she said slowly, "but I can't guess how your uncle would feel."

"I don't know, either. That's why I didn't tell anybody."

"Wasn't it more than that? Your mother was determined to keep the abuse a secret. Revealing the truth probably would have seemed like a betrayal, even after she was gone. The same with calling anyone else Mom."

Trent thought about the confused mix of anger and love and protectiveness he'd felt for Fiona Hawkins. Emily was right—the habit had been so engrained by the time of the accident, it would have broken him to have revealed the things his mother had wanted kept private.

"When did you hide your father's handgun?" Emily asked.

"He tried to keep it a secret, but I knew he had one," Trent said slowly. "The morning of my tenth birthday he was in one of his jovial moods, claiming we'd go out that evening to celebrate. I was sporting the black eye and split lip he'd given me and didn't care about doing anything, but Mom was thrilled that he was being so nice."

"The honeymoon," Emily murmured.

"Honeymoon?"

She looked embarrassed. "I've heard abusers may be affectionate for a while after doing something dreadful. And how it builds false hope."

"Well, the honeymoon never lasted long with Gavin. He returned late that afternoon and slugged Mom when she asked where we were going for dinner. It terrified Alaina, but he just laughed and sprayed beer all over her. When she started screaming, he said to keep her quiet or else."

Trent stared through the windows into the backyard, thinking how it had looked that long-ago day.

"Then what happened?" Emily prompted.

"Gavin stumbled out to the yard and drank a six-pack before leaving again. I was picking up the empty beer cans when I found the gun. He must have been too drunk to realize it had fallen out of his pocket."

Emily nodded, her eyes wide and attentive.

"Seeing it scared the hell out of me. Sooner or later he'd forget my threat and start hitting Alaina as well, and if he did…?" Trent shuddered. "I could actually see me pointing that gun at my own father and pulling the trigger."

"So you picked a hiding place where nobody could get to it, even you."

"I didn't know what else to do. I wrapped the thing in plastic and stuck it in the wall I was patching."

"Why the plastic?"

Trent released a harsh breath. "By then I was willing to believe the worst about him. I wanted to be able to threaten Gavin with evidence that might send him to jail. After the accident I heard about a string of armed robberies in the area and wondered if he was responsible. The only thing that got me through those days was thinking that no one else had to know what he'd really been like. The secret was finally safe."

"Safe most of all from Alaina," she guessed softly.

Pain went through Trent, even after all these years. "My sister was so small and giggly and happy. I didn't want her growing up with everyone knowing she was the daughter of a violent drunk who may have also been a criminal."

EMILY'S HEART ACHED. Trent had learned all too well how to be a tough little boy, and he'd become a man who was just as tough and strong.

"The McGregors are a respected family in town," he said, almost in a monotone, as if reciting a litany.

Maybe that's what he was doing, listing everything he'd told himself over the years, reminders that no one else had to get hurt as long as he kept his mouth shut.

"People would have whispered when Uncle Parker went to sell cattle at the stockyard," Trent continued. "Aunt Sarah would have faced gossip at church and the supermarket. They didn't deserve that. As for my cousins…they already had to share their parents with Alaina and me. Who knows what kind of mean stuff the other kids in school might have done or said to them?"

"So you kept quiet to protect everyone." Emily understood, but she didn't think it was right that a child should have to protect the adults in his life.

He snorted. "Don't make it sound heroic. I was protecting myself, too. Besides, I relished every minute of hating Gavin on my own. For one thing, nobody was telling me to forgive him, something I had no intention of doing."

Emily chuckled at the rueful glint in Trent's eyes.

"How…human," she managed to say.

She cocked her head, thinking about the comments people had made when she was checking Big Sky's references. It had come up more than once, how much Trent looked like his father.

"I'll bet you didn't appreciate people saying you resembled your father," she took a chance on saying.

Seeing the muscle ticking in his jaw, she'd clearly hit a sore spot.

"Yeah," he admitted, "and think how they would have reacted if they'd learned I hated Gavin Hawkins, and even my mother in a way because she'd stayed with him."

"Maybe you should tell them now," Emily suggested tentatively.

"It's in the past," he returned in a tone that didn't brook argument. "Dead and buried with my parents."

Emily wasn't sure about that.

CHAPTER FOURTEEN

WHEN TRENT USED that tone of voice, his employees knew better than to continue the debate.

Emily just stuck up her chin.

"That's garbage," she shot back. "It isn't dead and buried. Well, it might be buried, but it isn't dead. And since you've buried something that stinks so much, it's in danger of turning your brain into a massive abscess. You and Alaina are adults now. It's time to tell the truth."

Trent stared at her belligerent face. Emily's colorful imagery was too apt. It *had* been like an infection, abscessing in various ways, pushing him further and further from his family and friends. But at least that had been a place where he had some sense of control.

"I'll think about it," he said.

She cocked her head and he knew the inquisition wasn't over. All at once he thought of the time when he'd had an abscess in his leg when he was fourteen. Aunt Sarah had rushed him to the clinic and he'd put on a stoic face, not wanting them to touch the painful swelling, at the same moment hoping it would feel better after the procedure. If this was the same as that, maybe he should consider it.

Emily leaned forward. "I bet you were also afraid that if Schuyler found out about your father they'd wonder if you'd turn out the same way,"

How could she so accurately locate his wounded spots? Once again he felt the sucking energy of the tornado.

"I suppose," he admitted grudgingly. "People always wanted me to be like Gavin—charming and sociable and fun—but I knew what a louse he was, so I never wanted anyone to say I was charming like him."

"Don't worry," Emily advised drily, "there isn't much danger of that."

Trent chuckled, feeling as if the joke had slapped him back into normality. *Almost*.

Lord, here he was, sitting in a kitchen with a woman who'd turned him upside down and forced him to look at his life in a new way. But he was also being whipped by two emotional storms, torn between the ancient one from childhood and the force of nature that was Emily. There *had* to be a way of putting her into a more manageable category in his life.

Would another night with her help or hinder that attempt? And could he resist either way?

"Where is the gun now?" she asked.

"In my private safe. I'd planned to dispose of it, but couldn't. I don't know, maybe it *is* time for the truth to come out." The admission gave him a curious sense of release. "Besides, if the weapon was used in the robberies, the authorities would probably appreciate closing the book on those crimes, even if the statute of limitations has passed."

EMILY SAW THE resolution spreading over Trent's face as he made his decision. She hoped it would give him some of the peace he deserved.

"What about your family?" she asked. "You can't speak to the police and leave them out of the loop."

"I'll think about it."

"That's good," she managed to answer through the tightness in her throat. She stirred her spoon in the pool of chocolate syrup left in her bowl, then went to the freezer to get more ice cream. She served herself another scoop and put a couple more in Trent's bowl. Something about Trent's expression had subtly shifted and it was making her heart pound harder.

They finished their dessert in silence, then stood. Trent tugged her close.

It was heavenly to have his arms around her. *We fit together,* whispered a traitorous voice in her head, a voice she crossly told to shut up. After a few more minutes, she felt his lips moving at the side of her neck. Delicious shivers danced down her spine and rushed into her abdomen.

"Why don't we take up where we left off this morning?" he asked in low, rough tone.

"I thought that's what we've been doing, discussing what needs to be...discussed."

"Actually, I was thinking about what happened *before* we started talking." His hand moved down, into the small of her back.

One more night, she thought. It wasn't too much to ask for someone who'd been stupid enough to fall for a man way out of her league. She still had questions, but she'd rather spend the night making love with Trent than talking.

His lips moved to her mouth and she realized he'd somehow disposed of her blouse. "I like these lacey bits you wear," he murmured. "But I like you even better without them." The bra quickly followed the blouse to the floor.

"It's too bad the hot tub hasn't been installed," Emily gasped as he played with her breasts, teasing them to plump attention.

"We'll make do," he breathed, lifting her easily into his arms and striding toward the bedroom.

MIKE SAT ACROSS from Alaina at a table outside the Roundup Café. She'd agreed to meet him for a cup of coffee, refusing to treat it as a date.

After stirring cream into her cup, she leaned forward. "I don't enjoy games and I'm tired of wasting time. I'll go to dinner with you, but it can't be a one-time thing. I want to know the real Mike

Carlisle, and I want you to know who I am, not just who you think I am. The only way to do that is to spend serious time together."

He blinked. "Were you this direct with the guys you dated in New York?"

"No. I was never that interested in anyone there."

Energy pricked at him... Did that mean she was interested in one Mike Carlisle?

"It still seems strange that you'd leave a good career and come back to Schuyler. I've wondered if it was a bad relationship you wanted to leave behind." It wasn't the smartest thing he could have said. New York seemed to be a sore point with Alaina, and now her eyes flashed once more.

"You don't get it. Over and over you just don't get it. I wouldn't let a guy run me off from a job I enjoyed and which, I might add, I continue to do as a consultant. The only thing I gave up was location."

Wow, he'd walked into that one.

"Okay." Mike held up his hands in surrender. "Then why did you come back to Schuyler?"

"Because you did. I was hoping you'd finally pay attention to something right in front of you."

Astounded, he stared at her. Alaina had left New York because of him?

"How... I mean, you wanted...?" he stuttered into silence.

"I want you to notice me. I'm the dumb player who goes for the long ball, same as you always did.

And by the way, I know exactly what happened at your last game. You were showing off, like usual, this time for a slinky redhead. It was stupid and I was so mad at you I could have spit, but I loved you anyway."

"You...loved me?"

"Yeah."

It suddenly hit him that she hadn't said how she felt *now*. "Loved," he repeated, "as in past tense?"

"I don't know. I'm trying to figure out what's real and if you're the person I always thought you were. I never cared about Lightning Carlisle. Now I'm wondering if anyone else ever existed, except in my imagination."

The enormity of what she was saying slammed through Mike's head. Apart from his parents, Alaina and her brother might be the only people who hadn't cared if he was a hero. Yet he'd never paid much attention to Alaina, first because she was too young, later because he was too involved with being a hotshot baseball star, and still later because he was bitter over the loss of his career.

"By the way," Alaina continued heatedly, "you had a decade in the majors. That's more than most guys. It's too bad it ended earlier than you wanted, but deal with it. You ought to feel lucky, not bitter."

A rueful smile tugged at his mouth. With the possible exception of her brother, Alaina was the only person he knew with the guts to tell him the truth.

"Okay," he said finally, "where do we go now?"

"First I need to know if you're interested in getting to know me the way people are supposed to know each other. If you're not, that's the end of it. I'll leave you alone to stew in your own juices, though I should point out that those juices shouldn't be too many six-packs behind closed doors."

The skin around Alaina's lips was white and he recalled her uncomfortable reaction when he'd answered the door with a beer in hand, and another time when she'd seen a carton of ale on his kitchen counter. In actuality he didn't drink that often, despite appearances.

"I agree completely," he said quietly.

She looked suspicious. "About what part?"

"All of it. I've been blind and stupid. You're amazing and I'm definitely interested."

Alaina regarded him suspiciously. "Second," she said, "I have no intention of becoming your girlfriend simply because you feel lucky to get me under the circumstances."

He blinked, confused, and she made an impatient gesture.

"Put it this way, Mike. I'm not a consolation prize for what happened to you. I don't want that, any more than Emily wanted to be someone you settled for because you figured you couldn't do better."

Hell. Mike winced. If that was what Emily had thought, it wasn't any wonder she'd dodged a second date with him.

"It isn't how I saw her… I mean, she seems like someone who wouldn't mind being a teacher's wife…" He stopped, aware that he was making things worse. "What I especially liked is that she's new in town and doesn't remember me as the town baseball star."

Alaina narrowed her eyes. "Gee, what woman wouldn't be honored to be pursued for such a stellar reason? Emily is my friend and I resent your treating her badly."

"Give me a break. Lots of people get interested in each other because of something small or simple. It wasn't that she isn't attractive."

Alaina's lips pressed together, then she nodded. "Okay."

Mike frowned. "Emily is nice and I never meant to hurt her."

"Don't get bigheaded about that, either. Her ego is slightly bruised, but she was hardly in love with you."

"I'll still apologize."

"Don't you dare," Alaina snapped. "With your foot-in-mouth disease, you'll just make it worse."

He was about to protest when he decided to follow the old saw about discretion being the better part of valor. Anyhow, maybe he did have some shortcomings in the verbal department. He'd never intended to give Emily the wrong impression.

"Okay," he agreed. "As for the rest, I guess I don't know very much, except that I've been attracted to you for a long time. The main reason I didn't do something about it when you moved back was because dating a buddy's sister can get sticky."

"I'll always be Trent's sister," Alaina reminded him crisply.

"Now I don't care if it gets sticky. It's Trent's problem, not mine."

"Good. I want to clarify another issue. I'm interested in the whole enchilada—marriage, family and lifetime commitment—with someone, not necessarily you. Are you opposed to marriage and kids, or willing to consider it with the right person?"

"I'm willing to consider it," he answered firmly. The conversation reminded him of a contract negotiation.

"Then I'll put this in terms you understand… you'll have a lengthy spring training and tryout period while we get to know each other and decide if we should play on the same team. No shortcuts. I'm not interested in someone who can't last more than a couple of innings, and I don't want someone who can't see that new dreams are able to take the place of old ones."

"That's… Sure."

"I mean it," Alaina insisted. "Teaching isn't a dismal fallback position. Kids are the future. When I have children, I want them to have teachers who are excited about helping them, and that's what your students deserve right now."

Mike nodded, feeling as if he'd been jerked awake after a long, stuporous slumber. Alaina Hawkins was the kind of woman he should have been looking for all along. And if he had recognized that, he wouldn't have been showboating for every pretty face he'd noticed in the stands.

And while he could do without having a bum knee, the future could be pretty great as a high school teacher in Schuyler, Montana.

EARLY IN THE morning Emily slipped out of bed and went into the kitchen. They'd gotten plenty of exercise over the past ten hours and she was hungry.

"Any coffee?" Trent asked, walking in sleepily.

"It's almost done brewing. Help yourself to toast and cheese if you want it. I'm not in a breakfast-cooking mode yet, but I have eggs if you want to give it a go."

"I don't cook," he admitted, popping two slices of the whole-grain bread into the toaster. "The closest I can manage are those microwave breakfasts from the grocery freezer case."

"Whatever works."

Emily was determined to be sophisticated and not get stupid about Trent spending a second night with her. It had been one of those unique events, where emotions and events came together and the result didn't mean anything; she wasn't even sure she wanted it to have a meaning.

Was she in love with the guy? That would be a

disaster. She had neither great beauty nor, apparently, a personality he especially appreciated.

And even though she understood the tragedy behind his hard face and admired the way he protected his family, she wasn't necessarily crazy about *his* personality. Probably it was simply a case of full-blown lust.

Trent had gotten dressed, which was good because the sight of his still-tousled dark hair left her wobbly with renewed cravings.

"Uh… I guess it's obvious why you wanted Wild Rose Cottage," she said. "To get the gun."

"Yes and no." He poured himself a cup of coffee. "To be frank, I wanted to bulldoze the place into splinters. I've dreamed of doing it for years, but Webber wouldn't sell, and then you bought it before I knew it was on the market."

"Oh," she said, the admission sending mixed emotions through her. Curiously, she was sorry he hadn't got what he wanted, but the thought of Wild Rose Cottage being demolished was disturbing.

He shrugged. "I'm dealing with it." After finishing his coffee and toast, he stood. "I'd better get going. I've got some people to see."

Emily hoped those people included his family, but didn't ask. She wanted to keep the morning-after routine casual. That way there were no false hopes.

With so much of the downstairs completed and the second-floor renovations in progress, she should have been satisfied. The bedroom and bath she was using needed to be done, but things were in good shape. Once they finished the second floor and attic, she'd move up there and let them do the rest. Everything was going fine.

She was perfectly happy except for a few niggling feelings of guilt. If she hadn't bought the house, Trent could have erased the scene of his childhood pain. Part of her wondered if she should let him warm up the wrecking ball after all, but she really believed Wild Rose Cottage deserved a future.

At least he'd made some peace with it. She probably wouldn't see so much of him now that he didn't feel the need to personally knock down the walls. There might be a few nasty notes or odd bits that could surface, but hiding them only mattered if his father's behavior was a secret, and if he turned in the gun it wouldn't be a secret any longer.

"It's a good thing that he's laid some of his ghosts to rest," Emily told the house as she curled up in the corner window seat. She absolutely refused to let any tears fall.

It was time to be normal again.

ALAINA DRIFTED AWAKE as her golden retriever nudged her fingers and whined for attention.

"Morning, Shelby," she said, yawning. She was still having a few nightmares, but they'd gotten better lately.

She and Mike had decided to treat the evening as their first date, eventually going to the Chinese restaurant. They'd lingered after dinner, talking for over an hour. It might have gone on longer, but she'd felt it was wise to keep things to a reasonable length of time.

Mostly they'd discussed movies they liked, probably because it was a relatively safe topic and they'd needed a break from more intense subjects.

Mike's favorite film was *The Shawshank Redemption*, which she'd already known from the interviews he'd given over the years, and he had discussed the Stephen King story with thoughtful intelligence.

As dates went, it had been good. He'd even kissed her before saying good-night.

A satisfied smile curved Alaina's lips.

It had been a very nice kiss.

CHAPTER FIFTEEN

TRENT SHOOK THE sheriff's hand.

"Thanks, Carl," he said. "I should have told someone about the gun a long time ago, but believed it didn't matter that much because my father was dead. I didn't know someone had been killed in one of those holdups."

"You were a kid when it happened. Besides, it might *not* matter. Until we get a ballistics report, we won't know if Gavin Hawkins had any connection to the murder. This type of thing usually turns out to be a false lead."

Despite the assurance, Trent was certain Gavin had been involved in the death of a seventy-year-old grandfather protecting his convenience store. There wasn't any proof yet, but drunk or sober, his father had been mean enough to shoot anybody who got in his way.

It made Trent sick, but in some part of his mind he was glad the truth was coming out. Justice was important; now David Barker and his family would get their share.

Carl had pulled up the reports on the robberies and asked a number of questions, including one about tattoos. Apparently a witness had seen a single-color eagle tattoo on a suspect's upper right arm…the same as Gavin's own body art. Tattoos weren't uncommon, but it was another piece of evidence falling into place.

"I'll let you know once we learn something," the sheriff assured him. "But it could take a while. This is an old case."

Trent got into his truck, trying to imagine how Alaina would react to the truth. He still thought it was possible she wouldn't believe him. After all, Alaina had grown up hearing fairy tales about her charming, fun-loving father.

He started the engine. In a few hours the family would be gathering at the McGregor ranch for Sunday dinner. It was a tradition that included the extended family, but the initial conversation ought to be with Alaina.

He'd prefer waiting until the ballistics report was back, except rumors might begin flying. Generally gossip raced through Schuyler with the speed of stampeding cattle. In the meantime he should tell Emily what he had learned; the break-in at her house made him more uneasy now that he knew about the murder. After all, there'd been two men confronting David Barker in that convenience store.

As Trent drove toward 320 Meadowlark Lane he spotted a ratty truck down the nearest cross street, tucked between two bushes. His hackles rose. It was Webber's pickup.

Parking out of sight of the front windows, Trent approached the house. The front door was open but nobody was visible. Emily was from the city, so it was unlikely she'd leave it open for longer than a couple of minutes, particularly after the break-in. Just as much of a concern, her car was sitting in the driveway with the trunk up.

Trent slipped along the side of the house opposite the driveway, forcing his way through the overgrown bushes, getting more than one scratch from a wild rose bramble. A detached part of his brain made a note to have Caveman trim them back; they'd provided cover for the intruder to break the window, and the rose thorns weren't thick enough to discourage someone who was really determined.

He approached the door on the mud porch; luckily he had a key so he could close up the house when Emily wasn't there. The lock turned with only a faint click and the door swung silently on the new hinges. Ducking into the kitchen, he could hear Webber's voice.

"My, my," the louse was saying. "If I'd known how nice this joint could be, I would have fixed it up for myself."

"I thought you kept Wild Rose Cottage as a rental," Emily responded in a guarded tone.

"Sure, for tenants who couldn't afford something nicer. It seemed the right thing to do."

Ha.

Webber was trying to make it sound as if renting Wild Rose Cottage had been a philanthropic enterprise. Trent clenched his fists, remembering his mother's fear that they'd be thrown out because the rent was late or the property was damaged in one of Gavin's drunken rages.

"How nice," Emily said, the irony in her voice probably escaping Webber's less agile mind.

"Oh, yeah, I got a real soft spot for folks in trouble."

The man was chatting in his usual genial manner, but Trent wasn't convinced.

"You're sure gutting the place," Webber continued. "Walls moving, floors torn up... You know, I was surprised to hear Trent Hawkins took the lead on the job. The way I hear it, he ain't bossed a crew for years."

"Really?" Emily sounded indifferent. "They told me that Big Sky is booked more tightly than usual, so Mr. Hawkins needed to take charge on one of the contracts."

"But why this place?" The question was sharper, more insistent. "He could have worked a dozen different sites."

"You'll have to ask Mr. Hawkins."

"He ain't exactly easy to talk to."

Trent crept closer to the broad opening into the dining room and glanced around, looking for a reflective surface. The shiny front of the microwave showed that Webber was facing away from the kitchen.

Trent moved forward and put a finger to his lips when he saw Emily. Other than her eyes flickering she didn't react, which she would have done if she'd thought nothing was wrong. A paper bag sat on the floor next to her and Trent suspected Webber had slipped in while she was unloading groceries. She wouldn't have allowed him inside after the last time he'd shown up.

"So what is Hawkins doing here?" Webber demanded. "He's got no need to boss the job. I bet he's giving you a cut and you're looking for it together. He's been here the last two nights. I know because I've been watching the house."

"All I know is that it's time for you to leave," Emily responded firmly.

Webber turned toward the stairs. "Not until I've checked for myself. Trent Hawkins hates this place and me along with it. God, he was an obnoxious kid, always getting in my way. He'd love to spite me."

"If Trent got in your way, then you were headed the wrong direction."

Trent swallowed an urge to laugh. Emily's cool wit was wasted on the clod.

"That's none of yer business."

Fear shot through Trent as Webber's beefy shoulders tensed. While the guy must have gained at least sixty pounds in the past twenty-odd years, he was still dangerous, maybe even unhinged, and he was standing only a few feet from Emily.

"You're absolutely right," she said, sounding perfectly calm. "But I still want you to leave my house. Now."

If Webber went for anyone, Trent wanted it to be him. He crept closer, but something must have alerted Webber because he swung around.

"Working on a Sunday?" he asked, obviously making an effort to control himself.

Trent took another step forward, plastering a false smile on his face. "With the flu running around, I've got some catching up to do."

As much as he'd enjoy punching the guy senseless, for Emily's safety, it was better for Webber to leave quietly. After that, the authorities could deal with the creep whatever way they liked.

Webber's piggy eyes narrowed. "Really?"

"That's what happens when you're in charge... no days off when a contract is on the line."

"There wouldn't be any other reason?"

"No."

"Frigging liar. I should have figured it out a long time ago. You kept trying to buy this place, offering more than the dump was worth. Who'd have guessed that a snotty kid knew about the loot and gun? I've waited long enough. It belongs to me."

"You're too late," Trent said. "The sheriff has the gun. I gave it to him this morning. As for any loot? It probably went where every dime my father ever had went, to booze and gambling."

"No," Webber yelled. "Gavin was holding it while things cooled off, 'cause nobody'd suspect a family guy like him. Then he went and got himself killed. I searched this place top to bottom a hundred times and couldn't find the stuff. Never thought it could be in the walls until you started tearing them down."

"If you thought my father wouldn't spend the money, you obviously didn't know him that well."

"I don't believe you," Webber snarled. "That dough belongs to me and I've waited long enough for it."

He inched closer to Emily, sending Trent's blood pressure rocketing. The best option was provoking Webber into attacking him.

"The sheriff will be delighted when I reveal the identity of my father's accomplice," he taunted.

A switchblade suddenly appeared in Webber's fist and he lunged forward.

"Emily, run," Trent shouted.

Feinting to the left, he grabbed the other man's wrist and wrestled for control. But instead of running, Emily snatched one of her folding chairs and bashed it into Webber's ribs with a resounding thud. He screamed and fell to the floor.

Trent kicked the knife from his hand and got him in a choke hold. Emily threw the chair aside and nabbed the switchblade.

Trent grinned.

It was wonderful how efficient Emily George could be.

"ARE YOU ALL RIGHT?" Emily asked, seeing a streak of red on Trent's cheek. Her stomach rolled.

"Just a few scratches from the roses. You?"

"Fine." She hit the button to retract the blade and handed him the knife.

"Bitch," Webber moaned. "You broke my ribs."

"Watch your mouth," Trent warned.

"Don't worry about it," Emily said. "From some people, name calling is a compliment. Do you think I actually broke his ribs?"

"Probably."

"Good. I'll call the sheriff," she added.

Webber tried to twist away from Trent, who tightened his hold.

"Give me an excuse," Trent said softly, "and I'll give you what I promised when I was nine and caught you trying to feel up my mother. You broke my arm that day, but I'm not a kid any longer."

Webber instantly froze.

Emily dialed Carl Stanfield. The comment about Trent's mother was yet another piece of the puzzle. He'd dealt with so much garbage growing up; no wonder he'd developed a thorny personality.

After filling Carl in on the details, she disconnected and locked gazes with Trent. "He'll be here right away."

Within minutes a siren wailed down Meadowlark Lane. The sound panicked Webber and he scrambled upward again, hampered by both his girth and his injury. Emily snatched the chair once more while Trent kicked his legs out from under him; Webber tumbled back, cursing and clutching his side.

Carl charged through the open door, gun drawn, relaxing when he saw his suspect subdued on the floor.

"Robert Webber, I'm arresting you for the murder of David Barker," he announced, taking out his handcuffs. "I also want to thank you for being stupid. If you hadn't pulled this stunt, we might have never known you were involved. Unless your fingerprints are on the weapon, of course."

While the sheriff informed Webber of his rights and Webber moaned that he needed a doctor, Emily stared at Trent. "Murder?" she whispered.

"I didn't know until Carl told me this morning, but a store owner was shot and killed a few towns over during one of the robberies."

"It wasn't me," Webber yelled as Carl and his deputy pulled him toward the door. "Gavin did it. I said to leave the guy alone and Gavin threatened me, too."

"Tell your story to the jury," Carl told him.

"I'm glad you didn't say a jury of his peers," Emily said wryly. "You couldn't find twelve people that sleazy."

Carl chuckled. "This is a good day for Schuyler. We get to close several cold cases, plus we got a perp on breaking and entering and assault with a deadly weapon. Can you both come down to the office and make a statement?"

"Sure," they said in chorus.

Emily went to the door, Trent close behind, and they watched as Webber was loaded into the backseat of the cruiser.

She heaved a sigh and Trent put an arm around her waist.

"Are you really okay?" he asked.

Emily shrugged. "I'm glad I didn't know murder was involved when it was happening. Webber had a flimsy excuse for slipping into the house uninvited, but he must be dimwitted if he thought I'd believe him."

Trent drew her closer and Emily leaned into his warm, muscled strength. But she only allowed herself a minute before pulling away.

"We'd better go make those statements and get it out of the way as fast as possible," she said brightly.

"Sure. We can take my truck."

"What's the matter, do you think my car will die on the road?"

He groaned, though his eyes had a wry glint in them. "Couldn't resist, could you?"

"Wouldn't you do the same in my shoes?"

"You aren't wearing any."

Emily blinked and looked down at her feet. He

was right; she'd kicked them off after depositing her first bag of groceries in the kitchen. It was when she'd returned with the second bag that she'd found Bob Webber in the living room.

She slipped into her sandals while Trent relocked the door on the mud porch.

"It's lucky you had a key," she told him.

Trent seemed ready to hug her again, so Emily backed away a few inches. They'd just gone through a dramatic event, so it wasn't strange that he would react that way. She wouldn't let herself think it meant anything.

Two hours later they signed their statements about what had happened and Emily hopped back into Trent's truck.

"Sorry," she said. "I should have driven my own car so you wouldn't need to take me home."

"I'm headed your direction anyhow," Trent assured her. "I'll drop you off. I'm…going out to my folks' place to tell them everything." He released a heavy breath and Emily wanted to offer reassurance, but didn't know what to say.

"Bob Webber basically confirmed what you suspected about your father and the gun," she observed quietly.

"That's right. Now they'll have to hear every rotten detail."

Emily wished she could be there to offer support, but it wasn't her place. They might have shared a couple of nights together, but that didn't mean anything had changed. Trent's reputation was well-known in Schuyler—he was a loner who didn't get into permanent relationships. And if he ever changed his mind, he wouldn't choose a less-than-gorgeous oddball.

"I'm sure that Sarah and Parker's first thought will be concern for you and Alaina," she told him. "They love you both."

Trent didn't respond and his face was grim.

At Wild Rose Cottage Emily slid out, shut the truck door and leaned inside the open window. "Good luck."

"Do you want me to check the house?"

She shook her head. "Carl says the judge is tough on violent crime, so Webber will probably be denied bail. Besides, I wasn't kidding about those self-defense classes. I was always a top student."

"You're good with chairs, too. I assume you're going out to see Stella Luna later…?"

"Of course. She's a terrific listener and I want to tell her everything that happened, though not in a way that'll scare her."

Emily stepped away from the truck and headed up the front walk, refusing to look back. Inside the house she blinked tears away. From now on she expected to see less and less of Trent.

Lord, had it only been forty-eight hours since the barbecue fund-raiser? Webber must have been getting desperate, and with half the town at the park, including her, it would have seemed an ideal opportunity to break into Wild Rose Cottage. He'd found nothing, but by his own admission had kept watch on the house, getting even more suspicious when Trent spent the next two nights with her.

He was such a slimy crook, it plainly hadn't occurred to him that they might be doing something besides searching for his ill-gotten booty.

Still, everything had worked out, and she hoped Trent's life would take a turn for the better now.

Emily changed her clothes and drove to the Crazy Horse Ranch. One of the ranch hands waved.

"She's in the corral getting some fresh air," he called.

Emily waved back and circled the barn to the grassy paddock. Stella Luna greeted her with an excited whinny.

"Hey, girl." Emily climbed onto the high fence. "You're so beautiful," she murmured. The finer points of a horse's breeding were unimportant to her, though the affectionate Appaloosa was undeniably lovely—a silvery gray with white spots over her rump.

She stroked Stella Luna's neck, her thoughts inevitably circling back to Trent. It was a curious reality to think that if Bob Webber hadn't broken into Wild Rose Cottage, she would have slept alone the past two nights.

Emily made a face.

Sleeping alone would have been wiser, but it was still hard to regret it.

Stella Luna was nosing her pocket, distracting Emily, and she took out a bag of sugar cubes. "Carrot first," she said, holding one between her fingers.

The Appaloosa obligingly crunched it down before getting a sugar cube. All at once she sidestepped a foot or two, and Emily realized the ranch foreman had walked up to them.

"Hi, Greg," she said, rubbing Stella Luna's nose to reassure her.

"Say, you aren't doing badly for a city gal," he teased.

"I'm sure Kayla and DeeDee have proven that city gals are a force to be reckoned with," she retorted, referring to his boss's second wife and stepdaughter. Kayla's knockout looks still tweaked Emily's insecurities, but she was a nice person.

"They do all right."

Emily rubbed Stella Luna's nose again. "Trent Hawkins says I'm buying her affection with sugar and stuff," she murmured, glancing at the foreman. "He claims good horsemanship is someone who understands the barter system between humans and animals."

Greg gave her a kind smile. "Don't pay Trent any mind. Trent is Trent, and most of us give him a wide berth when possible. That mare loves you and it's got nothing to do with sugar cubes." He glanced at his watch. "I gotta go pick up my kids.

Don't worry about Stella Luna being outdoors. We'll get her stabled before dark."

"Thanks," Emily called after him, fighting an instinctive urge to defend Trent from a reputation he'd probably cultivated with grim determination. Besides, it wasn't totally inaccurate, and that was the problem.

She sighed.

"You know what?" she whispered to Stella Luna. "I've been back and forth about whether I love Trent. I'm pretty sure that loving him is guaranteed heartbreak because he doesn't trust people. Besides, I don't think he likes the real me."

Hopping down, Emily took the mare's halter rope to lead her around the large paddock. She had to stop thinking about Trent…because if she didn't, insecurity and sadness were going to drag her under.

Maybe she should move away from Schuyler, but moving was much more complicated now that she owned a horse. Besides, leaving town would be running away from her problems instead of dealing with them. In a way, that's exactly what she'd done after ending her engagement to Dennis—gone for a winter vacation in Montana of all places. Where was she supposed to go next? After all, a city girl couldn't go much farther than Schuyler, Montana, unless she bought a plane ticket for Tibet.

The Appaloosa's trusting eyes didn't hold any answers and Emily hugged her neck. She might be a dope of major proportions, along with being unrealistic and stupid on the romantic end of life, but she wasn't a sniveling coward.

So they were staying.

CHAPTER SIXTEEN

WHEN TRENT ARRIVED at the McGregor ranch, Jackson and Kayla were already there, having just returned from a trip to Seattle. The three kids from their blended family were playing a board game with Alaina.

He hung back, watching, thinking how well his sister got along with children. He didn't know if he'd made a mistake keeping the truth from her, but wondered if she'd still be the same bright, sassy woman who could so easily charm two teenagers and a quick-witted preteen after he told her.

"Can we take a walk?" he asked Alaina when the game ended. "There's something we need to discuss."

"Sure."

"But we were going to play Monopoly next, Aunt Alaina," DeeDee protested.

"Sorry," Trent apologized. "I wouldn't take her away if it wasn't important."

"Trent, darling," Sarah exclaimed, coming into the living room before they could escape. "I was afraid you'd be too busy to come this week. We're having shish kebabs. They're your favorite, aren't they?"

"You bet." He bent and kissed her cheek. "Do you think we could have a family discussion after dinner?"

"Of course," she said, obviously puzzled. "I'll tell everyone."

Let them know they won't be hungry for dessert, he thought grimly. Between the Montana news agencies and the internet, who knew how long the story would hang around? It certainly wouldn't stay private, not with Webber under arrest and screaming that his partner, Gavin Hawkins, was the one responsible for the death of the convenience store owner. The prominence of the Mc-Gregors would fuel the gossip.

Alaina stood waiting by the front door and they headed toward the creek that was shaded by box elders and black cottonwood trees.

Part of Trent's brain was occupied with finding the right words, but another part kept thinking about Emily, hoping she was all right—a certain amount of stress would be normal after what she'd gone through. He was uptight himself, especially when he recalled his fear that Webber would go for Emily.

It would have been his fault if she'd gotten hurt, which bothered him for the usual reasons…and for others he didn't want to question.

ALAINA COULDN'T IMAGINE what Trent wanted to discuss—he'd never initiated a family conference, so it must be serious.

At the creek they stopped and stared at the cool water that swirled across the McGregor land, even in dry years.

"If you're planning to fire me, you could have waited until we were at the office tomorrow," she joked to lighten the mood.

A faint smile quirked his lips, but it wasn't one of those odd, controlled smiles that Emily had mentioned.

"Are you going to tell me the real reason you left New York to work for Big Sky?" he asked.

"Okay, but don't give me a hard time about it. I wanted to get Mike Carlisle's attention."

"Pardon me?"

"You heard what I said."

"And is he, uh, interested?" Trent asked.

"It took a while, but yes. So tell me what's on your mind." Her brother's expression was so serious that Alaina began to get alarmed.

"There are things you don't know about our childhood," he began slowly. "Stuff that happened before the accident. I've never told anyone, because the truth isn't pleasant."

It was so unexpected she frowned. "What do you mean?"

Trent let out a humorless laugh. "Everybody

thought our father was the nicest guy in town—lousy with money, but charming and thoroughly fun."

"He was…wasn't he?"

"Yeah, until he was behind closed doors with his family."

Alaina knew about their father's problems with money. Decades earlier, the question of who would inherit the McGregor ranch had been resolved when Fiona McGregor married Gavin Hawkins, a man who wanted nothing to do with cattle and ranching. Her parents had given the newlyweds a huge sum, and later established an informal trust fund for their son. But within a few years, all the money was gone on a bad oil investment.

Alaina had learned about it after graduating college, though she'd known the McGregors controlled her own trust fund. Sarah and Parker had restored Trent's fund, but he'd refused to touch it, saying he wanted to succeed on his own.

"What was he really like?" she asked.

"He was abusive," Trent said flatly. "It was worse when he was drunk, but he didn't need much of an excuse to start swinging."

The air left Alaina's lungs in a whoosh. Suddenly a lot of things made sense…such as her recent nightmares, so reminiscent of the ones she'd had as a kid. Or the way she'd hated seeing Mike drinking beer, alone in his condominium.

"Mom and Dad don't know, which is why I need to talk to them and the rest of the family. Honestly, I didn't think anybody needed to know, but today…" Trent stopped.

"Today what?"

The expression on her brother's face contorted. "I knew Gavin was capable of doing anything. After the accident I heard about a bunch of armed robberies and suspected he'd been involved, only I thought it no longer mattered. But it turns out that Bob Webber was his partner…and they killed someone during one of those robberies."

Alaina's brain reeled as Trent explained about hiding their father's gun in a wall on his tenth birthday out of fear and spite…and how Gavin had threatened to start beating her, as well.

"I'm sorry there isn't a prettier story to tell about Wild Rose Cottage," Trent finished. "I know that's what you wanted, but anything else would have been a lie. I've wondered if you'd even believe what really happened."

Tears stinging her eyes, Alaina threw her arms around his neck. "You big dope. I care about you, not pretty stories that aren't true," she choked out. "But I'm mad, because you should have told me the truth a long time ago."

"I wanted to protect you."

She drew back and thumped the heel of her hand

on his chest for emphasis. "I mean it, Trent. I'm not a child any longer."

Then she hugged him again, her heart aching. No wonder he'd been a loner all these years.

TELLING THE REST of the family was as hard as Trent had expected.

"I'm so sorry," Sarah exclaimed when he fell silent. "I'd like to take that man apart with my bare hands," she added darkly.

Uncle Parker—*Dad*—was quiet, apparently in shock.

"The sheriff can't keep this from becoming public and I didn't want you to hear about it from the newspaper," Trent told them. "Or from a reporter asking questions."

Dad threw back his shoulders. "The local radio station may already have the story. They monitor the police scanner."

"And we all know how well the rumor mill works," Kayla added. She'd been through a firestorm of gossip herself when she'd returned to Schuyler with a teenage son obviously fathered by Jackson.

"I'd like to get my hands on him," Walt growled. "Never did trust Gavin. Too smooth for my taste."

The talk went on for some time. Jackson urged Trent to let him know how he could help, and the members of the extended family staunchly vowed a united front. Finally, in a subdued mood, everyone began leaving.

"I'd better go over to my office and email Josh and Madison," Trent told his folks. He didn't have internet at the Balderdash since his time was either spent at Big Sky or outside with his horses and few stock animals.

"Do it here," Parker said.

Trent spent over an hour composing emails to Josh and Madison. Mom had gone to bed by the time he was done, but Parker was waiting with more questions...ones he wanted to ask in private. At length he fell silent and Trent looked down at his hands. Dad was in a lot of pain, realizing his sister hadn't come to him for help.

"What about your folks?" Trent asked. Parker's mother and father were out of the country, traveling in Kenya. "How do you think they'll take it?"

Parker gravely shook his head. "I don't know. The accident report showed Gavin had a high blood alcohol content, so they already blame him for Fiona's death. I feel the same way, but I didn't want to say anything to you kids."

The revelation was another shock for Trent. He'd believed the McGregors knew little about Gavin's drinking. "I'm sorry."

Parker gave him a fierce bear hug. "You have nothing to apologize for, hear me, son?"

Trent wasn't sure, but he did know that he and

Alaina had been very fortunate when Parker and Sarah McGregor became their parents.

WHEN MIKE'S PHONE rang it was after 11:00 p.m. He wouldn't have answered except he saw Alaina's caller ID on the screen.

"Uh…yes?" he answered, half-asleep.

"I'm outside in my car. I know you're probably in bed, but can I come in and talk for a while?" she asked in a strained voice.

Mike bolted upright in bed, no longer groggy. "Sure."

He threw on clothes and hurried to the door as Alaina came up the walkway. Inside she sank onto the couch, her face pale and drawn.

"What's going on?" he asked, sitting on the hassock he used to elevate his knee.

"It's about my family. I just learned…" Her voice trailed and she bit her lip so hard a small bead of blood appeared.

Mike squeezed her hand; it was icy. "Take your time."

She started talking, haltingly at first, until the words began pouring out. "I can't help being angry," Alaina said finally. "I'm mad at Fiona and Gavin, but also at Trent. Not that he understands."

"He was a kid," Mike reminded her, not sure he understood, either. Trent had gone through a whole lot alone, and it didn't seem right to be mad at him.

"We grew up a long time ago. He should have told me."

"Maybe, but if you could spare a loved one from pain, you'd probably do it, too. He kept something really ugly to himself so it wouldn't hurt anyone else."

Alaina stuck out her chin. "I got hurt anyway. A barrier has always been there, something that's kept us from being close. It's the same with the whole family. Now I know it was because of that secret."

Mike sighed. He had to be honest. "Yeah, but Trent would have felt guilty for telling you when there wasn't any need to open his mouth about it."

Alaina looked suspicious. "Don't tell me you're defending him."

"No, but I'm a guy, too, and I can tell you he would have felt guilty. It's the whole macho male protective stuff that women complain about."

"Give me a break."

"I'm not kidding. I think it's genetic."

Alaina managed a weak smile.

Mike slid from the hassock onto the couch and pulled her against his chest. They'd just started sorting things out and he had almost missed his chance with her, but at least she'd wanted to talk to him, instead of Emily or another friend.

"This explains a lot about Trent," he murmured. "No wonder he's such a tough guy."

"Tough guy?" Alaina jerked away unexpectedly.

"What do you mean? Trent doesn't lose his temper or slap people around."

"That isn't what I meant," Mike said, bemused by the lightning shift from accusatory sister to champion of her brother's honor. "Take booze, for example. He never has more than a single beer, and he won't touch the hard stuff. He's got more self-control than anyone I ever met, no matter how much crap goes down. It takes a certain kind of toughness to do that."

"True."

She snuggled back again and Mike had a sudden thought. "Maybe you feel guilty, too, and that's partly why you're so angry…because Trent got the garbage, and you had a normal childhood."

Alaina nodded against his chest. "You may be right. It makes me feel awful to know what he went through while I was blithely being the tagalong little sister, without a care in the world."

Mike kissed the top of her head. "I'm hardly an expert, but that sounds remarkably similar to survivor's guilt."

She didn't say anything and Mike stayed silent, as well.

Not long after signing his major-league contract he'd come back for Christmas and Alaina had been visiting her folks, as well. It was then that he had realized she was special, but he'd been consumed with his rising career and the thrill of achieving his dream. No distractions, he'd told himself. There were plenty of women out there.

If he hadn't been so arrogant, things would be different right now. He could only pray that he wouldn't blow his opportunity this time around.

Alaina's breathing gradually slowed and Mike knew she'd fallen asleep. Leaning into the comfortable couch, he closed his own eyes and drifted away with her.

EMILY DIDN'T SLEEP WELL.

She kept thinking about Trent talking to his family and how they'd react. From what she had seen of Alaina and the McGregors, she knew there was plenty of love in that crowd. Too bad he'd never been able to truly accept it.

At 5:00 a.m. she dragged herself from bed, dressed and started the coffee.

After a long night of staring into the darkness, she had almost convinced herself *again* that she was wrong and didn't love Trent Hawkins.

Her heart was a yo-yo.

After all, they'd enjoyed two very pleasurable nights together, so it was natural that her heart would whisper she was in love. That didn't mean she had to listen.

Pushing the thought out of her head, Emily began making a coffeecake for the crew. It had just come out of the oven when Eduardo arrived, followed by Vince, Caveman and Mike.

But not Trent.

"Got a message from the boss," Eduardo told her. "He may be late, but when he comes, he'll fix that broken window."

She nodded, hardly surprised. Wild Rose Cottage was receding in importance for Trent. It was healthy for him, if hard on her.

Vince sniffed. "Something smells terrific."

"Come into the kitchen and have some," she invited.

The guys loved the maple-pecan coffee cake with bacon crumbles and she told herself everything was working out for the best. She could still be buddies with them, even if Trent never showed his face again at Wild Rose Cottage.

"This is the bomb," Vince enthused as he took a second piece.

"I've never had anything like it," Eduardo added. "My wife would love the recipe. Where did you get it?"

"I developed it myself," Emily replied, "and I'll be glad to share."

"Pure genius."

As Eduardo, Caveman and Vince headed to the second floor, Mike lingered for a last sip of coffee.

"Emily, I've been talk… That is, uh…never mind," he stuttered into silence before limping upstairs, as well.

She couldn't guess what it was about, though surely it wasn't another attempt to get a date.

The day seemed longer than usual. In the early afternoon Emily ran down to the Emporium, knowing the hours were passing slowly because she kept listening for Trent's distinctive knock on the door.

The crew left at four and she handed a copy of the coffee cake recipe to Eduardo on his way out to his truck.

Trent still hadn't come.

That was okay. The window could wait. She could have gone through her home insurance to deal with it, but with the deductible, it seemed better to pay the crew to do the repairs since they were already working on the house.

The doorbell rang a half hour later. Emily couldn't help a slight roll of her stomach, but shrugged it off and went to the door. Alaina was coming so they could go to dinner together; she'd probably left work early.

Instead it was Trent and she blinked, startled that he hadn't knocked as usual.

"Hi," she said with casual friendliness. "How did it go last night?"

"Fine."

He leaned forward as if for a kiss and she stepped backward, pretending she hadn't noticed. Anyway, a kiss might not have been what he'd intended.

"Eduardo told me you were coming to fix the window, but there isn't any hurry if you have something else to do," she explained.

"I spoke to him earlier. He mentioned you served a killer pastry for breakfast. I'd love a taste if there's any left."

"Sure, come on in."

Trent sat at the card table in the breakfast nook and Emily served him a square of the coffee cake.

"I have decaf in the pot," she said. "Caffeine late in the day makes me jumpy."

"Sounds good."

She poured him a cup. The polite trivialities were *also* making her jumpy.

TRENT WAS CONFUSED as he ate the tasty coffee cake. Emily's behavior at the front door didn't make sense.

Granted, his brain wasn't in top working order. He'd had a soul-searing evening, followed by a short night. While his intention had been to work the day as usual, between the phone calls and other stuff cropping up, he'd only just gotten free. Was she angry that he hadn't come sooner?

Finally, he put down his coffee mug and looked at her.

"Emily, I'm not sure what I'm supposed to do now."

She frowned. "What do you mean? You glazed most of the windows without Vince."

His eyebrows shot upward. "I'm talking about what happened between us."

"Oh. Sorry."

"The thing is, I usually don't sleep with women who live in Schuyler. Basically, no one I'm likely to see that often. But in your case, I'm going to see you quite a bit. And the other women...well, I haven't liked them the way I like you."

Though Emily had seemed edgy, she flashed one of her gorgeous smiles.

"It's nice that I wasn't simply convenient," she said. "But don't worry, I'm not expecting anything."

"I know that...*now*," Trent said, on more solid ground. "I've actually met a few women who wanted to be my girlfriend just to get a free kitchen or bathroom."

"Wouldn't that make them high-priced call girls?" Emily asked wryly.

Trent laughed. "My question exactly, though I only asked it once." He pointed to a small scar on his forehead. "See that? When I was younger and even less diplomatic than I am now, I asked a date about her ambitions in prostitution. She threw a plate at me."

Emily's eyes twinkled. "Sometimes the truth hurts."

"In more ways than one. Anyway, what I'm trying to say—somewhat clumsily—is that I've realized you aren't devious or grasping."

Her brow furrowed as if she was thinking hard about something, then she nodded. "I'm grateful for your high opinion."

High opinion?

It was an odd response, but before he could figure it out, the doorbell squawked. He winced.

Emily stood. "You don't like that bell, do you?"

"I can't believe it's still torturing this house."

"In that case, give me an estimate for replacing it."

She left before he could say that he'd throw the doorbell in as a gift. It was just as well. Considering their earlier discussion, it might have come off wrong. But he was relieved that they'd settled things between them. Friendship with a woman was an odd category, but it wasn't a tornado that could rip him apart.

EMILY OPENED THE DOOR; this time it was Alaina.

"Hi, come on in."

"Hey, sis," Trent said.

He must have followed her from the kitchen and Emily hoped Alaina wouldn't get the wrong idea about her brother's presence after regular work hours.

"I didn't know you had plans," he said. "I can do the window tomorrow if you prefer."

"We're just going to Roundup Café," Emily told him. "It isn't a problem if you want to stay, but as I said before, there's no hurry."

"Nah, having a board over a window is gloomy." He looked at his sister. "It's the one Bob Webber smashed."

"Oh," she said. "Emily, you're a saint to try to let Trent off the hook. I would have had a glazier replacing the glass ten minutes after I found it was broken."

Emily carefully avoided looking in Trent's direction. In other circumstances she might have called a glass repairman. Instead they'd ended up in bed. Sex was life affirming, or something, and a natural reaction to intense emotions.

That's my story and I'm sticking to it.

Grim humor went through her. It might be the story she'd tell herself, but she wasn't eager for anyone to know she'd slept with Trent, no matter what the trigger. Certainly his casual explanation to Alaina about being there to do the repair had been a relief.

Of course, he wanted the whole event put behind him, even more than she did, so sorting everything out between them was probably the primary reason he'd come. What she should focus on was the fact he'd said he liked her. That had brightened her day considerably...until she'd considered the possibility he was being polite, brushing her off gently. Thinking about it gave her a headache.

At least he'd stop believing she was out to get something from him...well, for the moment. His general distrust would probably return.

"I DIDN'T EXPECT to see my brother tonight," Alaina said to Emily as they walked downtown.

Trent had told her to take the day off and she had come in late to the office, but mostly because she'd needed to go home from Mike's place to shower and get fresh clothes.

Emily shrugged. "The guys said he'd be over to fix the window, but when they went home and he hadn't arrived, I figured he'd do it another day."

"Trent didn't work with the crew today?" Alaina asked, surprised. "Where was he?"

"He didn't say."

Alaina shot a sideways glance at her friend. "I guess you know what hit the fan last night at the McGregor ranch, seeing as it hit your place first. Webber didn't hurt you, did he?"

"My war wounds are minor. You know those old wood folding chairs I've been using? I got a splinter in my palm when I whacked him in the ribs with one of them."

The image made Alaina laugh. If anyone else had bought Wild Rose Cottage, it could have been a disaster.

At the Roundup Café she hesitated, suddenly remembering the town's rumor mill. Her sister-in-law was right, it worked overtime, and the patrons had likely already heard about Gavin Hawkins's secret life as a larcenous murderer. She squared her shoulders; the people who counted would handle it the right way. The others weren't important.

As they sat down, Alaina smiled determinedly at the waiter, who was a former classmate.

"Hi, Tom. How's Barbara?"

"Morning sickness."

The usual pang went through Alaina. She was thirty now and her biological clock was ticking louder all the time. "Still? She's almost through her second trimester."

"Yeah. I can't even bring burgers home."

"That's bad. Say hi for me, okay?"

"Sure."

After they both ordered a buffalo chicken salad, Emily leaned forward with a concerned look in her eyes. "You seem uptight."

Alaina let out a breath. "Until we walked in here, I didn't truly understand what Trent tried to protect us from all these years."

"Sorry."

"It's okay. I'm tough—not as tough as Trent—but tough enough to take it. Besides, I need to take more charge of my life. I headed back to Schuyler hoping for the best, only to sit around for an entire year, waiting for Mike to notice me. It wasn't until I began harassing him to be a bachelor in the auction that I actually *did* something."

"How did your talk go the other night?"

"Good. We're going to work on properly getting to know each other. No more romantic hazes—if we head toward marriage, I want to be sure Mike can hang in for the hard stuff."

Deep down Alaina was starting to hope that she and Mike could work everything out, particularly after the previous night. He'd been supportive and honest, but they still had a long way to go. Ironically, her own heart was now one of the biggest question marks.

CHAPTER SEVENTEEN

EMILY LOVED FAIRY-TALE ENDINGS, but Alaina's caution was wise…and so much better than how she'd handled her own situation with Trent.

Impatiently she shook her head. It was tempting to pour out her heart, but Alaina had enough to deal with already.

The salads came, and by unspoken consent they changed the subject to something lighter, chatting about books and movies. After the meal they walked back to the house, enjoying the lazy summer evening.

Trent's truck was gone so Emily was able to relax. "You want dessert?" she asked.

"I was up late last night, so I'd better go home and crawl into bed."

"In that case, sleep tight and don't let the bedbugs bite."

Alaina laughed. "I haven't heard that one in years."

"Sue me. I'm a kid at heart."

Waving goodbye, Emily went inside and walked through the silent rooms. Suddenly it felt lonely, but that wasn't Wild Rose Cottage's fault.

"I know, you want a family living here," she announced to the house. "A happy family, with a husband, wife and kids, and grandparents stopping by, maybe a cat and dog…"

Hmm. Much as she loved Stella Luna, a horse couldn't cuddle up at night. Perhaps she should get a second pet, one that didn't live in a barn. Dogs were nice, but they required lots of time and attention to be really happy, so a cat would be best. Nothing purebred. A long-haired, mixed-up-parentage cat, maybe white and gray with a long tail. The image was so strong Emily peeked out on the porch, just in case it was sitting there, ready to come in and make itself at home.

No cat.

She showered, her brain replaying the brief minutes with Trent in the kitchen, unsure whether to laugh or cry. He'd assumed she'd been assuring him that she didn't expect free work on the house just because they'd slept together.

Plainly the possibility of an emotional commitment hadn't even *occurred* to Trent. Hope was hard to kill, but the humiliation of that realization should do it. The only consolation was that he'd completely misunderstood what she'd been trying to say.

Emily shivered, despite the warm water running down her body. Women who *weren't* supermodels fell in love every day, got married and had kids… so what was wrong with her?

TRENT ARRIVED AT Wild Rose Cottage at 6:20 the next morning, more energized than he'd felt in a long time.

"You're bright and early," Emily observed when she answered his knock on the door. She was wearing one of the flowing skirts she'd abandoned while helping with the renovations. The blouse was different, though, and the outfit was more provocative than before.

"I wanted to get a jump start," he said, controlling his thoughts, remembering that friendship was the right category to keep her in. "We're still behind schedule between the flu and the fire department barbecue," he explained. "I hope it isn't a problem."

"Of course not," she said. "And since you're here, I'll be able to go down to the Emporium. Tourists have been cleaning us out, so I need to order new stock and do other stuff."

"How long will you be gone?"

"Just a few hours, though I may go out to the Crazy Horse this afternoon. Jackson's daughter, Morgan, is teaching me to ride and she mentioned being available. I don't want to be a total novice when I get on Stella Luna for the first time. Anyway, the coffee is ready in the kitchen and the leftover coffee cake is on the counter."

With that, she grabbed her purse and trotted out the front door, leaving Trent rather nonplussed.

A few hours...?

The irony *wasn't* amusing. A month ago he'd fervently hoped Emily would leave for an extended period; now he was disappointed by her absence. The men clearly felt the same way when they arrived.

Caveman trudged upstairs without even getting a cup of coffee.

"I guess she has to keep her business going," Eduardo said with a huge sigh.

"But she still made coffee for us. What a peach," Vince declared. "Er…she's okay, right, Trent? That is, I hear they took Bob Webber out of the house in handcuffs."

Trent nodded. "She hit him with a chair."

"That's our Em." Eduardo chortled.

Mike agreed and seemed quieter than usual as they were working together on the new master bedroom.

"Something on your mind?" Trent asked.

"I was just thinking. Stuff about Alaina."

"I hear that you've started seeing each other."

Mike's face turned belligerent. "You got a problem with that?"

"No, not that it would make any difference. Alaina will have my head if I interfere with her life."

"Yeah, I've gotten a glimpse of her determination lately."

Trent decided not to ask if his sister had discussed the revelations about their father. It obviously wasn't a secret any longer, though some of the details might take longer to circulate than others.

As Parker had predicted, that morning the radio station had done a news report about Bob Webber's arrest and the alleged charges against him. The gossip train had probably moved even faster than WCBY Schuyler, so if anyone didn't know the story already, they'd probably had their heads in a horse trough.

THE MORNING CRAWLED by at a snail's pace and Trent finally admitted to himself that it was because he kept listening for Emily's return. Finally he heard the front door open.

"Hey, Em," Eduardo's voice called down the staircase. "We missed you."

"That's nice. I bought sandwiches."

"Boss, it's time for lunch!" Caveman yelled instantly.

The atmosphere returned to normal while they ate. Emily tossed off questions about Bob Webber, making a joke out of the whole thing. While it was possible she avoided looking his direction, Trent couldn't be sure.

He ought to be grateful she wasn't behaving differently toward him. The men regarded her the way they would a kid sister and didn't need the complication of thinking she was involved with their employer.

After the meal, Emily changed into jeans and joined the crew upstairs. "I'm going out to the Crazy Horse later, but I can help until then. I'll work the garbage detail," she offered.

"Terrific," Mike told her. "We need you on the payroll—you volunteer for the jobs we hate."

"Nah. You couldn't pay me enough to do some of this stuff, but I enjoy helping in my own house." She grabbed a chunk of debris and tossed it into the wheelbarrow they'd been using. It filled quickly and she rolled it into the hallway, headed for the window chute that led to the Dumpster below.

Trent and Mike continued knocking out the rest of the wall. Almost with indifference, Trent saw a piece of paper float out and down.

Vince reached for it. "Wonder what that is?"

"Most likely something I stuck in there as a kid," Trent said.

Emily had returned with the wheelbarrow. She glanced at him with concern and he lifted his shoulders a fraction of an inch.

Vince whistled as he read the paper. "This was written when you were a kid? I didn't know some of these words until I was twenty. You had an impressive vocabulary, boss."

"I still do."

Vince chuckled and tossed the scrap into the wheelbarrow.

This time when Trent caught Emily's gaze, he detected a faint smile in her eyes.

As the days passed, Trent pushed the renovations forward as quickly as possible. The crew griped, good-naturedly, about the hurried pace, saying that the sooner they finished on Meadowlark Lane, the sooner they lost their sixth team member.

Curiously, everything was now progressing with uncanny speed; it was almost as if Wild Rose Cottage was cooperating with the renovations. But he didn't agree with Emily's fanciful notions, did he?

"It won't be that long before we release you from construction-zone hell," Trent assured Emily the following Tuesday. The crew was gone for the afternoon, but he'd been staying late to get additional work done.

"Things are much easier now that I have a kitchen," she assured him, "but I know you're anxious to put it behind you."

Considering they'd slept together, some women might have been insulted by his rush. Yet once again, Emily had gone straight to the core of what was going on in his head.

"Hey, are you a psychic?" he asked with a joking air.

"Heavens, no. I get feelings about places, not people. But it makes sense. You've been dragging this house around on your shoulders for most of your life, and it would be a relief to finally drop it and forget everything connected to the memory."

"I suppose," Trent acknowledged. "By the way, Carl called. They found Webber's and Gavin's fingerprints on the gun, though the bullets inside only contained partial prints from my father—which of course sounds as if it's out of a *CSI* episode. Preliminary ballistic tests indicate it was the weapon used in the shooting."

"Where did they get your father's prints to compare against?"

"From his service record. It turns out he was in the army briefly, only to be dishonorably discharged for striking a commanding officer."

"Ouch. Sorry. I mean, before you just wondered if he was involved, and now you know for sure, and it's even worse because someone died. Of course, since you already knew what kind of guy he was, I guess it… That is…" Emily stuttered to a stop and her nose wrinkled. "I'm not saying this very well."

"That's okay."

She looked cute with a streak of paint on her cheek and he had an urge to kiss her. Controlling himself, he said good-night and hurried out to his truck. That's what happened when he broke his rules and got personally involved with a customer—the dividing lines blurred.

Trent gripped the steering wheel. It was well and good to talk about friendship, only what did he do with the desire that still gripped him?

MIKE PULLED OUT the lesson plans he usually ignored until shortly before the start of fall term.

Curiosity pricked at him—there had to be better ways to teach this stuff to blasé teenagers.

When the timer buzzed on the stove he tucked the lesson plans away so Alaina wouldn't think he was trying to impress her with a renewed dedication to teaching.

They were having dinner at his condo. At first he'd been uncomfortable revealing that he knew his way around a kitchen. While lots of athletes cooked, Schuyler's expectations were traditional when it came to men. He'd considered getting takeout, but what was the point? If he and Alaina wanted to make it together, they had to be honest. Besides, it would be a relief to stop putting on an act.

Everything was ready by the time she arrived.

"Hi," he said, kissing her cheek.

She half smiled; it would probably take a while before they were comfortable as a couple.

"Is everything okay?" he asked.

"They're pretty sure my father's gun was used to kill that poor man. I…wrote a note to tell his family how sorry I am. It doesn't seem fair to make them meet with me, though Carl says there's just his granddaughter left."

Mike squeezed her hand. "I'd want to apologize, too, but don't forget that Gavin Hawkins, not his children, chose to hold up that store."

"I know. Maybe I'm just wishing that Mr. Barker had more people who remembered him."

Cold reality hit Mike in the stomach. He was an only child and his parents didn't have relatives in the area. The guy who'd died could have been him, leaving only a footnote in the baseball records.

He wanted to kick himself for the opportunities he'd wasted at the high school. Alaina was right. Kids deserved the best teachers. A number of them had helped him along the way—two had even called in favors to get college scouts to Schuyler, helping him to score a scholarship. Teachers might not go in record books or have screaming fans, but he was increasingly intrigued by the possibilities.

"Dinner is ready," he said. "I'm not a gourmet chef, but I can put together a mean chicken enchilada casserole."

"Spicy, I hope."

"Naturally. I saw the hot sauce you used the other night, so I figured your mouth could take it."

She grinned and he loved the way her eyes crinkled in the corners.

They ate out on his small private patio.

"Mmm," Alaina said after a minute. "This is first-rate."

Mike ate another forkful. "Not bad. Maybe instead of working construction next summer, I should teach cooking class."

"You have other options, too. Big Sky sponsors a Little League team that will need a coach next year. Jack Embry is retiring."

She stopped and looked down at her plate, possibly afraid she shouldn't have mentioned baseball. But he didn't want her to censor what she said— nobody talked baseball around him.

"I'll consider it," he told her easily. "I didn't enjoy coaching Triple-A ball, but it would be different working with younger kids. Truthfully, I got so caught up in being a star before I came back to Schuyler that I forgot why I started playing in the first place—because I love the game."

She relaxed and continued eating.

"By the way," he said, "thanks for jumping on my ego and beating the crap out of my delusions."

Her eyes widened. "Uh…yeah?"

"Yeah. I was acting badly and deserved to be called on it," Mike continued. "Don't get me wrong, I miss playing, but I'm more than a former major leaguer or a guy who got hurt showboating for a woman."

Alaina grinned. "To be frank, you always went for the big play. It wasn't just because of that slinky redhead."

True, but the reason hadn't always been dedication to the game. He'd liked the cheering and how the sportscasters would applaud him for going all out, whether the team was winning or losing. No matter how or when his career had ended, he would have had trouble adjusting.

It had taken someone who'd never cared if he was a star in the first place to show him there was something better. Because Alaina didn't give a flip for his former fame, his injuries hadn't changed her expectations of what he could accomplish. Now she wanted to see if he was still a man she could love and he was eager to work on it with her.

TRENT BROUGHT IN three additional crews the following Monday—one to build the decks in the back and restore the porch, another to finish the roof and paint the outside of the house and the third to finish repairs on the storm cellar.

Caveman and the others grumbled about it all week, saying it was their job. But they kept quiet around Emily, who was excited to see everything coming together.

By midmorning on Friday the exterior work was completed. Emily went outside with Trent to survey the results.

"It no longer looks like a set out of a horror movie," she exclaimed. "And it will look even better when the surrounding jungle is under better control." Her nose wrinkled. "I haven't dared check whether the wild roses or honeysuckle survived."

"Some did," he said, "although it may take a while for them to look their best. I'm not sure whether they're native species, but one of my guys is good at preserving plantings, so I put him on it."

Trent followed as she walked to the backyard by way of the new gate. She surveyed the rose pergola that had been erected, set far enough from the house that the walls could be kept free of the brambles.

"That looks great," she exclaimed, giving him a fast hug and bouncing away before he could react—the imprint of her body lingered.

The construction crew had cut paths and trampled down the growth nearest the house and they went around to the patio, now enlarged to include decks with multiple levels, one with a sheltered hot tub, and another with the new outdoor kitchen.

"It's fabulous," she said simply. "Thanks, Trent."

"You're welcome. I shou—"

"Yoo-hoo," a voice interrupted. "Is anyone home?"

It was his mom, though he had to remind himself to call her that in his head. But she deserved it and that's who she really was.

They walked around to the front of the house and found half of the McGregor and Nelson clan had pulled up in various trucks and SUVs.

"Hey, what's this about?" he asked.

"Alaina said the work out here would be done this morning, so we came over to give Emily a jump start on taming the jungle."

Emily stared. "That's awful nice," she said, "but you really shouldn't… It's too much."

Sarah put her arm around Emily's shoulders. "Don't be silly. Trent has told us how wonderful you've been about everything. We want to show our gratitude."

"Besides," Parker added, "how else can we have a barbecue in your yard tonight?" He turned and looked at Trent. "Hope you don't mind us horning in, but once the idea got started, it charged through the family the way a stampede clears everything in front of it."

"You guys are amazing," Emily said, choking up.

"Nah, we're just stubborn, EmGee," Morgan declared. With Stella Luna being boarded at the Crazy Horse, Emily had gotten to know Trent's niece quite well, though the nickname, EmGee, had actually been devised by her younger sister, who loved to make up new words.

Jackson took over directing family members to various locations around the yard, leaving Trent with Emily.

"I know you have ideas for landscaping the place," he said, "but I doubt they'll do anything that interferes. They just want to show their appreciation."

Emily's smile peeked out through her tears.

"You don't realize what they're doing, do you?" she asked. "There are a dozen ways to tell someone 'thank you,' but they came to show that you're no longer alone with all the horrible things that happened here. Your family is saying they love you."

Warmth flooded him. It was true; he just hadn't seen it immediately.

Emily sniffed. "I'm a sentimental dope. Tell the

crew inside I'm sorry I can't do anything right now, but I'll be working on the yard today."

Again, before he knew quite how to react, she dashed away.

EMILY DOVE INTO trimming bushes, not wanting to get overly emotional. The McGregors were the nicest people. She knew they had oil money, but despite their wealth, they worked hard and seemed to enjoy doing it.

When she tried to order something for lunch, Sarah stopped her. "We're all set. We've got coolers filled with cold drinks, and boxes of food to munch."

"Grandpa Parker also brought a gas grill on the truck," DeeDee told her. "Trent said you have one in your outdoor kitchen, but Grandpa thought we'd need extra cook space for such a big crowd."

With that, Parker fired up the grills and began cooking hamburgers and hot dogs for the family and Big Sky crew alike.

"Sure missed you inside today, Em," Caveman told her as he ate his third burger, loaded with two thick patties.

"Big-time," the other members of the crew affirmed.

Trent stayed silent and Emily swallowed her disappointment. What did she expect, protestations of undying devotion?

Friendship without romance *was* possible—

Nicole was chums with a male model who worked for the same agency she did, and there wasn't a speck of romance between them. But Trent didn't have many friends in the first place, and no matter what they'd discussed about friendship, he wasn't likely to become buddies with a scatterbrained woman who talked to houses and hung crystals in her windows.

Besides, it might be easier if she didn't see him often.

Emily shook the speculations away. Thinking about Trent was a bad habit and she didn't want it turning into self-pity. Friends might think about each other occasionally, but they didn't constantly wonder what every nuance meant. Though that didn't mean she was in love with him.

Drat. Even after telling herself not to, she was still thinking about the guy.

"Did I see tree-trimming equipment in the truck?" Trent asked Parker as the other members of the crew disappeared inside the house.

"You betcha." Parker turned to Emily. "I assume you want that black cottonwood taken out since it's long dead, but what should we do with the rest?"

Emily shook her head. "You've all been wonderful, but that's too much for you to do. I'll hire a tree service."

"Dad, if you'll do the pruning Emily wants, Jackson and I can deal with the dead cottonwood," Trent said to Parker, ignoring the protest.

Parker winked. "Sounds like a plan."

The family returned to work and Emily was amazed anew. She'd expected to spend weeks clearing the yard, but by the end of the day, the wilderness had been transformed into an orderly space, with heavy mulch laid down to control growth where she didn't want it. There was even a rough lawn, the weeds having been whacked into submission.

Dinner in the early evening was as delicious as lunch had been—barbecued chicken and steaks, with side dishes from the coolers brought by the McGregors and Nelsons.

Trent was as cheerful as she'd ever seen him and Emily tried to be glad. She liked happy endings and he was probably going to get one, at least when it came to his family.

As for herself, Wild Rose Cottage was turning into a real home, and that would have to be her own happy ending.

CHAPTER EIGHTEEN

EMILY WOKE THE next morning trying to understand why she was depressed, then told herself it was ridiculous. The McGregors and Nelsons had done something extraordinarily nice for her. Now she could start landscaping the garden immediately with time to get plantings established before the onset of winter.

The crew gathered at the usual time for coffee and a snack before heading upstairs, but Trent stayed behind.

"I didn't get a chance to talk to you about this last night, but there's a problem with the master bath tiles," he explained. "When the shipment arrived we checked the top layers, but we should have gone deeper. Yesterday Eduardo found the ones below have quality issues."

With a sigh, Emily told herself she should have known better. Trent had warned her that the manufacturer wasn't reliable, but she'd liked the tiles, and at the time, she hadn't liked *him* that much. So she'd gone the opposite direction of what he'd advised.

"Go ahead and get it over with," she said, re-signed. "You must be dying to say, 'I told you so.'"

He grinned and it struck her that he was getting much better at smiling. "What about the adage 'the customer is always right'?"

"Except we both know customers can make de-cisions that really suck."

He chuckled. "Maybe, but we can fix this one. I'll take you over to Big Sky so you can see what we have in stock. If we have something you like, we won't have to delay finishing the master bath." He didn't have to tell her that specialty tiles could take weeks to receive.

"Okay." Emily wondered if the tile problem ex-plained why she'd been depressed earlier. Wild Rose Cottage could be sad about the tile problem... Yeah, that must be it.

Grabbing her purse, she followed Trent outside. "I could take my car," she suggested. "You don't need to drive me.

"I'm heading right back anyway," he said. "And if you like something we have in stock, I'll bring a pallet of the tiles with me."

He opened the door and she climbed into the high cab, trying not to look toward the truck bed where they'd slept under the stars. If she'd only stayed as strong the night of the barbecue and auc-tion as she had that evening at the farmhouse, she might not be fighting her heart so much now.

ALAINA SAW TRENT'S truck pull into the construction yard and came out to greet Emily, delighted for a chance to share her news.

"Trent told me what happened," she said first. "I've already contacted the company. They've apologized and issued a refund, claiming some sort of glitch."

Alaina followed Trent and Emily to the warehouse, where a display area showed which products they had in stock.

It was unusual for her brother to stand around while a client looked at samples—he really *did* have lousy social skills. Of course, with everything that had happened, the situation with Emily was far from normal.

"I can stay if you want to do paperwork in the office," Alaina told him. "There's a big stack of estimates waiting for your approval."

Trent cast a glance at Emily, who was carefully studying the samples. "All right. Emily, give a shout if you have any questions."

"Thanks." Once they were alone, Emily abandoned the tiles and looked at Alaina. "Okay, I can tell you've got something you're bursting to tell me about. What is it?"

"Mike has agreed to coach Big Sky's Little League team next year, and I don't think it's because he's trying to make me happy. He also has another appointment with the principal at the high school, so he may be considering *that* coaching job, too."

"Terrific," Emily exclaimed. "He'd be a great coach."

"That's what I think, and he wants me to be his assistant with the Little League team."

"Any particular reason?"

"He says it's to keep him balanced. I'm supposed to make sure he lets the kids have fun, and that they only enjoy winning because they've done their best and played fair, not because they're miniature Mike Carlisles in training."

Emily looked impressed. "He's come a long way in a short time."

"Yeah. But I still want to take it slow. It's easy to do and say the right things for a little while, and I'm interested in the long haul."

"You don't completely trust him yet, do you?"

Alaina frowned. It was a fair question. After years of waiting and hoping and being continually disappointed, she wasn't sure she trusted Mike *or* herself.

"I guess I don't," she admitted.

"The road to love has plenty of cotton bales in the way," Emily said in a credible Southern drawl. "At least that's what my great-grandmother Adele always said. She died when I was sixteen, but I adored her. She had an interesting edge to her personality that may have increased her romantic challenges." Emily laughed. "When she finally fell in love with someone who accepted her, she said the price was changing her name to Adele Philpott, which she didn't appreciate at first. But she later became proud of it."

They turned back to the tiles. To be sure her friend was seeing everything available, Alaina pulled out several catalogs with color pictures of bathrooms and the tiles used in them.

Her cell phone rang and Alaina glanced at the caller ID. It was Mike, so she went outside to answer.

"I just called to hear your voice," he said.

She melted inside. "I'm glad, because I wanted to hear yours, too."

While she wasn't sure if she was in love with the guy, this was a whole lot more fun than just sitting on the sidelines, wishing for something to happen.

TRENT QUICKLY SIGNED off on the estimates, wondering if it was really necessary. Maybe he should let Kenny make the final decision on jobs under a certain amount. Why hold up work just because he couldn't get to the paperwork?

He headed back to the warehouse. His sister was standing out in the yard, talking on her cell phone. Inside he found Emily thumbing through a catalog.

She glanced up.

"See anything you like?" he asked, hoping she would choose something they had in stock.

She pointed to a tile on the sample rack with a

dark and pale gray variation. "This one, I guess. Eduardo was going to intersperse random glass tiles of different colors, so this would work."

"We've got enough of those on hand to do the job, so he can start right away."

"That's nice." She didn't say it with her customary enthusiasm and he frowned.

"Emily, if this isn't the tile you want, don't go with it," he surprised himself by saying. "We still have the attic to renovate, along with the remaining bedroom and bath downstairs. We could do those while waiting for a shipment to arrive."

Her smile flashed.

"It's nice of you to offer," she said more cheerfully. "But this one will be like clouds on a stormy day and the small glass tiles will create a rainbow effect. Pretty, don't you think?"

"Sure. Not vintage, but attractive."

Her nose wrinkled and he realized she'd gotten a light tan from working in the yard the previous day. "I love vintage, but it isn't great for the business end of living—let's face it, early kitchens and bathrooms left a lot to be desired."

"There's something else to consider, though," he said carefully. "If you ever want to sell the house, having something too taste-specific could be a problem."

She shrugged. "Perhaps, but I doubt I'll ever want to leave Schuyler. It's too nice and I have

Stella Luna to think about—I don't think she'd be happy anywhere else."

"Then I'll get the tiles loaded on my truck."

Trent frowned as he headed out to speak with the yard foreman. It hadn't occurred to him that Emily might leave Schuyler, only that she could decide to live somewhere else in town. Yet leaving was the first thing she'd thought about when he'd mentioned salability.

In actuality, there wasn't much holding Emily in Montana—just her business and an affectionate mare, and Stella Luna could move with her.

He needed to think about it, because the possibility of Emily leaving Schuyler was seriously disturbing.

EMILY TRIED TO read Trent's face out of the corner of her eye as they pulled out of the Big Sky Construction yard. He'd gone moody while the tiles had been loaded into the truck.

Of course, moody was Trent's usual disposition, though he probably wouldn't appreciate the label.

She'd been on and off all day herself. It bothered her that she wasn't as excited as she had been about the renovations. She still felt Wild Rose Cottage was happy to have a new future, but she had the craziest idea it was saying that its future didn't include *her*. How was that for gratitude? She'd saved it from being bulldozed and was spending stacks of money to make the house splendid again, but now it was saying she might not belong there?

She was truly becoming an airhead. Before long she'd start having conversations with houseplants.

"Emily?" prodded Trent's voice. She had a feeling it wasn't the first time he'd called her name.

Criminy, she'd wandered off in her head again. "Yeah?"

"Do you mind if I stop to pick up lunch for everyone?"

"Not at all."

She went in with him at the deli, which was a mistake because it felt as if they were shopping the way a couple would shop together. He consulted her on what sort of sandwiches to buy and how much soda she thought everyone would drink. Not that it was so strange—she'd fed the crew a number of times from Simpson's Deli and also could tell him that Alaina was coming over at lunchtime. She was good at the practical stuff. Her dad had always claimed the family needed someone grounded in real life. *The rest of us need a lesson from Emily, our wise owl,* he used to say.

She'd recognized it had been an awkward attempt to bolster her self-esteem, but it had only made her feel more left out.

Darn it.

Why was she going over that old territory again? No parents were perfect, and compared with Gavin Hawkins, her mom and dad were saints complete with halos. Her dad would howl with laughter if she ever described that image to him—because even if they had nothing else in common, they shared the same quirky sense of humor.

Actually, it was nice remembering the times they'd laughed together. Perhaps she needed to take another peek at the past and remember more of the good things. When it came down to it, how many people could claim the Mona Lisa as a close, personal friend?

A WEEK LATER, Trent did a thorough inspection of the newly completed master bedroom and bath. Everything was in order. The bathroom with its gray tiles and splashes of color was attractive; the unorthodox design a reflection of Emily's personality. It wouldn't be long before she could move in so they could complete the last two rooms on the ground floor.

He checked his watch. It was almost seven. He'd continued staying late most evenings, getting extra licks of work finished after the others had gone.

Emily's behavior kept puzzling him, especially when they were alone together. She was bright and friendly, yet had erected an invisible barrier between them.

Was it regret from sleeping with him?

The whole thing could be his imagination, of course. Aside from his sister, he didn't spend much time with women.

He went down to say good-night, but couldn't find Emily. She wasn't in the basement and when he checked the yard, she wasn't there, either. Concerned, he searched the house again from attic to basement before returning to the backyard. Finally he peered into the new hot tub, fearful she might have hit her head and be floating in the water.

"Hey, Trent," Emily said from behind him. "Considering a warm plunge to ease those muscles?"

He jerked and swung around. There were smudges of dirt on her face and her clothing had bits of cobwebs all over.

"I was looking for you," he said, realizing he'd overreacted. "You usually say when you're leaving."

"Sorry, I was exploring the secret passageway. You never mentioned it."

"Huh?"

"Don't tell me you didn't know. It runs out from the house toward the storm cellar. I got curious when I was down there looking at the old shelves. It's seriously cool."

"Mind if I take a look?"

"Not at all. I came out to see if I could borrow your flashlight. Mine isn't bright enough."

He collected the flashlight and a high-powered headlamp from the truck and followed her into the basement.

"See?" she said, running her fingers along an

old wooden shelf. "There's a catch here. You pull it forward and the shelf swings open."

Trent examined the shelf. Strictly speaking, it wasn't secret since the catch wasn't hidden, though in the low basement light, it also wasn't obvious and could be mistaken for something else. He certainly hadn't realized it was there as a kid, or else he might have used it as an escape route. A few times he'd taken Alaina and hidden in the storm cellar when Gavin had been in a drunken rage, but had constantly worried about getting trapped.

"It isn't a secret," Trent said, pushing the unpleasant memory away. "Nothing like the ones back East where they hid slaves in the Underground Railroad."

"Spoilsport," she shot back with a grin.

"I'm just sulking because you found it and I didn't."

Emily laughed. "Maybe you can be the one to figure out how it opens into the storm cellar."

"It's possible the guys who did the repairs sealed the opening without realizing it was there."

Trent was very aware of Emily's scent and shape as they moved along the passageway. Though old, it was strongly built and seemed sound, but the latch at the other end didn't work.

"It must have been blocked," Emily said with obvious disappointment.

"We can fix that," he promised.

As she turned to make her way back, she bumped into him. Trent broke into a cold sweat.

"Sorry. Tight quarters in here," she murmured, slipping under his arm and moving swiftly back into the basement.

"Whew," she said, climbing the stairs. "It's a cool discovery, but a little claustrophobic."

So that was what it was, claustrophobic. He'd have sworn it was a torture chamber.

In the hallway she plucked cobwebs from her hair and shoulders.

"We'll fix the door," he assured her again.

"I know. To tell the truth, I hoped we'd find whatever Bob Webber was looking for. Wouldn't that annoy the hell out of him?"

Trent smiled wryly. "And it would be even more evidence to convict."

"I thought of that, too. But they have enough, don't they? I heard the judge denied bail, calling him a 'flight risk and potential danger to the community.'"

"Carl thinks they're okay on evidence, though the district attorney's office is always glad to get more. With two credible witnesses, they obviously have Webber on unlawful entry and assault. At the very least, he'll also be charged as an accessory to murder."

"Good."

The next day Trent didn't plan to stay late, but decided he needed to reputty one of the windows upstairs. Once it was done, the crew could finish painting.

He trotted downstairs. "Good news," he said, finding her in the kitchen. "They can finish painting the second floor tomorrow, and then we'll start on the attic."

"That's great."

She'd been to the Emporium that afternoon and was wearing the blue sundress with white piping. She looked incredibly good. Tired of resisting, he leaned forward to kiss her.

Emily laughed and backed away.

"Come on, Trent," she chided him, "you must have better prospects for the evening. Someone much more exciting."

More exciting?

Was she crazy?

"Emily, you leave any woman in Montana looking flat."

She just laughed again. "Honestly, there isn't any need to say things like that. I know the situation is new territory for you, but men and women really *can* be friends. Two of my sister's best chums are guys and there's nothing physical between them."

"That sounds very modern," he commented, "but not something we see much in Schuyler."

"I suppose. I'm just saying that you don't have to wonder if I expect sex now and then, or if I'm maneuvering for favors. We can be friends without that stuff getting in the way. In fact, I'd rather not be classed with the other women you've slept with. Okay?"

Bemused, Trent nodded and decided he'd better get out before his head exploded. Emily might claim to understand what was going on, but it definitely confused him.

LOCKING UP BEHIND TRENT, Emily leaned against the cool glass pane in the door and let tears wash her eyes clean. Maybe she was crazy. If she'd played her cards right, they could be making love right now. Instead, they'd had a nice rational discussion, and then she'd sent him out to find a hot date for the evening.

Finally she straightened and swallowed the rest of her tears. She wasn't geared for a relationship that included occasional sex, especially knowing it was only until the guy lost interest or fell in love with someone else.

Deciding to forego dinner, Emily crawled into bed and curled up tight, hugging her pillow for comfort and wishing she had already found the cat she'd envisioned.

At least she wasn't accepting a mediocre relationship, which is what she'd done with Dennis without even realizing her mistake.

In the growing dim, Emily ticked off the facts of life on her fingers. She wasn't the gorgeous George sister, but it was okay—she would have hated being a supermodel. She was reasonably smart, her current quandary notwithstanding. She had two businesses that provided a generous income. And she'd made a bunch of new friends in Schuyler, despite her quirks.

So she was doing fine.

CHAPTER NINETEEN

TRENT WENT STRAIGHT to the Balderdash and took
a cold shower in the ancient bathroom.

How could Emily think he'd had better prospects
for the evening?

He slapped his hand on the cracked tile wall, furious with how blind he'd been. The very first time
Emily had made one of her self-deprecating comments he should have told her that she was beautiful and didn't need to compare herself to anyone.
But *nooooo*, he'd figured it was a feminine game
to fish for compliments.

He was a fool.

Emily didn't play games and her ego had taken
a beating growing up. Then there was her asinine
ex-fiancé, who obviously wouldn't recognize a gem
if it was thrown in his face.

Trent was embarrassed at how long *he'd* taken
to see what an amazing, sexy, fun, honest, caring
person Emily was beneath her mix of whimsy and
practicality. He might have recognized it sooner if
it hadn't been for his general distrust for people,
but that wasn't much of an excuse.

As he got out and rubbed a towel over his hair, a

whinny blew in from the barn and Trent suddenly realized he hadn't gone riding in over a month. Speakeasy and the other horses were becoming more accustomed to the ranch hand he'd hired than they were to him.

It had never occurred to him to make a life, and not just a successful business. Succeeding had been his way of proving that he was nothing like Gavin Hawkins, but at the end of each long day, he returned to an empty, ramshackle house. Hell, he didn't even have a dog; he had horses he didn't ride.

Coming home to Emily...that would mean something. *She* was home. The place didn't matter.

He had shared his dark secrets with Emily and she'd remained generous and caring. Now he wanted to share everything else with her. Love had crept in day by day and he'd been an ass not to see it sooner. She'd even opened his eyes to other kinds of love—the parents who'd raised him, his siblings...the possibility of children that he and Emily could have together.

You just have one tiny problem, chided a voice inside Trent's head. Right, a tiny problem. He'd realized the truth rather late, a dumbass move that left him with the most important question of all: Would Emily ever believe him after all his accusations and declarations of mistrust?

Trent went out to the barn to bed down the animals, mapping out his next steps. He'd stop pushing the men to hurry—it was working against him—and he'd spend as much time with Emily as possible.

He needed her to start trusting him.

EMILY WAS PROUD of the way she'd handled things with Trent. Despite the temptation, she hadn't leaped at him like a lovesick rabbit. Instead, she'd kept her dignity...and spent the night aching with need.

When Trent arrived alert and energetic the next morning, she didn't know what to think, except that he'd plainly gotten more rest than she had. *The louse.* If there was any justice in the world, he'd look as tired as she felt. Of course, then she'd be left wondering if he was tired because he'd enjoyed an active night with a sexy bombshell.

"I'm intrigued with the basement," he announced immediately. "It isn't on your list of renovations, but do you really want to leave it as is?"

She blinked. "I guess not."

"Good. It could be an interesting challenge to see how nice the space could be made. And who knows? We might find more evidence for the DA to use against Webber."

Emily's confusion subsided. It made sense that he wanted to be thorough.

"Good idea."

"This one is on the house," he said with a grin, "unless you want solid-gold knobs and eighteenth-century mahogany paneling."

"Don't be silly. Just give me an estimate."

"We can debate it later. Let's go down and see what might work."

In the gloomy space he measured the size and then turned to her. "Do you want a hobby room, an extra bedroom or a well-designed storage area?"

Emily looked around. The basement was large, though support beams broke up the area. She almost said to forget it, but the house seemed to whisper *finish me.*

"If I was planning for a family," she murmured, "I might say to put in one of those man-caves they talk about in house-hunting programs."

"It should be what you want."

"Then let's do it mostly as storage and still put in the man-cave thing," she said, wanting to get upstairs. For some reason the low light seemed too intimate for comfort. "You're right that I should consider future salability, and I can always use it as a woman-cave."

Trent's smile suddenly seemed pained for some reason.

"Storage and a woman-cave it is," he said. "Now, do you want to help install the hardwood flooring in the attic? That's one skill you haven't mastered yet."

"Okay." Puzzled, Emily headed up the stairs. Trent had consistently discouraged her helping on projects, though he hadn't ordered his crew to do the same. Now he was inviting her to work with him?

He first showed her how the tongue and groove boards fit together, even handing her the mallet to tap the next piece firmly into its place.

Running a finger over the smooth fit, Emily grinned. "This is neat."

"Sure is." He leaned close while he pulled the next length out and she swallowed, enjoying the feel of his hard muscles as he brushed against her.

"Hey, Em, boss, are you up there?" Eduardo called from the second floor, interrupting them. "We knocked, but nobody answered."

"We're both here." Trent straightened. He glanced at Emily. "Shall we take a break and have coffee with the guys?"

"Uh, sure."

The entire day was like that. The rest of the crew worked on the second floor, but Trent urged her to stay close, helping install the new flooring. When the lengths he'd already cut had been used, he plugged in the small table saw he'd brought up and measured the next board.

"Want to give it a shot?" he asked.

"Oh. Okay."

She stood in front of the saw and reached out, trying to emulate the moves she'd seen Trent make a thousand times over the past weeks. But then he put his arms around her and laid his hand over hers.

"I don't want to take a chance that there'll be an accident," he said softly. "Is this okay?"

She nodded mutely and he turned on the saw. They cut an entire stack that way, leaving Emily pulsing with more than the saw's powerful vibrations. He was aroused as well, and didn't try to hide it from her, but she didn't think it meant anything other than a guy being a guy.

When the crew left for the day, Trent stayed behind as usual, but didn't go off to work on his own. Instead, he sat at the card table in the breakfast nook.

"Shall we go over ideas for the basement?" he asked.

His smile was friendly and the warm glint in his eyes had to be her imagination.

MIKE SHOWERED FAST and dressed for an early dinner with Alaina. They were driving to a nearby town where there'd be fewer people they knew to come over and visit...curiosity burning in their faces.

When she opened her door, he let out a wolf whistle.

"Sorry," he apologized. "You'd make a burlap sack look good, but that black number is ruthless on a man's blood pressure."

She smiled mischievously and he knew he was in deep trouble. There was no longer any question that he wanted to spend his life with Alaina

Hawkins. But any thought he might have had about a calm family life while teaching school was getting shot to hell. Alaina would keep him on his toes.

The meal was delicious, but Mike barely noticed as they talked, and he discovered an entrancing streak of whimsy in Alaina that he'd never encountered before. She claimed it was Emily's influence.

"Say, is something up with Trent?" he asked as they lingered over coffee and dessert.

Her eyebrows shot upward. "Other than our family skeletons getting rattled? Not that I've noticed. Have you seen something?"

"It isn't a big deal, but for one thing, he asked Emily to help him install the hardwood floor in the attic. They worked all day together. Emily has pitched in all along, just not with Trent. So now I'm wondering if he's interested in her, and I'm not the only one. The rest of the crew is wondering, too."

Alaina grinned. "That would be amazing. She's good for him and he *has* seemed different lately. Give me details."

He described everything he'd noticed, including how Trent had stopped pushing every minute to get finished and had mentioned adding the basement as another project.

Alaina finally shook her head. "It would be a weird courtship for most people, but who knows with Trent? We'll just have to wait and see."

Mike nodded.

It would make Alaina happy to see her brother fall in love, and her happiness was what mattered most to Mike.

EMILY DIDN'T KNOW what to make of Trent's behavior. They talked about the basement and he sketched several designs without pressuring her to accept any of them, seeming quite happy to keep suggesting new ones. She was getting hungry when Trent took out his phone and ordered a large pepperoni, mushroom and onion pizza. Her mouth watered.

"We might as well eat while we work," he explained after getting off the line.

Except they didn't actually work—they talked about house designs in general. Then he invited himself out to Jackson's ranch with her to meet Stella Luna "properly."

"My God, she's a different animal," Trent murmured, staring at the calm, playful mare.

It would be easy to feel smug about it, but Emily knew the transformation had been a joint effort, with both Jackson's family and his ranch hands playing a big part.

She expected everything to return to normal the next day, but when Trent arrived in the morning, he told her the crew wouldn't be there until early afternoon.

"I hope you don't mind, but we had an emergency job at the retirement home. Do you want to help paint the corner bedroom upstairs?"

"I could do that."

A while later she was on a ladder, painting around the window frame, when her elbow caught the edge of the pan and paint sloshed onto Trent's shoulder.

"Oops," she said. "Sorry."

"It's artistic," he said glancing at the way the paint was making long slow drips down his sleeve. "If I don't smudge it up, it might look deliberate."

"I can throw it into the washing machine if you want."

"Nope, I'd rather have it this way. More of a fashion statement," he said with a grin.

She didn't understand. She didn't understand at all.

That evening Trent ordered her favorite dishes from the Chinese restaurant to eat as they talked, followed by another trip out to the Crazy Horse Ranch. It was the same story, day after day. There were only a couple of afternoons he left when the crew did, saying he needed to do a favor for his brother.

Inside Emily was trying to prepare herself for the time when the work would be done and she wouldn't see him so much. His current behavior was making that a challenge.

On Wednesday a couple of weeks later, the crew

left early because the plaster work in the basement needed to dry before the next step could be completed.

"It's looking good," Trent told her, sitting at the kitchen table drinking a glass of iced tea. Though it was autumn now, the weather had remained warm.

"Yes. But I wish we'd found more evidence for the DA." Fun as the secret passageway had been, it really *had* just opened into the storm cellar and everything else in the basement had been anticlimactic.

He shrugged. "It was a long shot, but it didn't hurt to try."

"I guess not."

Trent drained his glass. "Come on," he said, jumping to his feet. "Let's take a ride."

Emily figured they were going to the Crazy Horse as usual, but he drove past his brother's spread and turned after another half mile.

"Don't worry, we aren't trespassing," Trent said. "The Balderdash belongs to me."

"I didn't think you'd do anything illegal."

"And certainly not in the broad daylight with a witness." He smiled and winked.

Considering everything, being able to relax and joke about something like that showed he'd begun healing.

They drove past a collection of ranch buildings and over a rise that looked across a stunning view. The wide sweep of rolling, tree-studded grass with the arching sky above called to her, whispering a welcome.

Trent pointed. "That's part of the McGregor ranch, and to the south is Jackson's place. I wanted the Balderdash when it came up for sale, partly because it was adjacent to their spreads."

"So you're into ranching, too."

"Not really. The Balderdash is what Schuyler calls a hobby ranch," he explained. "It's enough for me. I'm a builder, but it's satisfying to run a few cattle and have horses. The existing house and barn aren't great, so I'm trying to decide where to build a new place. This is my top choice."

"I can't imagine anything better," Emily agreed. A few clouds floated lazily overhead, casting shadows on the ground. It was so vast and beautiful that she sighed with pleasure.

"What sort of house do you think would be good here?" he asked.

"Something that fits into the landscape," she said, "with lots of windows so you can see in every direction."

"How about facing the living room that way?"

He pointed toward the McGregor ranch.

She nodded thoughtfully. "I like it, but the hills to the west are special, too."

They sat in the truck debating which view properly belonged to the living room, until Trent proposed a round house made of glass.

"If that's what rings your bell, go for it."

He chuckled.

Finally they headed over to the Crazy Horse and spent time with Stella Luna before returning to Wild Rose Cottage, where Trent insisted on walking her to the door. He kissed her cheek and hurried back to his truck.

Emily swallowed. Trent had been dropping quick kisses when he left in the evenings—sometimes on her cheek, more often on her lips. It was always so fast that she didn't have a chance to react. Even if he was still figuring out how to be friends with her, she wished he'd stop the kisses—they always left her aching for more.

And it was difficult not to start hoping, because Trent wasn't treating her like a friend, he was treating her like a woman he loved.

TRENT DROVE TO Wilson's Jewelry Store for his evening appointment.

"Good evening, Trent," Jarvis Wilson greeted as he let him into the back door of the store.

"Thanks for making a special time for me," Trent told him. "I want this to stay confidential for the moment."

"I understand," said the old man. "This isn't the first time a fellow didn't want the whole town knowing what was going on in his heart."

Mr. Wilson unlocked the safe and pulled out a velvet-covered box. "What do you think?" he asked, placing the platinum ring on a black cloth.

It was one of a kind, just like Emily.

Trent picked it up. The center sapphire was as intensely blue as the early evening sky, while sapphires in rainbow hues descended on either side. He'd spent hours choosing the gems, wanting something as unique as Emily. The center gem's Montana origin was sure to delight her.

His fingers closed over the ring for a brief, fierce moment. It hadn't been easy finding the patience and self-control to court her, when all he wanted to do was sweep her into his arms and lose himself in making love. Yet he also enjoyed their conversations and the quiet moments that came when they were painting or doing something else together. And he might be making progress. Emily didn't push him away as much, and seemed less wary when he touched her.

Trent put the ring back on the cloth. "This is just what I wanted," he told the elderly jeweler. "I'd like to take it with me tonight."

"Of course." Mr. Wilson returned his creation to the velvet-covered box. "Good luck," he said simply, handing it back.

Trent put the box in his pocket. He was determined to convince Emily that they were right for each other, and that he would be the luckiest man in creation if she agreed to marry him and have a family together.

Now he had to find the right moment.

CHAPTER TWENTY

ON SATURDAY MORNING Emily brought the last of her belongings upstairs. The day before Eduardo and Vince had moved her mattress to the new master bedroom and she'd slept there for the first time. With the renovations nearly completed, she could go hunting for furniture. While the prospect didn't energize her the way it had a few months ago, surely that was a temporary condition.

Once Trent was no longer there every day she'd get her equilibrium back. But for the moment, Saturday stretched long and empty ahead of her.

She grabbed the phone and dialed. "It's me," she said when Alaina answered. "Would you like to go shopping for furniture?"

"Oh." Alaina was silent for a moment. "What about your stuff in Los Angeles?"

"It doesn't fit here. I'm considering mission style. What do you think?"

"All for it, but this is Schuyler. Our furniture store is basic, to say the least. You'd have better luck finding what you want in Helena. You should go with Trent. His truck is huge and he can bring back anything you want."

Trent…furniture shopping?

"He's far too busy," Emily objected. "You said he's even behind on signing estimates."

"He's working that out. Why don't I call and see if he's free?"

Emily hesitated. The suggestion was bizarre, but Alaina was so involved with Mike, she probably hadn't thought about what she was saying. "Maybe another time. Do you want to look at the local store, anyway?"

"Sure, but let's have lunch at the Roundup Café first. Around noon?"

"Sounds good."

ALAINA HUNG UP the phone and shook her head in amazement.

"What's up?" Mike asked.

"Emily wants to shop for furniture with me."

"What about Trent? I doubt he's into shopping, but he's into Emily."

"I think she still doesn't get that he's interested. Or can't let herself believe it, which works out the same."

Mike snorted. "Then she's the only one who doesn't get it. The crew is practically stuffing sawdust into their mouths to keep from saying anything."

Alaina frowned. "They wouldn't, would they?"

"Nah, they'd never embarrass Em."

"Good." Alaina leaned across the bed and kissed

him. "I'm counting on you to keep me posted on what's happening."

He tugged her down for a more thorough kiss and she felt his hand on her breast.

"You have amazing stamina," she murmured.

"Athletes usually do," he said, his fingers teasing her.

"Mmm."

Four hours later, she dragged herself away and met Emily at the Roundup Café.

"Hey," she said. "You look as if you didn't get much sleep last night."

"I didn't—probably just excitement because the house is nearly finished."

Alaina doubted that was the reason. She envied Mike's front-row seat to the strangest courtship in Montana history. And to think she'd never believed her brother would let down his guard enough to fall in love.

"Are you sure it's the house?" she asked innocently. "I mean, Trent can be overwhelming and he's obviously been zeroed in on you lately."

Though her cheeks reddened, Emily just shrugged. "I'm probably the first woman he's had as a friend. He has to get used to it. So, what's going on with you and Mike?"

"We're doing okay."

"Glad to hear it," Emily said with a faint smile. She'd probably guessed where Mike was spending most of his nights.

Alaina felt her own face go hot. She was having trouble taking the last step with Mike...agreeing to forever.

The night before Mike had told her he'd wait as long as she needed, but he'd also reminded her that fantasy was usually more prettily polished than reality.

She knew what he was trying to say.

All these years she'd had a glowing vision of them together...rather like a wedding photo. But life was what happened after the flowers faded and the wedding dress was turning yellow in the back of the closet.

For her first parents, life had disintegrated into violence and alcohol and disappointment. Outside of fairy tales, happily-ever-after wasn't perfect. Even for Parker and Sarah McGregor, things hadn't always been easy.

If she married Mike, life would be messy and imperfect. He would be irritable at times, sometimes from the pain in his knee, sometimes for other reasons. She might have trouble getting pregnant the way Jackson's wife was having trouble... All sorts of things could come along. Still, they'd have each other to help deal with the imperfections, and Mike had promised to put their marriage first as long as she kicked him in the butt if he fell into bad habits.

He was doing his best to be up-front and honest. *This isn't fantasy baseball, and we aren't a fantasy team,* Mike had said before she'd left that morning. *I want the real thing.*

Alaina shook herself.

There was a difference between being realistic and procrastinating. She loved Mike. The grown-up Mike, not the boy from her childhood fantasies. And with that acknowledgment, the dream faded and reality came into focus, with a brighter, fuller vibrancy that any dream could ever hold.

EMILY WAS ABLE to fill her Saturday with activity, but after an early-morning visit with Stella Luna on Sunday, the rest of the day loomed long and lonely. At length she decided to work on the yard, so after church—where Sarah McGregor urged her to come to Sunday dinner—she went to the nursery and bought several fruit trees.

She was digging her third hole when Trent arrived.

"Take it easy," he said as she wiped a drip of perspiration from her jaw. "I can plant those for you."

She gave him a tight smile. "So can I."

"Uh, yeah, sure. I came to take you out to the ranch. We usually arrive early for dinner."

Emily shook her head. "It was nice of Sarah to invite me, but I can't intrude."

"Mom will be hurt if you don't come. She's expecting me to bring you."

"Oh. Um…can you wait while I get cleaned up?"

"Take your time."

He eyed the shovel, so Emily took it with her. She didn't want to come back and find the trees had all been planted in the time it took to wash her face.

TRENT KNEW IT hadn't been fair invoking his mother, though nothing he'd said was a lie. He'd mentioned wanting to bring Emily, and Sarah had been delighted. Of course, Mom had also gotten her hopes up because he'd never brought a woman to Sunday dinner…or any family event, for that matter.

I must have been waiting for the right one, Trent thought, *even if I didn't know it.* It might sound sappy, but somewhere, deep in his heart, he must have known Emily was the right one from the beginning, or she never would have gotten through his defenses.

EMILY LAY IN bed that night, again unable to sleep.

Hope, stubborn and intractable, kept rearing its head.

Trent had stayed close at the weekly McGregor barbecue, even convincing her to go riding with him after the meal. He hadn't joined in with the family merriment, but he was less standoffish and seemed more at ease.

As for Mike and Alaina?

From what Emily had seen, it was obvious they were going to be okay. No doubt another family announcement was coming, a far more pleasant one this time.

It wasn't light yet outside, but she got up and decided to wear some of her new clothes—it turned out that form-fitting T-shirts and shorts were just as comfortable as skirts and blouses that billowed like curtains in the wind.

Emily was putting the ingredients together for chili when Trent knocked at his usual time. She hesitated, abruptly self-conscious about her outfit, but it was too late to change her mind.

"Hey," she said casually, opening the door.

"Uh, yeah. Good morning." Trent gazed at her figure longer than usual and Emily gritted her teeth. If he was still attracted to her, why didn't he do something about it? The excuse that he was adjusting to having a female buddy was growing thin, but he hadn't made any effort to *really* kiss her in weeks. Just quick little pecks. It was discombobulating…a word that usually made her smile, except she was too exasperated to find anything amusing.

That evening, as usual, Trent stayed after the others had left.

"How about Mexican for dinner?" he asked. "Manuela's has started delivering, but we could go out if you want a change of pace."

She'd had enough.

"Stop it," Emily said. *Loudly.* "Stop paying so

much attention. Stop ordering dinner. And stop looking at me all the time!"

He didn't stop. Instead he looked at her all the more closely, his chest rumbling with a low, gravelly laugh that sent electric pulses down her spine.

TRENT HAD WONDERED how long Emily's patience would last.

"Why should I stop?" he asked. "I love you and I won't stop until you agree to marry me."

Shock flashed across her face. "That's ridiculous."

Trent shook his head. "The idea of living without you is ridiculous, and it's just as ridiculous that I took so long to figure it out. You're the best friend I've ever had, and what could be better than loving my best friend with all my heart? What's wrong with wanting you in my bed every night and making babies and raising our children together? Is there something bad about finding you more desirable each time I look at you?"

She stared and he laughed again.

"Hell, Emily, I thought my heart would fail when I saw you in those shorts this morning. You're gorgeous no matter what you wear, but—"

"Don't say that," she interrupted.

"I said *gorgeous* and that's what I meant," he told her firmly. "For God's sake, stop listening to that nonsense you grew up hearing. You're stunningly beautiful, from the top of your head to the tips of your toes. I don't want a boring blonde Barbie. I want you."

A sober expression crossed her face. "I'm flaky. Don't deny that's what you think, or that you don't consider it a compliment."

Panic tightened his gut. He took a deep breath and decided to be honest. "Okay, I went through a time…a lot of times, maybe, when I was trying to figure things out. You're different than anyone I ever knew in Schuyler and I kept trying to put you in a category I could handle, or at least understand."

"Like a woman who uses people."

He swallowed. "Yes. I also wondered if you were one of those people that always need to be rescued, unable to deal with real life. People like that suck you under. Now I know better."

"How do I know you wouldn't start pigeon-holing me again?"

"Because I expect our relationship to grow. Most of the reason I was doing it in the first place was to keep myself from envisioning a relationship. You turned my world upside down, or so I thought. Now I know you turned it right-side up."

EMILY'S HEAD WHIRLED. Trent was saying the kind of things she'd dreamed of him saying, but she needed to stay rational. *Maybe this isn't the time to be the smart George sister,* a voice whispered. Perhaps it was Wild Rose Cottage talking, or maybe just her wishful heart.

He reached out and tugged her close, his lips brushing her cheek, her neck and finally her lips.

"You say you get feelings about places, not people," he murmured. "Yet when you saw me taking that gun from the wall, you trusted me, before there was any reason for trust. Please listen to your heart again. Please have faith in me, the way I have faith in you. Please love me."

The hope that had been growing inside of Emily went bounding out of control. She *did* love him. As for trust…maybe she mostly needed to trust herself and the honest certainty she saw in Trent's eyes.

"I'll always love you," she whispered.

His kiss was fierce, stealing her sanity for an endless minute. After a long, long time, he pulled back a few inches and stared at the smile on her face. She saw the excitement in his…not only the surge of desire, but a joy that went deeper.

He took a velvet box from his pocket and opened it. Inside was the most beautiful ring she'd ever seen.

"They're all sapphires, but the center stone is from Montana," Trent explained, slipping it on her finger. "I wanted something unique, just like the woman I love."

Emily hadn't known sapphires came in different colors and her eyes widened; he'd chosen something exactly right for her.

"You're the only future I will ever want," Trent promised. "We can build our dream house on my ranch, the place I showed you with the wonderful views, or we can live here and be Wild Rose Cottage's second chance."

"I think someone else is supposed to make it their home," she said slowly, finally understanding what the house had been trying to tell her... Wild Rose Cottage had been remodeled just for her, but they could build a home for both of them out on the ranch. "Let's build the other house. I have a really good feeling about that piece of land. I think it wants us there."

Trent smiled and kissed her. "You're right. Absolutely and wonderfully right."

* * * * *

LARGER-PRINT BOOKS!
GET 2 FREE LARGER-PRINT NOVELS PLUS
2 FREE GIFTS!

◆ HARLEQUIN®

Romance

From the Heart, For the Heart

YES! Please send me 2 FREE LARGER-PRINT Harlequin® Romance novels and my 2 FREE gifts (gifts are worth about $10). After receiving them, if I don't wish to receive any more books, I can return the shipping statement marked "cancel." If I don't cancel, I will receive 4 brand-new novels every month and be billed just $5.09 per book in the U.S. or $5.49 per book in Canada. That's a savings of at least 15% off the cover price! It's quite a bargain! Shipping and handling is just 50¢ per book in the U.S. and 75¢ per book in Canada.* I understand that accepting the 2 free books and gifts places me under no obligation to buy anything. I can always return a shipment and cancel at any time. Even if I never buy another book, the two free books and gifts are mine to keep forever.

119/319 HDN GHWC

Name	(PLEASE PRINT)

Address		Apt. #

City	State/Prov.	Zip/Postal Code

Signature (if under 18, a parent or guardian must sign)

Mail to the **Reader Service:**
IN U.S.A.: P.O. Box 1867, Buffalo, NY 14240-1867
IN CANADA: P.O. Box 609, Fort Erie, Ontario L2A 5X3
Want to try two free books from another line?
Call 1-800-873-8635 or visit www.ReaderService.com.

* Terms and prices subject to change without notice. Prices do not include applicable taxes. Sales tax applicable in N.Y. Canadian residents will be charged applicable taxes. Offer not valid in Quebec. This offer is limited to one order per household. Not valid for current subscribers to Harlequin Romance Larger-Print books. All orders subject to credit approval. Credit or debit balances in a customer's account(s) may be offset by any other outstanding balance owed by or to the customer. Please allow 4 to 6 weeks for delivery. Offer available while quantities last.

Your Privacy—The Reader Service is committed to protecting your privacy. Our Privacy Policy is available online at www.ReaderService.com or upon request from the Reader Service.

We make a portion of our mailing list available to reputable third parties that offer products we believe may interest you. If you prefer that we not exchange your name with third parties, or if you wish to clarify or modify your communication preferences, please visit us at www.ReaderService.com/consumerchoice or write to us at Reader Service Preference Service, P.O. Box 9062, Buffalo, NY 14240-9062. Include your complete name and address.

HRLP15

LARGER-PRINT
BOOKS!

LARGER-PRINT BOOKS!
GET 2 FREE LARGER-PRINT NOVELS PLUS
2 FREE GIFTS!

HARLEQUIN®

INTRIGUE
BREATHTAKING ROMANTIC SUSPENSE

YES! Please send me 2 FREE LARGER-PRINT Harlequin® Intrigue novels and my 2 FREE gifts (gifts are worth about $10). After receiving them, if I don't wish to receive any more books, I can return the shipping statement marked "cancel." If I don't cancel, I will receive 6 brand-new novels every month and be billed just $5.49 per book in the U.S. or $6.24 per book in Canada. That's a saving of at least 11% off the cover price! It's quite a bargain! Shipping and handling is just 50¢ per book in the U.S. and 75¢ per book in Canada.* I understand that accepting the 2 free books and gifts places me under no obligation to buy anything. I can always return a shipment and cancel at any time. Even if I never buy another book, the two free books and gifts are mine to keep forever.

199/399 HDN GHWN

Name	(PLEASE PRINT)
Address	Apt. #
City	State/Prov. Zip/Postal Code

Signature (if under 18, a parent or guardian must sign)

Mail to the **Reader Service:**
IN U.S.A.: P.O. Box 1867, Buffalo, NY 14240-1867
IN CANADA: P.O. Box 609, Fort Erie, Ontario L2A 5X3

**Are you a subscriber to Harlequin® Intrigue books
and want to receive the larger-print edition?
Call 1-800-873-8635 today or visit www.ReaderService.com.**

* Terms and prices subject to change without notice. Prices do not include applicable taxes. Sales tax applicable in N.Y. Canadian residents will be charged applicable taxes. Offer not valid in Quebec. This offer is limited to one order per household. Not valid for current subscribers to Harlequin Intrigue Larger-Print books. All orders subject to credit approval. Credit or debit balances in a customer's account(s) may be offset by any other outstanding balance owed by or to the customer. Please allow 4 to 6 weeks for delivery. Offer available while quantities last.

Your Privacy—The Reader Service is committed to protecting your privacy. Our Privacy Policy is available online at www.ReaderService.com or upon request from the Reader Service.

We make a portion of our mailing list available to reputable third parties that offer products we believe may interest you. If you prefer that we not exchange your name with third parties, or if you wish to clarify or modify your communication preferences, please visit us at www.ReaderService.com/consumerschoice or write to us at Reader Service Preference Service, P.O. Box 9062, Buffalo, NY 14240-9062. Include your complete name and address.

HILP15

YES! Please send me **The Western Promises Collection** in Larger Print. This collection begins with 3 FREE books and 2 FREE gifts (gifts valued at approx. $14.00 retail) in the first shipment, along with the other first 4 books from the collection! If I do not cancel, I will receive 8 monthly shipments until I have the entire 51-book Western Promises collection. I will receive 2 or 3 FREE books in each shipment and I will pay just $4.99 US/ $5.89 CDN for each of the other four books in each shipment, plus $2.99 for shipping and handling per shipment. *If I decide to keep the entire collection, I'll have paid for only 32 books, because 19 books are FREE! I understand that accepting the 3 free books and gifts places me under no obligation to buy anything. I can always return a shipment and cancel at any time. My free books and gifts are mine to keep no matter what I decide.

272 HCN 3070 472 HCN 3070

Name   (PLEASE PRINT)

Address   Apt. #

City   State/Prov.   Zip/Postal Code

Signature (if under 18, a parent or guardian must sign)

Mail to the **Reader Service:**

IN U.S.A.: P.O. Box 1867, Buffalo, NY 14240-1867
IN CANADA: P.O. Box 609, Fort Erie, Ontario L2A 5X3

* Terms and prices subject to change without notice. Prices do not include applicable taxes. Sales tax applicable in N.Y. Canadian residents will be charged applicable taxes. This offer is limited to one order per household. All orders subject to approval. Credit or debit balances in a customer's account(s) may be offset by any other outstanding balance owed by or to the customer. Please allow 4 to 6 weeks for delivery. Offer available while quantities last. Offer not available to Quebec residents.